The New Frontier

The Best of Today's Western Fiction

D0125089

The New Frontier

The Best of Today's Western Fiction

Edited by
JOE R. LANSDALE

A Double D Western
DOUBLEDAY
NEW YORK LONDON TORONTO SYDNEY AUCKLAND

A Double D Western
Published by Doubleday, a division of
Bantam Doubleday Dell Publishing Group, Inc.
666 Fifth Avenue, New York, New York 10103

Double D Western, Doubleday,
and the portrayal of the letters DD
are trademarks of Doubleday, a division of
Bantam Doubleday Dell Publishing Group, Inc.

Library of Congress Cataloging-in-Publication Data

The New frontier : the Best of the West 2
edited by Joe R. Lansdale.—1st ed.
p. cm. —(A Double D western)
1. American literature—West (U.S.) 2. American literature
—20th century. 3. West (U.S.)—Literary collections. 4. Western stories.
I. Lansdale, Joe R., 1951–   . II. Best of the West.
PS561.N45   1989
813'.0874'08—dc19   88-33998
CIP

0-385-24569-6

*This one is dedicated to
my friend and favorite Western writer,
Theodore V. Olsen.*

Contents

Introduction

I'll keep it short, but not real sweet.

In my introduction to the first volume of this series, *The Best of the West*, I said some real bad things about the state of Western literature—short stories in particular—about how predictable and stale the field had become, growing little since the pulp boom, and I blamed most of this on the writers, and I'm here to say those comments still stand.

But, there is good work being done. Innovative work using the Western motif in new and exciting ways, and herein are examples.

Last time I had to take a stick and beat the bushes for stories of the sort I was looking for, had to send back numerous shoot-'em-up reprints (I never asked for reprints; I asked for original stories), but this time I got all original material, and the quality was high. A number of the stories I passed up were so close that it made my back teeth ache not to buy them. I'm going to say up front that as fine a volume as I thought the last one to be, this one is even better. And let me brag about the first book in this series a moment, emphasizing that I'm not responsible for how good it is, but that the writers are, and the same goes for this volume. Last time, the nominees for the Spur (the highest honor the Western Writers of America can bestow) were all picked from *The Best of the West*, and the winner was Loren Estleman's fine story "The Bandit." Another story, "Sallie C," by Neal Barrett, Jr., was picked by Gardner Dozois for his *Year's Best Science Fiction, 1987*, and John Keefauver's "Cutliffe Starkvogel and the Bears That Liked TV" was given an honorable mention.

This anthology, like the last, is reaching for new horizons, new frontiers, and like the last, it succeeds. These stories have grace and guts and even meanness, and by golly, I think a few of these little buddies even break new ground, and I'm of the opinion both readers and writers want this. If they don't, let them look up the old, dusty pulps, brush them off, and reread the dull old stories about fast draws in the middle of the street and sweet schoolmarms and bad ranch foremen and the like. If that's what you like, then folks, this isn't the book for you.

But I think the writers are on to something here. Not only did a number of the stories in the last volume receive recognition, not only did the mail run highly pro for the volume (there were certainly a few who thought I should be lynched for being so bold as to insult the Western), there are currently in the works several more volumes of Western short stories, a number of them modeled on *The Best of the West.* This is the first time in years that there has been this much interest in the Western short story and certainly the first time in years that so many writers have taken such an innovative approach to the field, and this can only fuel the imaginations of even more writers, and in the long run, both they and the readers will profit.

So if you as a reader want to see imaginative sparks fly, want the fertile tinder of your imagination fanned to a blaze, then this, my friends, is the book for you.

Enjoy. And take a writer to lunch.

A First Blooding

MAX BRAND

William F. Nolan's special afterword to this Max Brand story covers most of what I could say, so I leave him to it. But I will add that Max Brand is one of the most popular Western writers ever, even if his work is more mythic than realistic, taking place in what can only be described as an alternate universe West owing more to Greek and Roman mythology than to our own, "true" Western history. "A First Blooding," however, is an odd exception.

Bill Nolan is an expert on Max Brand, and along with Robert Easton, Brand's son-in-law, is responsible for the appearance of this "lost" excerpt, which appears here for the first time anywhere. It's just the thing to start off an anthology like this.

Lieutenant Allan Loring was built after the true Yankee model, tall and heavy-boned, with the muscles fitted on hard and flat, like those of a mule. He moved toward the assembled patrol. The light from the open door of the guardhouse touched vaguely on shapeless uniforms and caps that sagged forward. The faces were dirty with new beards. Loring himself had tried to raise at least a pair of whiskers that might add dignity to his twenty-one years, but his mustaches grew in such irregular patches that he had to keep a clean skin.

Sergeant Means reported the detail ready, saluting with exaggerated precision.

Loring nodded, stepping smartly to the front of his patrol. In a moment he was striding at its head; the camp fell away behind him and its odors of woodsmoke, coffee, and burned meat dissolved and left him alone in the night with the detail slogging steadily in his wake. As he walked, with nine men keeping the rhythm behind him, Loring felt there was a glorious purpose in the discipline of war which teaches men both to serve and to be masters. To his rapidly enlarging spirit there were no proper dimensions in the geography of earth, the blurred mist of woodlands or the small undulation of the hills; he preferred to look up into the sky where the clouds were black mountains with the moon among them.

Here he struck up spray as high as his head by walking almost knee-deep into a puddle of rainwater, and Loring became aware that instead of a road, he was following random paths such as are bound to grow up near a camp. However, he had kept to a straight enough line, and yonder were the three tall trees which marked the outer limit of his patrol; the moon brightened them for an instant. He put his men in single file. In that formation they could make their way more readily through broken country. He noticed that they were panting.

"The men seem a little blown, Sergeant," he said, proud of himself and his long legs.

"They are accustomed to the regulation step, sir," said the sergeant, after a moment of pause.

"Ah, and my stride is too long?" asked Loring rather happily.

"By several inches, sir," said Means.

The soldiers looked darkly at their lieutenant, but still Loring felt very well about the matter as the march continued with the detail serpentining behind him through the brush. Usually, when he looked forward in his career, he found himself an officer beloved by his men, eventually scarred like an old mastiff but always considerately careful of the needs of his soldiers, in fact a father to them, but as he strode on again it seemed to him that there was a less democratic ideal which might be of greater service to war and warriors, for are not soldiers better led by men above them? The very root of the word "discipline" means docile willingness to learn from superiors.

Loring was resigning himself, now without pleasure, to this more Spartan conception when he heard the note of a night bird flying low on the wind so briefly uttered and so swiftly gone that he could not name it. He began to think of all the birds he had seen since he came to Virginia with the regiment, ruby-throated hummingbirds, crested flycatchers, kingbirds, Baltimore and orchard orioles, bobolinks, indigo buntings, scarlet tanagers, rose-breasted grosbeaks, the vireos, warblers, Maryland yellowthroats, and above all the veery thrush. Only once had he seen its cinnamon-colored wings, but often in the woods he had heard the mysterious sound flowing from all sides, like light. It was only now and then, for moments, that one could even listen to the birds, for as a rule, the mere thought of war was a deafening uproar in the mind.

At this, he roused himself from his thoughts to find that his long legs were carrying him through dense brush, so that in part he had been awakened by the soft cursing of the patrol which followed at his back. He was disturbed by something wrong in the scene before him, and he required a moment to discover what was missing: the moon had a clear moment in the sky but nowhere could he find the three trees which were to be the limit of his march.

When he ventured a glance back and from side to side he realized that he had lost his way utterly during those moments when he had been alone with his mind. Now there was nothing for it except to admit to the sergeant that he was lost. The moonlight showed the chunky figure of Means, his fleshy brows slightly shadowed by a scowl as he grimly endured the folly of his superior.

The ground now sloped down toward a marshland where water glinted among the patches of brush and high grass; in fact, they had come close to the river, beyond which lay the South. A light wind carried the odor of mold and sun-cooked slime.

The tall marsh grass in one place waved violently; a moment later a figure slipped out of the grass into a clump of shrubbery.

Loring halted his men with a raised hand. He pulled his revolver from its holster.

"Did you see, Sergeant?" he asked softly.

"Yes, sir," said Sergeant Means.

"Apt to be one of them trying to come through," said Loring.

His own breath was short now, and not because of the distance he had tramped.

He pointed, saying to his men: "Cover that patch of marsh grass with your guns. It's the big patch near the dead tree. Where the bushes are moving. Something is coming through."

"A wild pig maybe," said one of the men quietly.

Loring stood as though ready for target practice, with his left arm behind him and the gun held high, ready to be dropped on the mark. He had been very thorough in that part of his training, for every time he handled the revolver he could not help remembering that his skill with it might be life or death to him.

Except for himself and the sergeant, his command was on the ground, two kneeling, the others lying with their heavy muskets hugged to their shoulders, their heads twisted a bit to get the sights.

"Hold your breath when you aim," he remembered to tell them. "And don't shoot too high. Not too high, men!"

The wind was gone, so that the night had the familiar sense of silence which is like fear itself. They were so close to the marsh that Loring could follow the small ripple, where a fish swam or a frog, across the oily silver of the moonlit water and even into the shadows. Wherever those shadows lay, whether beside the marsh grass, tree stumps, or derelict branches, the black of them was more real than the rest of the scene, like holes cut through a bright painting.

The furrow that ploughed across the patch of brush now reached the edge of it, and a man appeared. From his slouched rag of a hat to his heels, he was so drenched that he looked more like a forked branch of a tree in motion than a human.

"Halt!" shouted Loring.

The figure whirled, leaping back into the bushes as Loring dropped the revolver on the mark. The sights came right on it, he thought, as he squeezed the trigger. The explosion boomed at his ear. The recoil jerked up the muzzle to readiness for the next shot, in perfect style; and then the muskets spat out little red snake-tongues of fire. The revolver had been like a terrier's bark; these were hounds in deep cry. The men were reloading, hurrying with their long ramrods, jamming the charges down the muzzles, while the smoke came bitter and sulphurous to the nostrils of Loring.

"Close in!" shouted Loring. "Close in!"

He began to run down the slope. He was slow on the level, but the pitch of the ground gave reach and drive to his striding. Even so, the sergeant got to the water before him, and Loring found himself thigh-deep, following. The ooze sucked at his ankles while man after man of his party got past him. He was panting as he dragged his weighted feet out of the slime onto the firm ground of the island. Breath came back to him when he saw his men standing in a circle like hounds around a quarry. The fugitive, in the center of that trampled place, lay back on his elbows with his hand over a shoulder wound. Blood leaked through his fingers.

"Name of Barnet, Todd Barnet, Twenty-seventh Virginia," reported the sergeant, who sat cross-legged, filling his pipe.

The wet slouch of a hat covered half the face of Barnet. A ten days' beard worked and bristled around his mouth as the pain put its teeth in him again and again. He had on shoes that looked homemade, and his attention seemed to be deeply fixed upon them. His trouser legs were worn to rags at the bottom. One shin, bared almost to the knee, was bone-white in the moonshine. "Turning up the toes" is a phrase for death; Loring thought of it as he stared at the Rebel, who was cursing Yankees and Yankee-land as though sure of his privilege.

"You damn fools," he said. "What you still carrying pistols for? A musket ball would of clipped spang clean through me, but this here pistol ball it took and jarred off the bone and slipped down inside and murdered me."

The last of the detail came up, crunching the bushes underfoot, but when they reached the place, they stood quietly. Some of them were masked by shadow, but the others looked the way Loring felt, very sick, for like him, the new recruits were seeing their first death. He could remember a voice somewhere in his past talking about fox-hunting and "blooding the pack."

Barnet took a long breath, half vocal and quavering. Pain snapped shut his open mouth, and the sergeant looked curiously at him. There was no more sympathy in Means than in a small boy who has pulled a leg off a frog. The smoke from his pipe entered the still air in round little puffs of brightness, and the smell of it reminded Loring of the tutor who had solved for him the mystery of "conditions" in Greek verbs.

"That was a good shot, sir," said Means. "A very good shot."

The sickness was leaving the stomach and throat of Loring. The odor of the marsh had become to him the smell of death, but there was a new and more cruel manhood in him which was untroubled. Men must die in war.

"It's a damn officer that done this to me, is it?" said the wounded man. "It's a dirty damn Yank officer that knocked a hole in me?"

"Shut your mouth, Johnny," said the sergeant. He spoke sharply, as one gives command to a dog. He was protecting his own dignity as well as that of his commanding officer, but this sign of devotion enlarged the heart of Loring. He became a merciful conqueror.

"I know something about medicine," he said. "Let me look at the wound. I hope it won't be so bad."

"You *hope*, do you?" asked the wounded man. "The hell you hope, you . . ."

The words choked off in such a way that he thought Barnet was about to break down into sobbing; instead, he commenced to vomit. Two of the detail, hurrying off into the brush, imitated the prisoner, but Loring mastered his own nausea. He kneeled, tore up a handful of the long marsh grass, and wiped the muck from Barnet's face and throat.

The wounded man's eyes closed and opened again. He glared up at Loring. "You boys is gonna catch a whoppin' from us Rebs," he said. "We're gonna whop you Yanks good an' proper." Then his eyes seemed to lose focus, and he began to speak as from a dream.

"We was in the lead of Jackson's column, and ole Stonewall was pulled up beside General Lee. It was the first time I'd ever seen Lee. His horse looked real small under him; that was my way of seein' that he was a big man.

"Stonewall had on that old cadet's cap, and he was all covered with dust and suckin' on a lemon. He had the visor of the cap drawn way down because the dust burned his eyes to bits, you know.

"It was getting late, an' the woods was sort of smudging together, and that seemed to let the Yanks get up close to us. A lot of our boys was passin' to the rear, wounded. A lot more lay here and there, as tired as dying. They'd get up and flop down and drag up again. Some of them wounded was pretty bad.

"A. P. Hill was up there on the ridge holdin' on, but he was bein' wore down. We went along toward the trouble in a double line with orders to trail arms and do no shootin' till the word came. A fellow beside me said, 'That means we're gonna charge.' "

Barnet's face was chalky, his breathing heavy and labored, but the words kept flowing . . .

"General Hood, he brought us up on the left of Law, and it seems that he saw a gap and open country in between Law and Pickett. He ordered us into that hole, and we went on the double through Hill's men. They didn't get up and join the charge. They just lay squashed into the ground and watched us go by. That's how much they'd been through. It was as though every one of them had been bled white. We come up over the ridge. Down below us was the marsh. Going downhill was easier for our legs. But the boys was droppin' pretty fast. You know how they fall sometimes, curling up small? It seemed to me that half our boys went down like that, shot right through the guts. I thought I was up toward the front, but somebody had been there before me. I remember him sittin' up and yellin' for water, water—there was too much noise to hear his voice, but his mouth was sayin' 'Water! Water,' and opening wide, like a frog. I didn't stop; but every step, I felt as though I was gonna die.

"We was close up under the Yanks, and then all at once we was in among them. I pushed a bayonet at one of 'em. He tied himself up in a knot around my gun. I kept pushin' but the bayonet was stuck and I couldn't pull it out till I fired into his belly. And when I'd reloaded, the Yanks was on the run everywhere. We went after 'em through the swamp with our legs mighty tired, but our boys was half crazy because we knew we'd cut through the worst of the trouble. Pretty soon, we could hear yelling, left and right, and then we was gobblin' up prisoners till there didn't seem to be any Yanks left. Well, that's about all. Guess it don't amount to much. Mostly beginning and not much end."

The wind began to rise and it blew the sweating face of Loring as cold as the marsh slime. Barnet, with every outward breath, was groaning.

"We're gonna whop you." It was hard to understand him now, for the loose slobber of his lips could not frame the words, and he seemed to breathe them forth without articulation. "Us Rebs is goin' to whop you."

Loring's left hand and sleeve were foul with blood. Behind him he heard the quiet voice of the sergeant saying "It's his first one. He's got to make the most of him." Then, "This here's a fine place to catch the marsh fever. Day's not so bad as night. The air's thicker at night. It lets the rot into you."

Todd Barnet was staring up at Loring. "You kin do a favor for me, Yank."

"And what's that?" asked Loring.

"You kin give me a drink . . . a wee swaller. Will you do that?"

And he slipped from his elbows and lay flat.

"Canteen," directed Loring.

"He don't need it," said the sergeant.

Loring looked down at Todd Barnet.

"He's done," declared Means.

The body of Barnet, diminished by death, seemed to be sinking into the marshy ground

"We ought to do something," said Loring. "We ought to bury the body."

"Nothin' to bury him in," said Means. "Just the damn marsh."

On their right, two men were advancing down the slope, one a pace to the rear of the other as though attending someone of importance. An army major, and yet his insignia of rank were so lost under the cloak he wore that he seemed more like a country gentleman who had chosen an odd hour for walking abroad. He was a large man, and as he moved, his long cloak swaggered from side to side. When Loring saluted, he answered with a wave of the hand which had nothing military about it. He stopped beside the body of Barnet and lit a cigar.

"Hello, Lieutenant!"

"Sir," said Loring.

"Did you do this?"

"Yes, sir."

"What's your name, son?"

"Loring, sir. Ninety-second Massachusetts."

"I'm Major Acton." He turned the cigar slowly in his mouth. "This your first dead man?"

"Yes, sir."

"I'll need a report."

"Yes, sir."

Major Acton lived in a cabin no better than any pair of soldiers in the Army of the Potomac might have constructed for their winter quarters. It was walled with logs chinked with mud and straw, and a tent made the roof; he had an Indian bed of springy willow, a fireplace, a table, stools, and a door made of hardtack boxes. There was not even a floor, which many a private soldier was at pains to build for himself, and the only distinguishing features of his furniture were the shelves of books, closely packed, above his fireplace and a closet which, when opened, offered a shining, thick display of bottles and cigar boxes. Four of the latter, empty, supported candles which were fixed in their own drippings. It was a dank, uncomfortable shanty. The wet clothes of Loring, as he sat at the table bent above his report, clung to his shanks and gave him a cold promise of chills and fever.

When his head grew heavy in the beginning, he had refreshed himself with a taste of the whiskey which the major put beside him, but he was not familiar with the stuff and it made him slightly ill. He could see that the major constantly was sipping from a tall glass, tilting a bottle now and then to replenish his supply, but the eye of Acton never grew bleared. Loring thought of the gossip that the army contained officers who were true two-bottle men: one for health and one for pleasure, as the saying went.

A knock at the door. The major called out and a sergeant entered the cabin, followed by three privates, two of them obviously keeping guard over the third, who was unarmed.

The sergeant saluted. He reported that the prisoner, picked up behind the lines straggling, had claimed to belong to the Fifteenth New Jersey. He gave the name of Christopher Hodge, but Colonel Collet carried no such name on the rolls of his regiment.

"Well, Hodge?" asked Major Acton. "Are you a New Jersey man?"

The prisoner scratched his head, screwed up his face comically, and winked.

"Nary hide nor hair," he said.

He was a tall young man, lean of flesh and large of bone. The layered tan of his face was weathered like old oak.

"Where are you at home?" asked the major.

"It kind of depends," said Hodge. "But mostly don't folks say that home is where your ma and pappy was born and raised?"

"Yes, usually," said the major. "And where *were* your mother and father raised?"

"Clean up to Vermont," said Hodge.

"That's pretty far north," agreed the major. "Where were you born?"

"The same, sir, sure enough. But they took and moved me down to Louisiana."

"Pleasant place, I'm told," said the major in the kindest of voices.

"Mighty pleasant some ways," said Hodge. "They got pretty fences down there at Louisiana, all Cherokee roses and sweetbrier, so's you can't find the rails of the fences inside the thicket, and the trumpet creepers and the grapevines and even cane grows right up through the roses, so's every foot of the way down a road is different from every other foot."

"Rich land, isn't it?" asked the major, growing more and more neighborly.

"It's fine and rich in the hollows and the flats, mostly," said Hodge, "but you see young pines on the high places, and where the pines come, it's sure that the soil has washed thin. But it's good earth."

"That's a hard country to leave," said the major.

"It is and it ain't," said Hodge.

Loring began to look more closely at Hodge and gather words with which to paint him in letters, knowing that this was a scene to be remembered, to be kept in hand when, after the storm, he found himself once again ashore among the long, long quiet days of peace. He had felt at first that the major was examining the man, drawing him out that he might at last make a false step, but now Acton seemed to drift into an attitude of acceptance, genially nodding agreement even before Hodge answered a question. This journey of one man among enemies through half the scope of the continent gave to Loring's imagination the materials out of which he already was building a whole odyssey.

"It's a long journey, Hodge," said the major.

"It ain't so short as to the schoolhouse," agreed Hodge, "but I got me a job teaming for the army, and I kept shifting north and farther north. Took me six whole months to get here. I been cussin' mules in Louisianian and Mississippian and Alabamian and Georgian, and I've had to take and fight some Carolina mules too, and they was the orneriest of the lot."

"So finally you wound up on the right side?"

"I sure did," said Hodge, his face growing bright. "I thought it was going to be pretty hard to get through the lines, but it warn't so. I just kept walkin' till I seen some of the boys takin' a swim in a creek, and I heard them talkin', their voices comin' with an echo up from the water, and they talked Fifteenth New Jersey. So I just took and borrowed some of their clothes. I didn't borrow no whole man's outfit, but I lifted a coat here and a pair of pants there till I fixed myself up and didn't make nobody go naked. And so, then I just walked on until finally I was stopped and asked questions, and they brought me here."

"Why did you take the uniform at all?" asked the major. "Why not simply tell them that you were a friend coming over to the right side?"

"I ain't one of the bright ones," said Hodge, "but then I ain't simple neither. If you try to come over without no uniform, they take and shoot you first and ask you questions afterward."

"What will you do in Vermont?" asked Acton.

"Farm work, most any kind, sir," said Hodge.

"You've been used to that, eh?"

"Yes, sir. I can plough or reap or thrash or mostly anything on a farm, I guess."

"You're a brave, cool fellow, Hodge," said the major. "And the clothes you have on *used* to be the uniform for the Fifteenth New Jersey."

Hodge grew slowly taller. To the anxious eye of Loring he did not seem to change color, but the words of the major had straightened him, taking the slouch out of his back.

"Your friends have done a very poor job for you, Mr. Hodge," said the major. "They must have heard that this army is now composed of corps which use badges. The Fifteenth New Jersey is in the Sixth Corps, Mr. Hodge, and if you had stolen a uniform from one of them, you would have found on it a cross; the cross in the First Division is red."

Hodge laughed.

"That's what there was on the coat," said he. "And I took and tore it off, because I was afeared it might mean something special, like a medal for service, and I ain't nothing special, sir. Just a Louisiana farmer is all. I didn't want no hard questions put to me, because I right well couldn't of answered them."

Acton was shaking his head slowly, as though he were reluctant to disagree.

"If you'd torn off the cross, it would have left a mark on the cloth."

However mild his voice, he was calling Hodge a liar. The air which Loring breathed had a different taste. It sickened him. Hodge was trying to laugh again, but it was no good this time, for behind the laughter his eyes were wandering in a desperate mist. He was like an actor alone in the center of the stage with his lines forgotten.

"It's no good, old fellow, is it?" asked the major.

The laughter of Hodge stopped. It hushed suddenly, leaving his face distorted. After a moment he was able to say, "No, I suppose it's no good."

"Pour him a drink, Loring," said the major, "and have another yourself."

From the first, Loring now realized, Acton had seen through the spy but had not wished to cut the scene short; instead, he had been lingering out his enjoyment. The soldiers of the guard had come in like hunters with a trophy, their pleasure gradually fading as the major's friendly conversation was prolonged, but now they were keen again, handling their muskets and taking a new grip with their eyes on this quarry which had almost escaped.

Loring poured some whiskey and offered it to Hodge, the liquid shuddering in the glass.

"I'm sorry," he said.

The shock had brought out a fine sweat on Hodge. Perhaps this was the true agony and all that followed would be easy.

"You're a kind fellow," he said as he took the whiskey.

Loring watched the glass steady in the hand of Hodge; he felt relief like an intake of breath, for he saw that the man intended to die well.

"Well, here's health to everyone," said Hodge, raising the glass to them. And he drained it.

"Ah, that's good stuff," he said, and seemed surprised that chance had placed such excellent whiskey in Yankee hands.

"Get that sort of goods in Carolina?" asked Acton.

"You had me spotted all the time?" said Hodge.

Being about to die, he nevertheless was embarrassed that his deception had been so easily penetrated.

"No, that was mostly guessing," admitted the major. "It was the lack of the badge that hurt you."

"That's *their* fault, not mine," said Hodge.

"Entirely," agreed the major. "Will you have another taste of whiskey?"

"Another? No, no! That one took the chill out," said Hodge.

"It's necessary for me to tell you," said Acton, "that if you'll give us the information you have at hand, everything can be arranged for you."

"Information?" repeated Hodge; then, his ugly face flushed. "I haven't any information."

"Of course not," said the major, "but we have to make the proposal."

It seemed to Loring that there was a hint of apology from Major Acton.

"I'm ready now, Major," said Hodge.

Acton shook hands with him.

"They should have given you the right uniform," he said. "They really should!" And he nodded to the sergeant.

"Atten-SHUN!" said the sergeant, quietly.

His men fell in beside the prisoner.

"Goodbye, Mr. Hodge." The major saluted, and the party disappeared through the door.

"Does he *have* to die?" asked Loring.

"Naturally," answered the major.

He canted his head a little to one side, listening, sipping his drank rather furtively. Then someone shouted. Two or three guns exploded, and there was a yell of satisfaction.

"Ah, yes," said the major, smiling and nodding. *"That* was a rare fellow."

The outer night, in which Christopher Hodge had just died, was as black as a tar barrel with a faint streak of brightness at the top of it, as though the barrel were slanted toward the polar star.

Loring found his cabin and went into it as noiselessly as possible; nevertheless, he blundered before he got his clothes off, and Watrous cleared his throat with distinctness to let it be known that he'd been wakened. The need for talk ached in the throat of Loring, but he knew it would be foolish to speak. He lay in his blankets on his back and stared up at the ray of a star that managed to slide through a crevice in the roof. His breath grew a bit short from pressure across his shoulder blades, but when he turned on his side, he inclined his head downward and sank his thoughts into a thicker gloom.

All the distances and dates of his existence had altered. From Massachusetts to the Rapidan had seemed a great journey, and from childhood to the present had been a monstrous stretch of time; but now all the years could be put into the balance against the hours of this single day. He saw with the mind's eye, by that Homeric light which casts no shadow, what war would always mean to him.

Somewhere a detail was marching through a rhythmical sloshing of mud. The detail turned an invisible corner into silence. In a cabin nearby, a man moved in his bunk with a creak of boards; but again the silence fitted down quickly and closely, like a black woolen cap drawn over the ears.

And, at last, Loring slept.

AFTERWORD TO MAX BRAND'S "A First Blooding"

As most Western readers know, Max Brand's real name was Frederick Faust, the half-Irish, half-German phenomenon whose twenty-seven-year output exceeded a million words a year. He wrote 400 Westerns under several pen names (175 of which have been published in book format: *Destry Rides Again, The Untamed, Singing Guns,* etc.) and was recognized throughout the 1930s as "King of the Pulps."

By the 1940s, Faust had firmly established himself in the "slick-paper" markets *(Saturday Evening Post, Collier's,* etc.) and had created "Dr. Kildare" for MGM. (He wrote the first seven in the series.) Yet, with all this mass of popular wordage behind him, he had never published what he termed "a really serious novel." In 1940 he set himself the task of writing such a novel, which he would call *Wycherley.* It would be set in the Civil War. In fact, the War Between the States would form a crucible, a moral and physical testing ground, for the novel's protagonist, Allan Loring, a young officer serving with the Union Army.

The book called for in-depth research—and Faust's Civil War library eventually covered an entire wall of the study in his home in the Brentwood section of Los Angeles. Between magazine work and numerous screen assignments in Hollywood, he labored on his book, writing and rewriting. By early 1944 he had 209 pages of manuscript, perhaps a third of the book. (Contrast this slow, careful production to his pulp Western days for Street & Smith when he averaged a novel every two weeks!)

Then, in February 1944, late into his fifty-second year, Faust shipped off for Italy as a war correspondent for *Harper's.* Three months later he was killed by German mortar fire, having volunteered to accompany frontline troops during a dangerous night attack at the outset of the Italian offensive.

His novel of the Civil War remained unfinished. And, until now, no part of it has ever reached print. "A First Blooding" is therefore "new" Max Brand, excerpted from Faust's 209 pages of *Wycherley.* Concise and poignant, it is both a fine action tale and a superb character study. One can assume that Frederick Faust would be pleased and proud to see these words published at last, after more than four decades.

Here, then, one of Max Brand's finest stories—clear testimony to his talent as a writer of "serious" prose.

—WILLIAM F. NOLAN

Steam Engine Time

LEWIS SHINER

Lewis Shiner lives in Austin, Texas, and is developing quite a reputation in the science fiction world, though it doesn't look as if he's going to work in that field alone. His novel Deserted Cities of the Heart, *though containing science-fictional elements and marketed as science fiction, is a mainstream novel in the tradition of Robert Stone's* Dog Soldiers *and Peter Matthiessen's* At Play in the Fields of the Lord, *with a touch of J. G. Ballard thrown in for good measure. To say that it is in the tradition of these books does not mean that it is a clone. Shiner is his own man, as the following story about a musical prodigy ahead of his time will prove. As an added note, all the material about the blues was thoroughly researched and is accurate, and this includes the reference to* Rolling Stone *magazine, which, though quite unlike the current* Rolling Stone, *did exist.*

Whatever, I think this story breaks new ground in the field by being the first Western short story about popular music, the blues in particular.

The Kid turned up the gaslight in his room. The pink linen wallpaper still looked a little dingy. Ever since J. L. Driskill had opened his new place in December of '86 the Avenue Hotel had been going downhill.

There was a framed picture on the wall and the Kid had been staring at it for an hour. It was an engraving of a Pawnee Indian. The Indian's head was shaved except for a strip of hair down the middle. There were feathers in what hair he had, and it hung down over his forehead.

He compared it to what he saw in the mirror. He was pretty badly hung over from jimson weed and unlabeled red-eye whiskey the night before. His fine yellow hair went every which way and his eyes were mostly red.

He got out his straight razor, stropped it a couple of times on his boot, and grabbed a hank of hair.

What the hell, he thought.

It was harder to do than he thought it would be, and he ended up with a lot of tiny cuts all over his head. When he was done he took the razor and used it to cut the bottom off his black leather duster coat. He hacked it off just below the waist. For a couple of seconds he wondered why in hell he was doing it, wondered if he'd lost his mind. Then he put it on and looked in the mirror again and this time he liked what he saw.

It was just right.

There'd been a saloon at the corner of Congress Avenue and Pecan Street pretty much from the time Austin changed its name from Waterloo and became the capital of Texas. These days it was called the Crystal Bar. There was an overhang right the way round the building, with an advertisement for Tom Moore's ten-cent cigars painted on the bricks on the Pecan Street side. The fabric of the carriages at the curb puffed out in the mild autumn breeze.

The mule cars were gone and the streetcars were electric now, thanks to the dam that opened in May of the year before. They were calling Austin "the coming great manufacturing center of the Southwest." It was the Kid's first big city. The electric and telegraph wires strung all over downtown looked like the history of the future block-printed across the sky.

The Kid was a half hour late for a two-o'clock appointment with the Crystal's manager. The manager's name was Matthews, and he wore a bow tie and a starched collar and a tailor-made suit. "Do you know 'Grand-Father's Clock Is Too Tall for the Shelf'?" Matthews asked the Kid.

The Kid had kept his hat on. "Why sure I do." He took his steel-string Martin guitar out of the case and played it quiet with his fingers. " 'It was bought on the morn of the day he was born/And was always his treasure and pride/But it stopped short—never to go again/When the old man died.' "

I'm going to goddamned puke, the Kid thought.

"Not much of a voice," Matthews said.

"All I want is to pass the hat," the Kid said. "Sir."

"Not much of a hat, either. All right, son, you can try it. But if the crowd don't like it, you're out. Understand?"

"Yes sir," the Kid said. "I understand."

The Kid came back at nine that night. He'd bought some hemp leaves from a Mexican boy and smoked them but they didn't seem to help his nerves. It felt like "Gentleman Jim" Corbett was trying to punch his way out of the Kid's chest.

The ceiling must have been thirty feet high. The top half of the room was white with cigar smoke and the bottom half smelled like farts and spilled beer. Over half the tables and all but a couple of seats at the bar were full. The customers were all men, of course. All white men. They said ladies dared not walk on the east side of the avenue.

Nobody paid him much attention, least of all the waitresses. The Kid counted three of them. One of them was not all that old or used-up looking.

Some fat bastard in sleeve garters pounded out "The Little Old Cabin in the Lane" on a piano with a busted soundboard. The Kid knew the words. They talked about the days when "de darkies used to gather round de door/When dey used to dance an' sing at night." If there was anything going to keep him from turning yellow and going back to the hotel, that had to be it.

There was a wooden stage about three feet wide and four feet high that ran across the back of the room. Just big enough for some fat tart to strut out on and hike up the back of her skirts. The Kid set the last vacant barstool up on the stage with his guitar case. He climbed up and sat on the stool. It put him just high enough up to strangle on the cloud of smoke.

The piano player finished or gave up. Anyway, he quit playing and went over to the bar. The Kid took out his guitar. He had a cord with a hook on the end that came up under the back and let him carry the weight of it on his neck. It was what they called a parlor guitar, the biggest one C. F. Martin and Sons made. With his copper plectrum and those steel strings it was loud as Jesus coming back. Still, the Kid would have liked a bigger sound box. It would have made it even louder.

Somebody at the bar said, "Do you know 'Grand-Father's Clock'?"

"How about 'Ta-ra-ra-boom-de-ay'?" said somebody further down. The man was drunk and started singing it himself.

"No, 'Grand-Father's Clock'!" said another one. "Grand-Father's Clock'!"

The Kid took his hat off.

Maybe the whole bar didn't go quiet, but there was a circle of it for thirty or forty feet. The Kid looked at their faces and saw that he had made a mistake. It was the kind of mistake he might not live through.

There were upwards of fifty men looking at him. They all wore narrow-brim hats and dark suits and the kind of thick mustaches that seemed to be meant to hide their mouths in case they ever accidentally smiled.

They were none of them smiling now.

The Kid didn't see any guns. But then none of them looked like they needed a gun.

The Kid played a run down the bass strings and hit an E 7th as hard as he could with his copper pick. " 'Rolled and I tumbled,' " he sang, " 'cried the whole night long.' " He was so scared his throat was swollen shut and his voice came out a croak. But his hand moved, slapping the rhythm out of the guitar. The craziness came up in him at the sound of it, to be playing that music here, in front of these people, rubbing their faces in it, like it or not.

" 'Rolled and I tumbled, Lord,' " he sang, " 'cried the whole night long.' " He jumped off the stool and stomped the downbeat with his bootheel. " 'Woke up this morning, did not know right from wrong.' "

He pounded through the chords again twice. He couldn't hold still. He'd seen it, lived with it all his life, sharecropping in a black county with the families just one generation out of slavery, seeing them around their bonfires on Saturday nights and in their churches Sunday mornings, but this was the first time it had ever happened to him.

It was time for a verse and he was so far gone all he could sing was "Na na na na" to the melody line. When it came around again he sang, " 'Well the engine whistlin', callin' Judgement Day/I hear that train a whistlin', callin' Judgement Day/When that train be pass by, take all I have away.' "

Through the chords again. It was play or die, or maybe both. The song roared off the tracks and blew up on B 9th. The last notes hung in the air for a long time. It was so quiet the Kid could hear the wooden sidewalk creak as somebody walked by outside.

"Thank you," the Kid said.

One at a time they turned away and started talking to each other again. A man in a plaid suit with watery blue eyes stared at him for another few seconds and then hawked and spat on the floor.

"Thank you," the Kid said. "I'd now like to do one I wrote myself. It's called 'Twentieth-Century Man.' It's about how we got to change with the times and not just let time get past us. It goes a little like this here." He started to hit the first chord but his right hand wouldn't move. He looked down. Matthews had a hold of it.

"Out," Matthews said.

"I was just getting 'em warmed up," the Kid said.

"Get the hell out," Matthews said, "or by thunder if they don't kill you I'll do it myself."

"I guess this means I don't pass the hat," the Kid said.

He sat on the board sidewalk and wiped the sweat off the guitar strings. When he looked up the not-so-old waitress was leaning on the batwings, watching him.

"Was it supposed to be some kind of minstrel song?" she asked. "Like the Ethiopian Serenaders?"

"No," the Kid said. "It wasn't no minstrel song."

"Ain't heard nothin' like it before."

"Not supposed to have. Things everybody heard before is for shit. 'The Little Old Cabin in the Lane.' Songs like that make people the way they are."

"What way is that?"

"Ignorant."

"What happened to your hair?"

"Cut it."

"Why?"

"So it'd be different."

"Same with your coat?"

"That's right."

"You sure like things different."

"I guess I do."

"Where'd your song come from?"

"Back home."

"Where's that?"

"Mississippi."

"Well," she said. "I sort of liked it."

The Kid put the guitar back in the case. He shut the lid and closed the latches. "Thanks," he said. "You want to fuck?"

She looked at him like he was a dog just tried to pee on her shoe. She made the batwings bang together as she spun away hard and clomped away across the saloon.

They'd laid Austin out in a square. Streets named after Texas rivers went north and south, trees went east and west. The south side of the square lay along the Colorado River so they called it Water Avenue. There was West Avenue and North Avenue and East Avenue.

East of East Avenue was colored town. The Kid carried his guitar east down Bois d'Arc Street, pronounced "BO-dark" in Texas. Past East Avenue there weren't streetlights anymore. Babies sat barefoot in the street, and there was music, but it didn't seem to be coming from anywhere in particular. The air smelled like burned fat.

The Kid finally saw a bar and went inside. This time, it got quiet for him right away. "Son," the man behind the bar said, "I think you in the wrong part of town."

"I want to play some music," the Kid said.

"Ain't no music here."

"They call it 'blue music.' You ever hear of it?"

The man smiled. "Didn't know music came in no colors. Now you run along before you make a mistake and hurt you self."

He went back to his hotel long enough to pack his bag, and then he went down to the train station. He sat on a bench there and read a paper somebody had left behind. It was called *The Rolling Stone.* It seemed to be a lot of smart-aleck articles about books and artists. There was a story by somebody called himself O. Henry. The Kid didn't find anything in there about music.

But then, what would you write about a song like "Grand-Father's Clock" or "The Little Old Cabin in the Lane?"

An old colored man pushed a broom back and forth, looking over at the Kid every once in a while. "Waitin' for a train?" the old man finally asked.

"That's right."

"Ain't no train for two hour."

"I know that."

He pushed his broom some more. "That your git-tar?" he asked after while.

"It is," the Kid said.

"Mind if I have me a look?"

The Kid took it out of the case and handed it to him. The old man sat next to the Kid on the bench. "Pretty thing, ain't it?"

"You play?" the Kid asked him.

"Naw," the old man said. He held the guitar like it was made out of soap and might squirt out of his hands if he squeezed down. "Well. Maybe I used to. Just a little. Ain't touched one in years now."

"Go ahead," the Kid said. The old man shook his head and tried to hand the guitar back. The Kid wouldn't go for it. "I think maybe you could still play some."

"Think so?" the old man said. "Well, maybe."

He put his right thumb on the low E string and just let it sit there. After a while he fitted his left hand around the neck and pushed at the strings a little. "Oooo wee," he said. "*Steel* strings."

"That's right," the Kid said.

The old man closed his eyes. His head started to go back and for a second the Kid thought maybe the old man was drunk and passing out. Then the old man took a jackknife out of his pocket and set it on the knee of his jeans.

It made the Kid uncomfortable. He didn't think the old man was actually going to knife him over the guitar. But he couldn't see any other reason for the thing to be out.

The old man didn't open the blade. Instead he fitted the handle between the ring finger and little finger of his left hand. Then he ran it up and down the strings. It made an eerie sound, like a dying animal or a train whistle gone crazy.

Then the old man started to play.

The Kid had never heard anything like it. The notes howled and screamed and cried out bloody murder. The old man played till his fingers bled and the high E string broke in two.

When it was over the old man sat for a second, breathing heavy. Then he handed the guitar back. "Sorry about that string, son."

"Got me another one." Tears ran down the Kid's face. He didn't want to wipe them off. He thought maybe if he just left them alone the old man might not notice. "Where . . . where did you learn to do that?"

"Just somethin' I figured out for my own self. Don't mean nothin'."

"Don't mean nothin'? Why, that was the most beautiful thing I ever heard in my life."

"You know anything about steam engines?"

The Kid stared at him. A couple of seconds went by. "What?"

"Steam engines. Like on that locomotive you gonna be ridin'."

The Kid just shook his head.

"Well, they had all the pieces of that steam engine lyin' around for hundreds of years. Wasn't nobody knew what to do with 'em. Then one day five, six people up and invent a steam engine, all at the same time. Ain't no explanation for it. It was just steam engine time."

"I don't get it," the Kid said. "What are you tryin' to say?"

The old man stood up and pointed at the guitar. "Just that you lookin' for a life of misery, boy. Because the time for that thing ain't here yet."

Just before dawn, as the train headed west toward New Mexico, it started to rain. The Kid woke up to lightning stitched across the sky. It made him think about electric streetcars and electric lights. If electricity could make a light brighter, why couldn't it make a guitar louder? Then they'd have to listen.

He drifted back into sleep and dreamed of electric guitars.

Trooper Story

LENORE CARROLL

Lenore Carroll lives in Kansas City, Missouri, and has a new novel forth-coming, as well as more short stories. She is one of the up-and-coming writers in the Western field. She writes realistically of the Old West, going bravely where few, if any, Western writers have gone before. That's certainly the case with this story. Though its framework is realistic, the core of the story's subject matter, to the best of my knowledge, has never been approached in Western fiction, least not with serious intent. If I'm wrong about that, let me know. In the meantime, read this groundbreaking story by Ms. Carroll and watch for her future work.

Shanley said he never got used to how dry it was in Arizona. Dry heat so you don't even know how much you need water because the sweat dries in your shirt. Dry cold that sucks the warmth out of your chest when you breathe. It's clean, and you get so you feel like a dried tobacco leaf, wrinkled and brown. I felt dried out and half dead when my Mary died, so feeling that way outside just suited my state of mind.

This morning when I walked to the creek it was so foggy I couldn't see a hundred yards ahead. Frost coated tall weeds beside the path. I sucked the ice off a hawthorn bud, curled tight waiting for spring. It's not like that out there. It's dry and clear and when I first got there, what I thought was ten miles away was twenty. There's cactus and mesquite, bunchgrass and grama, and the trees are mostly cedar and pine.

I got to Arizona a little ahead of General Crook. He was the famous Indian fighter. I lied about my age and enlisted and got sent to Arizona in '70 for a hard five years. I'd not trade it for millions. After "Gray Wolf"

Crook got the lay of the land, we started chasing Apaches around the Tonto Basin during the winter of 1871–72.

When it looked like they might have to fight, the Indians melted into those harsh mountains and scattered. Shanley said they drifted over the Sonora border where we couldn't chase them, raiding as they went. They knew hundreds of miles of desert and mountain the way I know the path to the creek. They swooped down out of nowhere, stole and killed and ran off cattle, then disappeared.

If you could catch them unawares—when they had their guard down after a raid—they'd fight. We had Indian scouts who could find them. "To polish a diamond there is nothing like its own dust," old Crook said.

We were on our way back from a scout. We separated from another company at Fort Grant and were making our way south to Fort Bowie when we must have cornered a small band of Apaches. They holed up on a ledge halfway up the mountain and we had to advance under fire. Our rations were low and our horses showed the strain. When the first rifle reports reached us, Sergeant Finerty shouted orders and we stopped and ran for cover. I never saw a single Indian, just puffs of smoke when they fired. I was the fourth man and I led my mount and three others out of range and picketed them, then crawled back to join the others.

Sergeant Finerty was a solid old campaigner, curly hair gone gray under his flop-brim hat. If you told him Crook was God, he would have saluted and said, "Yessir." I never thought he was much for brains, but he deployed the troops, and our Springfields peppered the rocks, although not with much effect. We did a sight more riding than we did shooting and this was one of the first fights I'd been close to since I'd been in the territory. I got a belly full of Indian fights before it was over.

Clouds were building up over the mountains to the west as the sun went down and gnats swarmed when a man sat still for a moment.

I crawled toward the rocks where the troopers took cover, staying low in the thin grass. My heart pounded and I hurried to join the fight. I was twenty yards back when a lucky shot tore through my arm. It didn't hurt much at first, but the blood dripped down my arm and I felt light-headed, but with the heat, that wasn't unusual. I kept crawling. The mountains always shimmered in the heat and that day they shimmered, ran red and started to slip sideways.

Corporal Shanley ran up and grabbed me as I went face-first into the dust. He threw me on his back like I was a sack of oats and half carried, half dragged me behind an outcrop where I could bleed in peace. He turned and fired a few rounds, then pulled my neckerchief off and tied it tight over the bullet hole so the bleeding slowed down.

Shanley wasn't my bunky. He had no reason to look out for me in particular, but while Finerty was a solid man who went by the book, Shanley was the one who got things done. He should've been sergeant and might once have had the stripes, but he was just a trooper now. He was somewhere close to thirty and enough older that I looked up to him. He was all nervous coiled muscle, rawhide stringy, with hands callused hard as boot leather. You don't get fat on beans and hardtack.

One night when I first arrived he had found me sleeping on guard duty. He could've had me arrested, but instead he told me how to keep awake, to move around and watch the stars and listen for night sounds. After that, when I had a question, I'd ask him. He was the best man with a Colt in the company and kept himself in tobacco winning unofficial target shoots.

That day in the valley the Apaches kept us troops pinned down behind the rocks, but they were well protected and come dark, we'd counted no coup. The Indians would be gone by morning, out a back canyon or over the top of the mountain. You or me, we'd never find a toehold to climb; only mountain sheep and Apaches could scamper over those rocky places.

We had no ambulance, just a couple of pack mules, so come morning, Shanley tied me on my horse and the company headed on to Bowie. We were eating dust, Shanley and me, at the rear of the column and I was half out of my head. I noticed Shanley had his arm in a sling, but he wasn't fading in and out as much as I was. The mountains shimmered across the hot plain, shimmered and turned black and there was Shanley, shoving me upright.

"Don't lounge in the saddle, you tinhorn frail."

I tried to rear up at the insult. I caught the McClellan's saddle horn and pulled myself straight, found the offside stirrup.

"Think you're still riding a mule?" He said anything low and mean, to get a rise out of me and keep me going. We were the only casualties and I hadn't even drawn my Colt. We trailed behind, didn't find camp until after dark.

That night Shanley rolled up in his blanket beside me and dribbled a little water into my mouth when I started talking, gone off my head by then.

The next morning, he helped me piss, then brought a pan of water from a spring and wiped my face and head. I was burning up with fever by then, when I overheard him and Finerty.

"I can't hold the whole company for the two of you," said the sergeant.

"You going to leave us here for the 'Paches?" asked Shanley.

"I'm going to the fort. It's another day's ride. I'll send the surgeon and an ambulance for you. It'd be better than trying to move him."

"Leave us some rations. I need to keep my strength up," bargained Shanley. "And extra rounds in case we need them."

That morning Shanley and another trooper moved me into a shallow cave by a spring. White minerals ringed the water, but I wasn't particular just then. Besides rations and rounds, Shanley got some oats for our mounts and a couple of extra blankets. I came to long enough to hear the jangle and creak of the saddles and gear fade as the company rode off.

We stayed by that spring for three days and no wagon or surgeon arrived.

Shanley looked after my bullet wound and cooked a little for us over a small Indian fire. He forced me to drink and eat a little. He soaked me down when the fever was bad and my clothes got caked with the water's minerals. I was off my head most of the time. If he hadn't taken care of me, I'd've died from dehydration or from the bullet. His wound was a long, shallow trench down one shoulder—not deep, but dirty—and it began to fester after a day and give him trouble.

The morning of the fourth day Shanley said, "No help's coming. We'd better start back."

"Go on without me, Shanley," I said. "I don't think I can ride."

"You're coming."

"I'll just hole up here till help comes."

"No help's coming," he repeated.

"How'd you know?"

"Just a feeling." He packed up our gear, then barked, "Get up!" I almost did. He helped me stagger from the spring, then got me on my horse. His arm must have pained him some, but all I ever heard was his breath going in through clenched teeth. He tied me to my saddle, then stepped into his. We rode all that day and along toward sunset we found out why they forgot us.

Signs of an Indian raid marked the trail. It looked like Finerty's company had taken off in a hurry. Cookpots lay tipped into the fire and mess tins and cups lay scattered on the ground. Shanley found blood spots in the dust, but the troopers got away. There were no bodies. Tracks led in the wrong direction—off into the mountains, instead of back to Bowie. They must have taken days longer than they expected and they forgot about me and Shanley.

"We'd better keep going," said Shanley. "Never know if Lo is still around."

We rode all through the night, stopping to stretch and rest the horses. I'd fade out, then come to when I started to fall off.

"Cut me loose, Shanley," I begged.

But he wouldn't. He'd trickle some of that gyppy spring water down my throat and get the horses moving.

I was sick-tired and riding-tired. I didn't know if I was awake or asleep most of the time. Streaks of red began to run down Shanley's shoulder and he wasn't too clear in his head, but he kept us on the trail to Fort Bowie.

We drug up the hill after nightfall the second day. I heard tattoo floating down the mountain. It carried a long way in that dry air, so we spurred our jaded mounts up the trail and tried to sit straight when we rode in.

They told me I fell off my horse when they untied me. Somebody put me to bed. Shanley and me, we stayed in hospital cots for a week, in the cool, adobe building. Laundresses brought soft food and helped us eat it, nursed us because there were no men to spare for hospital orderlies. Finerty came in but never looked Shanley or me in the eye once.

After that, if you'd've told me Shanley was God, I'd've saluted and said, "Yessir." After we were up and around, we had some leave coming. Shanley was heading for Fort Grant with a packtrain and I offered to tag along, but he said he had business there and would go alone. I was disappointed, but bided my time at the post. I still didn't feel first-rate.

Later that year, when we were patrolling the border, we'd overlap troops from Fort Huachuca or Fort Lowell or Fort Mason. Sometimes we'd have a high old get-together, two or three companies bivouacked, troopers seeing friends, playing music, pooling rations and trading for fresh vegetables. Come to find out, I wasn't the only one who'd lied about his age. Others re-upped under different names after deserting under their own. Lots of stories of who'd been where.

It's hard to remember because it's nearly as hot during the winter as it is in the summer down there, but it must have been along about February, we camped with a company from Fort Grant. We'd been chasing Apaches to the mountaintops where we'd ride up from heat into cold, shivering in our canvas uniforms.

I'd been on picket duty the first night. I was so tired the second I couldn't keep my eyes open for another song or another story, so I took my bedroll and carried it off, down near some barrel cactus in a low spot before you got to the creek bed. If it rained, the creek would fill to the banks with fast-running, reddish brown water, but it was dry that night.

There were a couple of cottonwoods—they seem to be able to thrive even if they only get watered once a year. I heard other troopers scattered through the paloverde, smoking and talking, and I was close enough I could hear the picketed horses stamp and fart and snort in the dark. But they weren't my responsibility that night.

I was just drifting off, looking up at the stars and catching a whiff of the woodfires and horses, feeling the night breeze in my hair when I caught the sound of a familiar voice.

"This'll be the only chance we have for months."

Then another voice I didn't know: "It's too risky."

"That ain't what you said the morning we swooped down on those Comanches."

"That was different."

"My feelings are the same."

"Oh hell."

Then I heard the sound of two men rolling up in their bedrolls. Then I heard them moving around again.

I knew I shouldn't, but I crept over to where they lay almost hidden behind a cluster of chaparral. There in the dim starlight I saw two naked men with their arms around each other. I didn't want to see it, but I did. I knew about men like that and I always thought they were womanlike with prissy ways. But these were two troopers, leather tough and ready for a fight. And one of them had a long, shallow scar running red down his shoulder.

I crept back to my blanket and couldn't sleep. I couldn't make the two ideas go together—that Shanley and that other man were that kind, and still regular troopers, too.

I still get a funny feeling, thinking about it. Here I'd been alone with him for four days and he never did a thing off-center. He cared for me like a baby, no liberties taken. I just couldn't put it together—he was strong and wiry, rode all day without a complaint. He'd saved my life. Yet, there he was, rolling around, doing God knows what with that other trooper. It made me nearly sick to think about it.

After that I kept my mouth shut and listened to see if the other men in our company knew about Shanley. Maybe I was just too green to cotton to him. But I heard nothing.

Shanley went along as he always had—getting things done, helping the new recruits, showing them how to keep warm in the mountains, winning shooting matches. I watched him, trying not to show I was watching. There was nothing priss about him.

The next time we had leave, I rode to Fort Grant with him. I wanted to say something, to ask him, to tell him what I'd seen. But there didn't seem to be any way to start. We rode mostly in silence, kept an eye out for Apaches and separated when we got there.

I went to a Mexican whorehouse not far from the fort. I'd bedded a few girls back home and I was hungry for the sight of a woman's flesh after living with men. Two of those little dark women were having at each other. It took me aback, but I didn't stop looking. I could see how women would like women because I like women. Just couldn't wrap my brain around the idea of men. I took the one with the curly hair and it was fast but friendly. Never made love to a woman who didn't speak English. I don't know what she was saying, but the words were soft like her body and her voice was high and sweet.

After a couple of days, my poke was gone, so I rode back to the fort to see if anyone else was heading to Bowie. A packtrain was leaving the next morning, so I slept where the packers spread their bedrolls. Early the next morning, they harnessed the mules and were ready to leave by nine. As the line of mules started out Shanley came riding up with another trooper.

"See you next chance I get," said the other trooper. It was the one who had been in the chaparral.

"If the Apaches don't see me first," said Shanley.

The other man slapped Shanley on the back with his hat and Shanley, looking seedy, trotted up to join the packtrain for Bowie.

The second day, Shanley and me, we decided to ride ahead of the train so we'd be at the fort that night. The train wasn't expected to get in before midday the next day.

I tried to think of something to say. I'd decided that as long as Shanley kept his preference to himself and didn't bother anybody in the company, I'd not say a word. But I wanted him to know I knew. I'm not sure just why. I owed him a lot for bringing me back when I was shot, but I didn't want him to think he could hold anything over me. That's mean, but there it is.

"Shanley," I began. Then I couldn't think what to say.

"What's that, button?"

"I know about you and that trooper at Fort Grant."

"What do you know?" He sounded cool and tough as always.

"I know what you and he, last winter when we bivouacked with all those companies that time, I know that . . ." I couldn't say it.

"That we're lovers."

"Guess that's about it."

He didn't say anything and I didn't say anything. Our horses trotted along in the dust. The sun was working its way behind mountains, throwing long shadows from the rocks. The desert smell, like a fresh broom, came up as the air cooled. The creak of the saddles sounded loud.

"Did you ever love a girl?" Shanley asked.

"I was right fond of Mary Bitterhagen, back home. We went to all the socials and church suppers together."

"Anything ever happen to her that made you feel bad?"

"You mean did she ever get hurt?"

"Yes." He waited and waited, so I went on: "One day she was riding along in a farm wagon. The wagon wheel hit a rock, and she and the driver almost fell, then the wheel came off and dumped her in the road. She broke her arm, but worse, she hit her head and never came to."

"That must've been hard to see."

"There she was, still looked like Mary, but she was gone. She breathed and they fed her and cleaned her up, but she was just a shell. Then she died."

"Did you love her?"

"Guess I did." I hadn't thought about Mary in a long time because it felt too bad. Now Shanley had brought all that back. I felt tears burn and the inside of my face hurt like it was all squeezed together.

"Picture this," said Shanley. "Someone, like Mary. And she saves your life, besides being the person you love the most."

"Like you saved me?"

"No. All I did was haul you back to the fort. Think of someone like Mary standing off a bunch of Comanches because your gun jammed. Shooting and covering you while you try to clear your Colt. And taking an arrow. And he kept on shooting, loaded and shot again. We ran off those Indians and waited all day in the heat without any water. Then he led the way, arrow in his leg and all, till we found the rest of the patrol."

He stopped and wiped his mouth with the back of his hand, and coughed. The horses clipped right along. We were a quarter mile from the post by now, trotting up the long hill.

"They liked to tore him to pieces, the surgeons, trying to get that arrowhead out. But he was too mean to die." Shanley coughed again. "Love's love and there's not so much in this world that I'm fool enough to turn my back on it."

"You never show nothing."

"The army don't take to men and men."

"You never did a thing when you were with me."

"Never will. This is just between me and my friend."

"I never said nothing."

"I know."

"I won't."

"Thanks."

"You did save my life, after all."

"Forget that horseshit. Think of me as the man who's going to beat you back to the post."

He kicked his horse's sides and took off for the corrals. It wasn't like him to push a tired mount, but I spurred my sorrel, too, and nearly caught him by the time we reached the watering tanks.

Uncle Harry's Flying Saucer Swimming Pool

JOHN KEEFAUVER

John Keefauver is unique. I said that last time, and I'm saying it again. The man is whacked-out—well, at least his writing is. John himself sounds like a pretty normal guy—almost. He lives out in Carmel and is not a personal friend of Clint Eastwood, the former mayor. He is that rare bird a professional short-story writer, and a good one. His story in The Best of the West *was one of the more popular ones, and I have a feeling the same will be said of this. Who else can mix ranch life, rubber, inflatable swimming pools, and flying saucers and make it work?*

Uncle Harry has done some screwy things in his time, like living in a bathtub one winter because he said it was cheaper to heat the water than the house, and another time collecting unemployment checks while he was in jail. And for a while there he was identifying himself as "a retired informed source." He wasn't what you'd call an average fellow. His latest, for example, was this flying saucer made out of a swimming pool.

He claimed that unidentified flying objects were portable rubber swimming pools he'd filled with helium and launched—not that anybody actually believed him, of course. Well, *we* didn't, anyway—Mom, Dad, and me. We knew better—or thought we did.

We first heard about his flying saucer swimming pool when he let out a bawl from the roof of our ranch house. He'd been sleeping up there for days, but he never would tell us why. We thought it was because he'd just come in out of the scrub and that he wanted to still live out of doors, even though it was on top a house. Dad had felt sorry for him and invited him in late summer to live with us on the ranch in exchange for some work, like keeping the snakes out of the pea patch and cattle inside fences he was supposed to keep mended. Uncle had reluctantly agreed to try it for a while; he must have been broke, or maybe his age was telling him that living in a lean-to wasn't smart anymore, especially during another Wyoming winter, which he knew was coming up.

Anyway, we didn't find out why he'd really moved up on the roof until one night when he let out a howl from up there. We ran up and saw him dancing around and cackling and bellowing, "There she goes! See it?" He was pointing off into the sky.

"See what, Uncle Harry?"

"My flying saucer swimming pool! Are you blind?"

We thought for sure he'd gone all the way off this time.

"Flying saucer swimming pool, Uncle Harry?"

"That's what I said—flying saucer swimming pool. I've inflated it with helium. You don't think a swimming pool can fly without being inflated with helium, do you?"

We said we guessed not.

He gave us one of his special dumb looks; then, real quick, he moved his finger a little bit, off toward a new direction. "Ain't she pretty! The only flying saucer in the world made out of a swimming pool! I'm going to use it to round up the cattle. I won't charge you a cent."

I looked where he was pointing. Don't ask me why. All I could see were stars and maybe a jet. I looked at Mom and Dad. They shook their heads —sorrowfully. They didn't see any flying swimming pool either.

"Do you need glasses?" he bawled when we didn't turn handsprings.

"But it's dark, Uncle Harry."

"Dark! Of course it's dark! That's why I've got it lit up with a red light. You think I want to get into trouble with the FAA? There! See that red light? That's my special flying saucer swimming pool navigation neon tube!"

We didn't see any flying navigation neon tube either.

"Don't you think you better get it down a little so the cattle can see it?" I said carefully.

"I will when I learn to aim it better. After all, this is my first one."

God help us if he went into mass production.

That was the beginning, and gradually we got the story. Uncle said he'd bought a rubber swimming pool, taken it to "my flying saucer lab on the roof," where he had attached an electrical gimmick to it that lit up a circular neon tube. Then he'd inflated the thing with helium instead of air and launched it in high glee.

That's what he told us, anyway, very seriously, and awful proud.

We didn't believe a word of it, of course. We're used to Uncle Harry. Although it's true we hadn't been up on the roof since he'd moved up there. He wouldn't let us.

Now, it didn't cause much commotion in town when Uncle started driving his beat-up pickup into town and going from door to door asking for cash donations. The local people all knew he was a little bit funny. But when he told them he needed the donations to buy swimming pools to make flying saucers out of, they thought they'd underestimated him for sure, especially when he started running up and down the main street, his finger pointed toward the sky, bellowing "There she goes!" Then often as not, he'd saunter into the local department store and say casually, "My last order for rubber swimming pools come in yet, Moe?"

"Not yet, Uncle Harry," owner Moe would say. (He knew what to say.)

"Well, when it does let me know. I'm running short." And he'd saunter out of the store as if he owned the place.

And we didn't mind his running up and down the street yelling so much. We figured it was better to humor him than to fight him. But when he nailed a big sign on the side of the ranch house—after first putting an ad in the town's little weekly, *Cowpoke Gazette*—that read, "See flying saucer swimming pool on inventor's launching pad—$1," we kind of re-volted. We didn't much care for all kinds of people—mostly strangers, too, because the town people knew better—banging in the house and up the stairs and onto the roof, especially when the only saucer they saw was the dirty one under Uncle Harry's coffee cup. We objected, and we let Uncle know it too.

He got all up in a huff about our objecting. Said we were just jealous because we didn't have any flying swimming pools of our own. Getting so a man couldn't even make an honest living anymore, he told us, drawing himself up to his full five feet three and trying to flatten his gut inside his jeans.

Well, our relationship went on for quite a time like this—sour—with him trying to get people on the roof and us trying to keep 'em off (and with snakes probably swarming through the pea patch), and it might have gone on for the rest of our lives if Sweetbread Monroe hadn't come to town.

Sweetbread was a gigantic fat woman about Mom's age, and every time I saw her she was dressed up in tons of jewelry, big jangly things dangling from her arms and back. She looked like the Queen of Garage Sales and smelled like a gallon of perfume had been spilled over her. Her face was painted up like a barber's pole, only more, especially her eyes. First time I saw her—at the front door—I backed up.

"I want to see the man who makes jewelry out of wisdom teeth," she said.

"Beg your pardon?"

She said it again—I'd heard her right!—but before I could tell her she was at the wrong place, Uncle Harry came busting down from the roof, which he was in the habit of doing when he suspected we were trying to keep a flying swimming pool customer from coming up. "Step right in, madam," said he, all smiles. "If you'll follow me up to my launching pad, you may see, with your own eyes, the only flying saucer swimming pool in captivity."

"Are you the man," said she, sort of gushing, "that makes jewelry out of wisdom teeth? I saw your ad."

That stopped him—but only for a minute. "That was last week," he said.

"Darn!" she said. "I've been saving mine for years for something special, and now I'm a week too late."

Then she gave our uncle a certain look and smile that made *him* back up.

He started to close the door but she barged right in, sort of giggling, and did everything but throw her arms around him. "Flying swimming pools! How delightful! I've always wanted to meet a different man. Let me *see.*"

Right then was the first time I'd ever seen Uncle Harry show any reluctance about his invention. "Closed up for the day," he told her. "Locked up tight."

She didn't make a move to leave. "Aw, come on, show Sweetbread."

Then she sort of cooed and grabbed him by the arm, and the next thing I knew she was pushing him toward the roof. Mom and Dad weren't home, and there was no way I could stop them by myself.

From that day on Uncle Harry would duck whenever he'd see Sweetbread Monroe coming. He'd bolt the door, run out the back. He even took down his $1 sign—which made us root for Sweetbread, all right. But she didn't give up. Even if she never got inside again, she came jangling up to the ranch almost every day—sometimes more than once—always with her wisdom tooth in her purse; she couldn't seem to get it through her head that teeth were last week. Hardest on Uncle Harry, though, was that he couldn't run up and down the street hardly at all anymore, yelling and cackling and pointing toward the sky, without running into her and having to have to run the other way.

I guess the battle between Uncle Harry and Sweetbread Monroe would have gone on into the fall, or forever, if she hadn't made the mistake of coming to the ranch one night with a bald wig for him.

Now, our uncle has pounds of thick, red, shiny hair on his head, of which he is awful proud. So when Sweetbread, at the door, gave him this bald wig to cover up his red glory with, you could tell she had made her final mistake as far as Uncle Harry was concerned.

"I like bald-headed men," she tittered, not noticing that his eyes were beginning to smoke and his face was turning as red as his hair.

"You do, huh?" he muttered.

"Uh-huh," she giggled. "It's something about the shine."

Uncle Harry's eyes got as black as poison. "You want to see my latest flying saucer swimming pool?" He didn't smile once, much less cackle. "It's the biggest one yet."

"I'd love to, Harry dear."

Without a word, and looking right through us, he took her elbow and, as she tittered and squealed, led her up to the roof. He was almost solemn. We didn't try to stop them. By now, Sweetbread was hardly a stranger.

We didn't go up, of course. We never went up. We knew what the roof looked like, and we didn't want to encourage him with any show of interest toward a swimming pool or flying saucer or whatever he had up there, if anything. Besides, he wouldn't let us.

We listened, though. A peaceful and solemn Uncle Harry puzzled us. It was quiet on the roof for maybe ten minutes. Then we heard this awful shriek from Sweetbread. "Harry, don't! EEEEEeeeee!" Then her voice gradually quieted—to be replaced by Uncle Harry's cackling and laughing and bellowing. He was back to normal, and we relaxed.

In a minute he came down from the roof by himself, all smiles.

"Where's Sweetbread?" we asked.

Grinning like a madman—or saint—he led us onto the empty roof and pointed toward the sky, awful proud. And, sure enough, in the distance there was a red light moving away.

Mountain Laurel

BETTY TRAYLOR GYENES

This is Betty Traylor Gyenes's first published fiction. Two years ago, she wrote her first short story, which won a first-place award at a local college where she was enrolled in a creative writing class, and another of her stories was a finalist for PEN Southwest. She lives in Texas, but is originally from Arkansas, which she describes as "the land of opportunity, poor folks, and glorious scenery." She has a husband named Paul, two daughters, Melanie and Kimberly, and she considers herself a romantic at heart—in fact, she has a heart collection. But I think it's telling that one of the hearts in that collection is made of barbed wire!

The following story, though somewhat romantic in feel, has a powerful undercurrent that flows through the best coming-of-age stories. And if it isn't a literary barbed-wire heart, I don't know what is.

My sister Laurel was sixteen when she met the outlaw Jesse James. Ma had named Laurel after the wild bush that clings to the mountainside and fills the rocky crevices with pale, pink blooms. Wild and tenacious—that was Laurel—like her namesake.

It had been a stifling day. Dry-mouthed birds chirped wearily in the dusty August shadows when my younger brother Jeb and me spotted riders on the mountain. We ran straight as an Indian arrow to the shed where Pa was stacking wood for the bleak Ozark winter hovering just around the corner.

Jeb was hollering so loud that Pa grabbed him by his scrawny ridged neck and shook him like he was a Sunday-dinner-chicken. "Pa!" I said. "There's riders in the woods—up on the mountain—a gang of 'em!" My lungs were heaving from the sliding run down the mountain.

Pa stared out at the green, dense trees and knotted up his bushy brows. We watched a whitetail doe venture to the edge of the clearing. Her shiny nostrils quivered briefly in the sulky breeze before she bounded back into the cool, dark depths of the forest. Strangers on the mountain might mean trouble. Thieves or robbers or outlaws maybe. My rusty toes scrunched in the dust, and I shuddered.

"Tell your ma," Pa said and ruffled Jeb's corn-silk hair. "Git on now!"

In the house, Ma smoothed down her apron like she was getting ready to meet company and carefully took down the Winchester from off the pegged wall in the bedroom. She patted the rifle with her flour-streaked hands, bits of biscuit dough still embedded in her worn nails. "Ben, go fetch Laurel," she told me quietly. I could see the restless fear in her somber eyes, could even smell the sour odor. I'd hunted in the woods too long not to know the smell of fear.

I couldn't find Laurel. She wasn't hoeing weeds in the garden like she was supposed to, and she wasn't dallying in the outhouse neither. Laurel was always sneaking off from her chores. Most likely, she'd be down at the rock-infested creek picking wildflowers and peering at her watery reflection in the shady, murky mirror. I caught her doing that once, and she knocked me for a loop. I told Jeb I fell down and split my lip on a rock. But Laurel wasn't at the creek—and my heart started hammering, scared. Outlaws in the woods and Laurel missing!

It wasn't long before she came traipsing into the house and clutching a bunch of wilted Shasta daisies. Ma rushed over to Laurel and slapped her. The flowers fell from Laurel's fingers and spattered the wooden floor with scarlet petals.

"Now, Lula, calm down," Pa said; then he scowled at Laurel, his eyes narrowing to sober slits. "Where you been, girl?"

"In the woods, Pa," Laurel was always stubborn and tight-mouthed as a jar lid. Why, you had to pry anything out of her; she hid her thoughts to herself like precious secrets. Ma said she was maturing, but I thought that sounded disgusting—like a heifer getting ready to breed. I was fourteen then, and living on a scratched-out hillside farm, we weren't dumb about the birds and bees and honey, so to speak. Laurel's shirtwaisted front used to be flat as a corncake. She had stretched up tall and willowy, and her neck was long and white and swan-like, and little peachy freckles speckled her nose and thin, angular arms. She used to wrestle with me and Jeb in the barn, slinging loose hay in our hair, her eyes laughing, bright and blue as a barn cat's. But now, she sat outside, alone, on hot summer evenings gazing at the sparkly stars. "Why, I feel like I could reach up and pull one down," I heard her whisper once, her voice all full of shy wonder. She looked frightened now, a loose muscle twitching beneath a hollowed-out dimple in her flushed cheek where Ma had struck her.

"You seen any men in the woods?" Jeb asked.

Laurel's eyes got big and round as a china saucer, and the blue depths flickered with pinpoint yellow flames. She pursed her white lips even tighter. Then the dogs let loose a howling racket, and we heard horses neighing and stomping nervously. Next came a knock booming at the stout wooden door. We all jumped like jackrabbits. All except Laurel. She stood there swaying, her long hair draped like brown lace across her sloping shoulders.

A man called out, "Hey, you folks! Got a favor to ask . . . Anybody home?"

"I met them in the woods, Pa," Laurel said quickly. "They asked who owned the farm, and I told you did, Pa. They don't mean us any harm . . . I believed them . . ." Her words flew out suddenly like a startled dove in the brush. Laurel hadn't talked that much in months and months.

Forty years of mountain living were etched on Pa's face as he nodded to Ma and walked straight-backed to the door. Jeb hollered, "No!" I put my shaky arm around his hunched shoulder. Ma mumbled something—prayer, I think—and I was real glad she knew God pretty good.

Pa wrenched the door open and stepped outside into the thick heavy heat. There were five men astride fine-blooded horses lathering in the sickly haze. "I'm Frank James," said one bearded man who looked, to me, like a bookish schoolteacher. "This is my brother, Jesse." He waved a rifle toward a dusty, dandied fellow bowing hypocritically to us from atop his white-legged sorrel. Jeb and me looked like two idiots with our mouths hanging wide. We had heard whispered tales about these outlaw Confederates turned bank robbers. Why, even trains weren't sacred to them. "We want to camp yonder ways," Frank said, while Jesse sat there, silent as a snake. "Don't want any trouble, just be around a few days." Five pair of hard eyes glittered at us.

I could see on Pa's upper lip sweat blisters dripping onto his handlebars. He wasn't no stupid man, and he showed his manners too. "No trouble atall," he said in a tone flat and smooth as a creek-bed rock. And that's how we all met Jesse James and his outlaws. Only I wasn't no moon-eyed girl falling in love with him.

Jesse was good looking for a murderer, with a sweet boyish face and a short-sawed nose and eyes that were blued steel, reckless. As his horse danced around the dog's feet, Jesse studied Laurel with his long-lashed gaze. He reminded me of a fox about to pounce.

She lowered her eyes, and behind that demure droop of lids, there was a flash like lightning in a blue, blue sky. I knew there would be trouble.

It didn't take long for Pa to set us straight. Later, over Ma's best cracked bowl brimming with butter beans and wedges of salt pork, Pa warned us tersely, "Boys, stay away from those men. They're like hunted animals, and they're liable to lash out at anybody who gets in their way." He pointed a long brown finger at us. "I'll get the strap to you, I will, if I catch you near them." Pa was a deacon at the Baptist church in the holler, and he never lied. But that didn't stop Laurel.

The day after the James gang rode up to our house, I caught Laurel sneaking out to the woods. I followed her. She climbed the hillside, nimble and fleet-footed as a bobcat with a hungry purpose. The hot wind whipped at her long-tailed hair and flapped her calico dress like crows' wings. I hid behind some brush as Laurel, breathless and shy-eyed, came up to the waterfall spilling over the mossy ledge into the creek below. Behind the fall there was a cave, an old Indian hideout. It was cooler in the sun-dappled shade, green and glowing with hushed light, and the gentle moans of the tumbling water were soothing to my strained, craning nerves.

From behind a glistening screen, a man ambled out waving a mean-looking six-shooter. "Whoa there," he yelled. "Oh, it's the little girlie from the farm." A gap-toothed leer crawled onto his bristled face. "Hey, Jesse," he called from over his shoulder. "You got a vistor!"

Mosquitoes fought for territory on my arms and legs as I wriggled in agony. Then out swaggered Jesse James, with his gun belt cinched tightly around his waist and four long-barreled revolvers peeking out of their fancy embossed holsters. He carried a surly looking shotgun. Why, he was a walking arsenal! I ducked lower and slapped at a whine near my ear. A fine sheen of mist covered his tanned face as he smiled at Laurel. Ah! What a smile! Jesse had a Sunday-going-to-meeting innocence and a devil-don't-care grin all shoelaced into one smile. He threw back his flowing black hair and laughed at something Laurel said, and the sound blended with the music of the water, echoing against the red, ragged cliffs. He was a gentleman, he was, right down to his string tie dangling from his neck, and he entertained Laurel like she was in the grandest parlor. They perched on the lichen-covered rocks by the emerald creek with Jesse's rifle propped between them and talked till the dying sun had melted into buttery streaks in the russet sky. Finally, Laurel stood up and lifted her soggy skirt hem and hurried away. She glanced back once, almost coyly, but Jesse was a ghostly wraith disappearing behind the cascading curtain.

I stayed put for a while, till I noticed a hot-tongued copperhead slithering near my bare foot. Slowly, ever so slowly, I eased my stiffened body away, wishing I could move faster. Jesse's six-shooters would come in handy right then. I could picture blowing that snake's fangs to Kingdom Come, I could. I hobbled after Laurel, my mouth dry as bitter dust.

At the supper table that night, the flickering coal-oil lamps cast a shadowy luster on Laurel's quiet face. She looked different. Ma spoke sharply. "Laurel, I said to pass the biscuits down." Laurel started, her secretive eyes colliding with mine. I grinned, my mouth full of hot bread. She blushed pink as those flowers she's named after, while Ma groped for a biscuit like a blind woman.

Outside the crystal moon shimmered like a grand lady's brooch pinned to a dark velvet gown. Awhile later on the porch steps, with her arms wrapped around her knees, Laurel stared upwards; and there was the touch of the moon on her shoulders and through her hair and the look of the moon in her eyes. And I was afraid.

The next day it was a burning yellow noon, and Jeb and me were splitting logs on the hillside when we saw plumes of dust rising off the trail from town. We ran for the house, then stopped in our tracks when we saw the sheriff and a rowdy posse culled from the riffraff that littered the hills.

Sheriff Holt shifted in his saddle to greet us. "How do, boys." He tipped his beat-up hat graciously in our direction and scratched his wadded hair. "Mr. Joiner," he said to Pa, who had come up behind us, "I declare you got a couple of long-legged scraps here! Growing like weeds, ain't they?" He grinned sourly as his handsome bay swished his tail at some ornery flies. "I heard tell that the James gang was seen hereabouts . . . thought to warn you." He hawked out some oily tobacco juice right on top of Ma's zinnia patch. "Robbed a bank up in Missoura, and Jesse kilt the cashier . . ."

Jeb tried not to look at me. It felt like a hard fist had been shoved in my throat—suffocating, tickling. I choked on a cough, and Jeb giggled. Sheriff Holt stared at us like a sloe-eyed lizard. Near the corner of the house, I saw a wisp of brown gingham, and I knew Laurel had heard. "Probably hiding out in some caves around here," he said. The posse was getting restless, horses trampling, snorting in irritable excitement.

Pa nodded quickly and said, "I'll shore keep a lookout." The posse left a gritty cloud of dirt filling our eyes. Back on the porch, Pa leaned back in his ladder-back chair and whittled on a knobby stick and stared out at the white-hot sky.

Toward evening, Ma called Laurel to help with supper. She stood out in the yard, her squinched eyes fighting the glare. Her face reddened, the color of old blood. One of the hounds begged on his belly to her, hoping for a scrap. "Ben, you seen Laurel?" She ignored Blue's pitiful look, and there was a hoarse struggle in her voice, almost a resignedness.

"No ma'am," I said, my eyes shifting away. Had Laurel gone to warn Jesse? Ma sighed and shuffled on her tired feet. "But I'll find her, Ma," I promised, jumping off the porch and shooing all the dogs back.

Halfway up the mountain, I spotted the posse tracking the trail toward the waterfall. Their quiet stealthiness was more menacing than a gunshot. I hightailed it through the woods and took a shortcut.

The crickets had started their nightly gossip and fireflies courted on flaming wings when I crawled up close to the outlaw camp. The breath of the mountain filled the cooling twilight with the scent of sassafras. In the distance, an owl blinked moon-bright eyes and hooted nervously.

There Laurel stood, near the waterfall, with her shawled arms tightly hugging herself. Her stricken face held all the anger and grief of a withered flower corrupted by the first frost. A lone horse and rider suddenly appeared out of the darkening trees, a darker silhouette against the garnet and gold of the horizon. Laurel's hair was streaked with mist and fire. She was as still as death.

Other horsemen followed. The gang was leaving! Laurel! I almost ran towards her. Don't go, I wanted to scream, but my voice was as silent as the shifting light. Jesse rode up to Laurel and reached down, hauling her slender bones all the way up the side of his prancing horse. Jesse's black brimmed hat sheltered their faces, but I thought they must be kissing. Then, he dropped her slowly back down to the packed clay, and a puddle of pine needles splashed against her ankles. The horses turned and felt their way gingerly down the blackening mountain; their hooves clumped dully on the mossy rocks. Hunched forward in his saddle, Jesse never looked back.

Laurel swayed like a willow branch in the night wind. The fringe of her shawl wrapped its white fingers around her clenched arms. I edged closer and whispered loudly above the haunting voice of the waterfall, "Laurel!" I caught my breath when she looked at me. Her eyes were no longer moon-soft, but cold and clear and wise as those stars popping out of the purple sky.

"Let's go home, Ben," Laurel said finally, her voice a sluggish feather brushing the air. I shivered and stumbled after her, and she reached out and clutched my hand. We braced ourselves against the mountain wind. Laurel never looked back.

Distant Thunder

GARY L. RAISOR

Gary L. Raisor has made his reputation in the field of horror and dark fantasy. His work is best exemplified by very short, tightly constructed, twist-ending stories that use humor in the most brutal of ways, "Cheapskate," which first appeared in Night Cry, *being a prime example. What follows, however, is not short. It is a horror Western right out of the* Weird Tales *tradition, but with a modern sensibility. And it's also much better written than the bulk of those pulp stories. So settle back and enjoy.*

Kansas, the Summer of 1872
It was hotter than hell in July.

Matt Thomas, employed by the Santa Fe Railroad, sat his horse and stared into the distance, watching the herd of buffalo he had tracked to a small, meandering creek. His fingers drummed a tattoo on the rifle butt that jutted from its scabbard. A trickle of sweat wormed its way down his forehead, causing him to pull out an already soaked handkerchief and mop at his face, causing him to swear at the heat that was making an unpleasant job even more unpleasant.

His job was killing buffalo.

He'd been a trapper, a scout, a prospector, and a few other things he didn't particularly care to dwell on. A large man, he had been eroded a little by time, but like the mountains he called home, he expected to stand a while longer.

Matt waited quietly and finally his patience was rewarded as the herd tired of wallowing in the creek and moved out to graze. He swung down, hobbled his horse, and reached across the saddle to ease out his .50 Sharps along with a tripod to rest it on. Even though the rifle weighed nearly sixteen pounds, there had been a day when he hadn't needed anything to hold it steady. The years were taking his strength, and he guessed, maybe, they were taking his mind, because the last several nights he'd been having dreams. Bad dreams.

Once again he played out the scene in his mind, and fear laid icy hands on his back, causing him to shiver.

Remembering how . . .

It was so much clearer than any dream he'd ever had before.

Remembering . . .

. . . standing on a vast plain that was without life of any kind, and beneath his feet, the earth was cracked and dry, untouched by even the memory of rain. Overhead the sky was a sullen brass color, cloudless, holding a sun that burned down much too brightly. When he stared at the mountains on the horizon, he saw a distant shadowy figure that was no larger than a speck moving toward him. The figure appeared to be walking slowly, yet it closed the distance between them with incredible speed as though each step covered many hundreds of miles. Then somewhere, farther back, came a sound like distant thunder rolling across the plain, and Matt could make out clouds of darkness billowing up behind the walking man. A huge storm was brewing out there and, it, too, was coming toward him with unnatural speed . . .

. . . and Matt had awakened before he could quite make out the distant figure or the blackness moving his way. He was glad of it, because there was something unnerving about the whole thing, something that left the taste of dust in his throat.

Maybe his mind was going, maybe he didn't sleep too good at night, but right now, he had a job to do. He laid the rifle on the tripod. With a motion born of long practice, he licked his thumb, rubbed it across the bead and sighted in on the shaggy old bull that led the herd.

He squeezed the trigger, hearing the rifle give a flat crack that raced across the prairie. A puff of dust erupted from the hide. The bull, mortally wounded with a bullet through the heart, staggered forward a few feet. Streaks of red spurted from the animal's nose before his legs gave way and he collapsed into a boneless heap. The rest began bawling and milling around, spooked by the smell of blood.

They kept milling, and Matt kept shooting, picking off the ones standing at the edge of the herd with an almost mechanical accuracy, until they were all dead. He felt no pride in what he had done. A lot of meat was needed to feed the railroad work crews; he was paid to deliver that meat.

Before riding back to camp and sending out the skinners, he thought he

might ride over and get himself a tongue or two for cooking. He was tired
of beans. His movements were slow as he swung down and hobbled his
horse. Too many winters spent wading through icy streams during his days
as a trapper had left him with a touch of rheumatism that sitting on the
ground aggravated something fierce.

He picked out a likely animal, pulled out his knife and started cutting.
A sound floated through the stillness.

What?

Pausing, he straightened up and looked around. Nothing. His ears must
be playing tricks. He went back to work and after he had the first tongue
wrapped, he started in on the second. A feeling of unease curled up
between his shoulder blades.

"Damn it, something's wrong," he muttered, jabbing the knife into the
hard ground and raising up from his task.

Scanned the area.

Didn't see anything.

Wiped the sweat from his eyes . . . and saw a huge bull staring at
him.

The animal was hurt, hurt bad, the fur along its right side was soaked
with blood, welling up from a jagged tear on the shoulder like water from
an underground spring. Dazed, Matt watched as it trailed down to spatter
softly into the dust . . . *pat* . . . *pat* . . . *pat.* Somewhere, far removed, he could hear the sound of flies buzzing. It was a lazy hum. Not
real.

Matt risked a look at his horse, calculating the distance. Too far. Besides, he'd never get the hobbles off in time, but if he could get closer, he
might have some chance. He took a step in that direction. It was enough
to goad the animal into action.

He yanked the .44 out of his belt and thumbed back the hammer.
Taking aim at the bull, he realized there was no chance for a killing shot,
especially with his old revolver. He'd be better off throwing rocks. To
make matters worse, the animal had its head lowered, protecting the heart
and lungs with a skull that was massive bone and almost impossible to
penetrate. But it was the only target he had. The pistol jumped in his
hand and the bullet smacked into the head with a thud, like an ax biting
into hardwood. He would have taken a moment to admire his own shooting—except that old bull was still coming on like a highballing locomotive
and he looked like the next stop.

"Matt, old son, looks like you done stepped in it good this time." He
leveled the pistol back onto its target, pulled back the hammer, and

squeezed the trigger again. The bullet struck home *and still it came forward.*

The animal's ragged breathing filled his ears as it chewed up the distance between them.

Matt had three shots left. Taking careful aim, he placed them as close as he could to the first two. No good. He was going to be gored, or most likely trampled . . . when it missed a step, staggered, missed another step and pitched forward. The old bull almost recovered for a moment, then faltered and sank to its knees, a felled tree swaying in the wind before finally toppling over onto its side. Dust geysered upward.

"I'm getting too old for this," Matt slowly breathed into the silence, letting his body uncoil as he sank to his knees. He yanked off his hat and wiped his forehead with a sleeve, letting a sigh of relief pass through his clenched lips. That had been close. Too close. He stood there with the pistol dangling from fingers that twitched and jerked with a life all their own.

After a few minutes, his breathing returned to normal and his hands quit shaking enough for him to shake the cartridge casings out of his revolver. To hell with the tongue; he wasn't that hungry anymore. He started toward his horse when . . .

. . . the impossible happened . . .

. . . and the blood-splattered animal lurched upright and came lumbering at him again. A precious moment was lost as he stood nailed to the spot, staring in disbelief before his hand darted into his pocket, trying to dig out more shells.

Wrong pocket.

He always put them in the left pocket.

Did he even have any more shells?

His fingers closed around one.

Racing against time he desperately tried to reload, fumbling with a cartridge that seemed too big to slide into the cylinder. He risked a look out of the corner of his eye and saw the animal was nearly on top of him. Cursing his stiff joints, he managed at last to jam a shell into the chamber. Snapping it into place, he raised the gun and fired, all in one motion. The bull was rocked back as though poleaxed, caving in at the knees, yet Matt knew the slug wouldn't be enough to stop the headlong charge.

Matt attempted to throw himself out of the way, but he was out of time and all he could do was watch. For some strange reason, he expected it to hurt more than it did, because he heard more than felt something snap in his right leg.

Darkness swallowed him . . .

. . . and Matt shaded his eyes and looked for the walking man, but the strange shadowy figure was nowhere to be found, and then to his amazement he saw the blackness gathering on the horizon wasn't a storm—it was a giant herd of buffalo, countless untold numbers of buffalo stretching across the prairie, a herd so large he couldn't see the end of it. The earth began to tremble as they swept toward him like wildfire driven before the wind, chasing the daylight from the sky.

Mesmerized by the enormity of what he was witnessing, he stood rooted on that dry, cracked earth watching their progress for what seemed an eternity, and all during that time the herd kept moving toward him, becoming clearer and clearer. Gradually they drew near enough for him to see there was something wrong with them, dreadfully wrong. As he stared at the animals, his gaze widened. Somehow, they were all wounded, terrible gaping wounds that streamed blood until the ground was soaked, until the very air became filled with the sickly sweet scent of copper. In a moment he would be crushed in the stampede. He raised his hands in an effort to fend off the inevitable, and when his fingers closed around the coarse fur of the first animal . . .

. . . his eyes jerked open . . .

. . . and he stared uncomprehendingly at the fur clutched in his hands. After a moment he realized it belonged to the buffalo he'd killed earlier. As he lay pinned beneath the carcass, he could still hear the thunder of the giant herd echoing in his head. Finally the sound died and he saw he had been unconscious for hours, because while he'd been dreaming, the night had crept close.

He took quick inventory. Everything seemed to be in working order, except his right leg, which no longer felt like it belonged to him. When he tried to move, he found he couldn't, and for the first time today a grim smile touched his lips. "This is a fine how-de-do," he said. "Just fine. I can see the marker now: 'Here lies Matt Thomas, kilt when a dead buffalo fell on top of him.' Probably get me in all the history books."

Matt spat blood and began working his leg from beneath the crushing weight, fighting pain so intense he bit into his lip to keep from crying out. It was slow going. But after nearly an hour of digging, he managed to work his leg free. He studied the damage. It was bad, no doubt about that; his foot hung at an unnatural angle, and when he pulled up his pants leg, he could see red-edged shards of bone poking through. The trip to his horse seemed to take slightly less than a hundred years and he was bathed in blood and sweat by the time he pulled himself into the saddle.

Each time his horse took a step, a slow rhythmic drumbeat of agony marched up his leg, and he couldn't say it was a tune he enjoyed. But at least it kept him from passing out. By the time the campfires swam into view, he felt like he'd ridden halfway across Kansas. When he went to swing down, he found he couldn't lift his leg.

"Would somebody mind getting me down from here?" he growled. "I think my ass is stuck to the saddle."

A buzz of indistinct voices was his answer, and then hands reached out and pulled him from the horse. As they lowered him to the ground, he tried to give them directions to the dead buffalo. If they didn't get there soon, a lot of meat would be ruined by scavengers.

A bottle found its way into his hands and he tipped it up, taking a long pull. When the whiskey hit bottom in his stomach, it felt like a fire had been built down there. Warmth spread through him and the pain was starting to recede a little when somebody grabbed his arms. Somebody else began tugging on his broken leg. White-hot agony lanced through Matt, and he did the only sensible thing he'd done all day; he fainted dead away . . .

. . . *and the herd of wounded buffalo passed right through him—a dark, swiftly flowing river that could be seen but not touched. He realized they were no more than shadows, yet the earth shook and he heard the heaving sounds they made when they galloped past. Fear drove them. Their eyes were rolled back, showing only the whites, and strings of saliva dripped from their straining mouths.*

From out of their midst the shadowy speck he'd first seen appeared, moving toward him like a swimmer fighting a strong current. As the speck neared, he saw it was an Indian dressed in nothing but gray tattered buckskins and a stovepipe hat, like some kind of make-believe wooden figure that shopkeepers put out front to hold cigars. No tribal markings of any sort decorated the copper-skinned body, and when Matt looked at the face, he saw it was rigid and unmoving, as though it weren't real, as though it were a mask meant to conceal what the figure really looked like. The Indian, neither young nor old, approached to within a few feet, doffed its hat and began capering and prancing about like some kind of puppet operated by a clumsy child. The effect should have been comical, yet there was nothing funny about the disjointed scarecrow who confronted him.

And there was nothing funny about the knife that caught the rays of the sun in a blinding flash. At first Matt thought the man meant to attack him; instead the Indian placed the blade against his own chest and slid it downward, slicing off a strip of skin which he held out to Matt. There was still no expression on the man's face, though Matt somehow sensed great anger.

Matt turned away from the grisly offering, and when he looked back he saw the Indian now had no features. While he stood there staring, the face of the stranger began taking shape. And as the face continued to form, the figure walked toward him with its arms open wide, as if it meant to embrace him. When they were almost near enough to touch, blood began welling from the corner of its eyes and started rolling down the cheeks . . . like tears.

Matt wheeled around to run, but something held him to the spot. A quick look over his shoulder and, to his horror, he knew the face—his own blood-stained features stared back.

The figure smiled and beckoned. Matt redoubled his efforts to escape, but now they were only inches apart. The face began to melt, bubbling up like wax from a hot candle, revealing the skull beneath, revealing empty black eye sockets that watched him hungrily. Matt fell to his knees in mindless terror. The figure loomed over him, and an instant before the skeletal fingers closed around his arm . . .

. . . he awoke . . .

. . . to the familiar but deafening din of railroad construction: men yelling, harness creaking, pickaxes and sledges pounding loud enough to raise the dead. That was an apt description of how he felt when he sat up. Fragmented, murky images from the nightmare chased across his mind; then remembering, he looked down to see his leg bandaged, splinted, and that he was lying on a cot in the track boss's car. Throwing back the blanket, he gingerly swung his legs around and sat them on the floor. Darkness obscured his vision as he fought to remain upright. After a bit, his head cleared and he looked down at the purple discolorations that stood out around his ribs. They didn't feel busted. But his leg was a different story, throbbing like a bad tooth as he balanced himself and began hopping toward the door.

He pushed it open and peered out, wincing at the heat that slammed into him. His eyes fastened onto the track boss, a beefy Irishman with receding red hair by the name of John Kirkpatrick. Matt tried to call out, but all that came from his throat were croaks.

"Well, it's about time you got your lazy butt out of bed," John said, relief plainly written on his face as he walked over with a canteen. "We was about to give you up for dead. What the hell happened? Your horse fall on you?"

"No," Matt laughed, lowering the canteen, "I ran out of cartridges and I had to throw the last one by hand."

As Matt finished relating the incident, John said, "You're a lucky man. Sounds like you damn near met your match out there. If that bull had got hold of you, there wouldn't have been enough left for a good Christian burial. Not that," he concluded with a grin, "anybody ever mistook you for a good Christian."

Matt rubbed a hand across his bristly face and looked down, trying to hide his unease. "Did Doc say anything about my leg?"

John didn't answer right away, and when he did, he wouldn't meet Matt's eyes. "I got to get back to work. I'll send the doc over and he can tell you all about it. You need anything?"

"Yeah, ask old Corky if he could send over some grub."

After a while, one of the mess boys brought over something that vaguely resembled beans. Matt took one look. "Shit, ain't these the same beans we had day before yesterday?"

"Yep, the same. Corky says he ain't cooking nothing else till they're all gone."

"You try feeding them to the dogs?"

"They won't touch 'em neither."

Matt had almost choked down the last of his beans when Dr. Marigold Fraser appeared, quiet and dark as a raincloud on an autumn day. The mournful doctor was something of a mystery around these parts. A lot of folks in camp had their own ideas why the small, portly man had come west. Some said the doc'd killed a man back East in a duel over a rich dowager and was fleeing the rope; some said he'd sobered up enough to get a good look at her and had decided he didn't need the money that bad. Still others claimed a few too many snorts of peach brandy before an amputation had led to some slight misunderstanding about which of a patient's legs was supposed to come off.

It was a source of endless speculation. What the truth was, nobody knew.

Doc didn't say anything at first, just slapped some dust off a black suit that had more shine to it than a newly minted silver dollar. He eased his bulk into a chair that groaned in protest.

"How's business?" Matt inquired, to be polite. He knew Doc had few patients. The fact that he owned a half interest in a funeral parlor might've had something to do with it.

"Been pretty good lately," Doc said, cleaning his glasses. "We buried three last week."

Matt glanced up from his plate to see if his visitor was kidding. Doc's face never changed expression, and Matt was glad he didn't play poker with the good doctor.

"I got good news and I got bad news," Doc continued, putting his glasses back on. "Which one you want first?"

"The bad."

"That leg of yours is busted in three places," the dour man replied. "I set it as best I could, but with a break that bad and your age being what it is, I can't make no guarantees. You should be able to walk, but you can count on having a bad limp."

"What's the good news?"

"You'll always know when it's going to rain." Doc smiled—and the smile vanished quicker than a rabbit down a hole, so quick Matt wasn't sure he'd even seen it.

Matt gave up on the beans and pushed them aside. "How soon before I can travel?"

"Like I said, a lot depends on how fast you mend." Doc pushed up his glasses. In the blink of an eye, they returned to their former position on the tip of his nose. "Let's just say you'll know when you feel up to moving around." With that he got up, slapped some more dust off his suit before advising Matt to keep his wounds clean.

As Doc left, Matt pulled out his pipe, letting his thoughts turn inward, back to the days when he had lived among the Oglala, back to the days before everything had gotten fouled up between the red man and the white man. Sometimes he longed to go back, but he knew there would be no welcome for him now. Of late he had begun thinking a lot about old places, old times, and old friends.

And dying.

When his eyes closed, his sleep was without dreams.

The days passed, and Doc assured Matt that he was healing up good for a man his age. Matt spent most of the time whittling himself a walking stick. He was sitting in an almost nonexistent patch of shade working on it when John Kirkpatrick came over.

"I talked to Mr. Simpson this morning, and he says you can stay on till you're fit enough to go back to work." He waited for Matt's response, eager as a puppy that had just spied his first rabbit.

"Well, John, you can kindly thank Mr. Simpson for his offer. But soon as I'm able, I'm going into business for myself . . . the hide business," Matt added, folding up his knife and putting it away. "Way I figure, one good season and I can retire."

John shook his head sadly and looked at Matt as though the older man had gone simple. His voice was dead earnest. "You'll get yourself kilt for sure. There's a war on, in case you ain't heard. Your hair'll end up decoratin' the lodgepole of some young buck."

"I got the answer to that," Matt said. "I'm going to take you with me, John, 'cause it's for damn sure no self-respecting Indian would ever be caught with *your* scalp."

Red-faced, John ran a hand across his head, smoothing down the few strands of hair that still sprouted there. "I can see it ain't no use trying to talk sense to you, Matt. When you set your mind, you have got to be the most stubborn, mule-headed son of a—"

"I hate to interrupt," Matt said, " 'specially before you get to the interesting parts. It ain't often I get a good Irish cussin', but I think I'm going to need a partner."

"You serious?" John asked.

Matt nodded. "You know anybody might be interested?"

"Yeah, I might know of someone. He's a new man, name of Kyle McCreedy. He ain't been here no time and he's already making noises about quittin'. Says the work's too hard for the money. Been complainin' about the cookin' too." John looked perplexed. "I don't know what he's hollerin' about. We only work twelve hours a day, all you can eat, and thirty-five dollars a month—just like clockwork."

"Some people just don't know when they got it good," Matt agreed. He had to look down at his walking stick to keep from laughing. A moment later he was serious as he thought how he sure could use an extra pair of legs. "Would you send him over when you get a chance?"

The shadows were stretching toward evening, and Matt was cleaning his Sharps when he heard footsteps approaching. He gave no sign that he noticed. When his visitor's shadow fell across his legs, he looked up. Neither said anything as they regarded each other intently.

The younger man tipped his hat back and broke the silence first. "Name's Kyle McCreedy, and I hear you're looking for a man to go partners with you, Mr. Thomas."

Matt looked at him evenly, trying not to grin. The *man* John had sent him was a kid and not much over twenty-one by the look of him. He was a big one though. That counted some in his favor.

"No need to stand on formality here. The name's Matt. Why don't you sit down, Kyle, cause I'm getting a crick in my neck staring up at you."

"Thanks," the young man said, tucking himself into a piece of the shade, "laying track is hard work in this heat."

Matt agreed it was. They chewed the fat for a few minutes, listening to sounds of the camp settling in for the night, until Matt figured it was time to get down to it. "If you don't mind me asking, where abouts you hail from, son?"

"I don't mind you asking. Marion, Ohio, Mr. Thomas—" He caught himself and grinned sheepishly. "I mean Matt."

"You're pretty far from home."

"Yeah, guess I got what you might call itchy feet, but I figure you already know all about that. John says you been just about everywhere."

"You got any family back in Ohio?"

Kyle pulled off his hat and wiped the sweatband, looking like he didn't want to answer that particular question. "It's like this, Matt. My folks own a little farm, they got four kids counting me, and all my old man was ever good for was drinking and beating on us. There wasn't hardly enough for everybody to eat, so I did us all a favor and cleared out."

Matt figured he'd better see if he could turn the talk in a different direction. "I reckon John told you what I'm fixing to do. I need a man who can handle himself. The country where I'm headed can get pretty rough."

There was a definite glint in Kyle's eyes when he shot back, "And I know what you're thinking. You're thinking I can't carry my weight. That I'm too young. Well, you're wrong, mister. I been making my own way eight years now, and I can handle anything that comes along."

"Is that a fact?" Matt said, unperturbed by the outburst. "Well, soon as this here thing comes off"—he tapped the splint on his leg—"I'll be leaving for the Cimarron. I'm telling you, right up front, it ain't a safe place for a white man. If we get into a tight spot, we ain't gonna have time to sit ourselves down and take a vote on what to do." He stopped and fixed Kyle with an icy stare. "You got any complaints about taking my orders?"

Kyle flinched but didn't drop his gaze. "No sir, I can take your orders. Anybody as old as you has got to have learned a few things about staying alive." He draped an arm over his leg and studied Matt with unabashed curiosity. "To hear John tell it, you done killed more buffalo than old

Buffalo Bill hisself." His gaze dropped down to Matt's leg. "Though Bill didn't generally ride in and finish 'em off with nothing but a knife."

In spite of himself, Matt smiled. There was something about the kid's spunk that appealed to him. A little voice in his head said he was a damn fool for making snap judgments, that the only reason he was doing this was because the kid reminded him of himself when he was younger. He thanked the voice very kindly when it was through, then leaned over and stuck out his hand.

"Kyle, I'm willing to take a chance if you are."

The young man stared at the hand for a moment. A huge smile split his face as he grasped it and shook.

Partnerships had been formed on a lot less.

The Cimarron

Things were going well as summer turned to autumn. Kyle and Matt were killing and skinning about thirty animals a day. It was a filthy, backbreaking job, but the pay was hard to beat. Matt held up his end of the bargain on the work, though it was obvious from the halting way he moved that the doctor's words had held true; he would never walk right again.

When they had enough hides cured to fill the wagon, they would drive to Dodge, and it seemed like they couldn't supply enough to the eager buyers. Both men had accumulated a tidy sum of money as autumn gave way to the first signs of winter.

They decided on one last trip before the bad snows came.

It was a mistake.

On December 18 the worst blizzard in years struck. The sky turned gunmetal as the temperature dropped far below zero. And if matters weren't bad enough already, the snow came, burying familiar landmarks beneath a blanket of white until they had no idea of where they were. They tried to make camp, but the wind was so brutal that all their efforts to build a fire ended in failure. Matt knew that if they didn't find shelter they would be dead before morning. He forced the horses on, knowing that it was dangerous, knowing he had no choice.

Sitting hunched over, trying to protect himself from the wind, Matt was jolted when the lead horse stumbled. "Whoa, you jugheads," he yelled, pulling back on the lines.

The team stopped and their labored breathing filled the air with plumes of whiteness. As Kyle bent down to have a look at the lead horse's legs, he thought he spied a small opening in the side of the hill. He pawed at eyes that were nearly frozen shut. Snow-blind, he must be going snow-blind.

Either that or it was his imagination showing him what he desperately wanted to see. As if to make him doubt, the swirling snow kicked up and he could see nothing.

"What's wrong," Matt yelled, trying to be heard over the wind that could drown a man's voice at twenty feet.

Kyle called back through cupped hands, "Hold on, thought I saw something." He plodded through the drifts on wooden legs, up to the entrance. The opening wasn't very large, not much larger than an oversized groundhog hole. He stared at it thoughtfully. Maybe if a man got down on his stomach, he might fit through.

"Looks like some kind of den or maybe a cave," he shouted in Matt's direction. "Better bring that cannon of yours, in case we run up on something that don't want company."

Matt grasped his Sharps in hands he could no longer feel and climbed down from the wagon. In his whole life, he couldn't ever recall being this cold. That wind cut into a man like a knife.

"Work your way inside and see if you can light a match while I cover you."

Kyle fumbled around in his pocket a few seconds before coming up with one, but his fingers were so numb he had trouble holding it. He scooted into the entrance, trying to protect the match from the wind. After five or six futile tries, he finally succeeded in getting it lit. He crawled the rest of the way into the opening with Matt following close behind.

Once they were inside, they saw that it was indeed a cave and bigger than they first thought. They couldn't tell how big from Kyle's match, only that they were able to stand. At first glance nothing seemed to be living inside, so they quickly turned and went back to the wagon to gather some firewood they had stored there earlier.

"If you don't back up, you're going to catch on fire," Matt observed, as Kyle hugged the blaze.

"I don't care. At least I'll die warm."

Grudgingly, the younger man moved away from the fire. "You stay here and warm up those old bones, and I'll go see about the horses. But first, one for the road." He backed up and stood over the flames until Matt swore he saw smoke curling up from Kyle's backside.

He returned a few minutes later with both arms full. "If you was to look around that mess, you might scare us up a bite to eat while I get some snow to melt for coffee."

They ate quickly and in silence, wolfing down their food, and when they were finished, Matt pulled out his pipe and worked on getting it lit. Soon fragrant smoke drifted across the fire. Outside the wind raged at the cave entrance, howling like a hungry animal denied its prey.

"I don't know about you, but I didn't think we was gonna make it there for a while."

"Yeah," Matt agreed around his pipe, "I was beginning to have some serious doubts my ownself. It must be twenty-five, thirty below out there." He gave his head a wry shake. "Guess maybe we should have quit a mite sooner."

Kyle cleaned off the plates while Matt worked on his pipe some more. After a few minutes Matt knocked it out and stuck it in his coat pocket. "I think I'd sleep better after a look around. Hate to have a grumpy old bear climb into bed with me. 'Less, of course," he winked, "she was female. We got any of those torches you rigged up?"

"Look under the wagon seat, over on the left side. Should be two or three still under there."

Matt reappeared a few minutes later. "I thought you were trying to hide them," he grumbled, stamping snow from his feet and backing up to the fire. After he warmed himself, he stuck the end of a torch into the fire, and when it flared into life, he handed it over.

"Kyle, my boy," he said, hefting the Sharps, "let's go have a look-see around."

As Kyle held the torch high, they treaded their way deeper into the darkness, pausing for a moment to stare at some boulders that circled the floor in an almost perfect ring. There was something about them that reminded Matt of silent old men sitting around a fire, brooding about a secret they would tell if they only had the ability to speak.

The cave went back a lot farther than either man would have thought. Their footsteps floated back with a ring that took some time dying.

Droppings speckled with white littered the floor.

"What do you think caused those?"

"Bats'd be my guess," Matt answered, a smile crossing his face as he warmed to the subject. "When I was down in Mexico, I seen bats that'd suck the blood right out of a man's body. Yes sir, do it while he was sleeping. I ever tell you about 'em?"

"No, and I wished you hadn't told me now." Despite the easy banter, the prospect of finding their way back caused the younger man's back to prickle with sweat.

They had taken several convoluted turns when the torch began to flicker. Matt handed over another. There was barely enough fire left to light the new one, and for an instant, the darkness moved in close, reminding them how far beneath the earth they were.

An anxious moment followed before the new torch caught.

"We only got one left," Kyle pointed out.

"I can count!"

"Shouldn't we be thinking about getting back?"

"What do you make of that?" Matt asked, pointing at a bulky object draped in shadow.

"I don't see a thing."

A dry, rustling sound carried, like the wind blowing leaves across the ground, before silence once again descended upon the chamber. Matt readied the Sharps, prepared to shoot at the first sign of movement. As he neared the object, it seemed as though a sliver of ice had been driven into his chest. An inner voice warned him of danger and his nerves were stretched tighter than wet rawhide by the time he was close enough to see what rested in the darkness.

Both men stared in disbelief. In front of them was . . . *an Indian burial platform.* The rustling sound had come from the wind moving around what was left of the blankets. Everything was rotted, and that accounted for the musty smell to the place. But beneath that, barely discernible, was another odor, one that Matt had never smelled before. Whatever it was, it was sickening.

Kyle was the first to speak. "What kind of Indians would put their dead in a godforsaken place like this?"

"None that I know of" was Matt's flat reply.

"I always heard they like to be buried on high ground so's their spirits could sorta watch over things." Kyle lowered his voice several notches. Something about this place made a man want to whisper. "You know, it don't make no sense why somebody would go to all that trouble just to put one man back here."

There was a reason that Matt knew of, but he said nothing. He started to turn away, but something caught his eye. Squinting in the dim light, he tried to make it out. Pictures. Lots and lots of pictures. The cave wall had been painted into one huge mural.

"Bring over that torch."

In the flickering light they studied the paintings, trying hard to understand why someone would go to the trouble to draw pictures that no one would ever see. They were crude slashes of color, barely more than stick men. Large portions were faded or gone altogether so that it was difficult to make sense of what they were trying to say.

"What's all this mean?"

"It means," Matt answered softly, "we're standing in the burial chamber of a medicine man."

"What in sam hill is a medicine man?"

"Indians believe there are some men who can heal the sick with magic, control spirits, that sort of stuff. They're held in great respect by the rest of the tribe."

"Yeah? Then why they'd stick him in here?"

" 'Cause they were afraid of him."

"That don't make no sense," Kyle answered. "He's dead."

"Indians are superstitious, that's all."

"You sure don't look too convinced from where I'm standing," Kyle replied, watching his face. "You sure there ain't more to this than what you're telling?"

"Come on, I'll show you there's nothing to be afraid of!" Matt angrily grabbed the torch from Kyle and walked over to the platform. Holding the light above his head, he studied the remains of the figure lying on the bare wood. Both men steeled themselves at the sight. It was impossible to tell how long the skeleton had lain there, but all the clothing had long ago rotted away, along with the flesh, and the only things that still clung to the yellowed bones were patches of skin.

But that wasn't the worst of it.

"Who could do something like that? Kyle asked, his face turning ashen. "Drive stakes through his hands and feet, and leave him in the dark. I bet he was still alive when they brought him here."

Matt saw that Kyle was getting scared and put a comforting hand on the boy's shoulder. "Don't get yourself worked up, son. He's dead and the dead can't hurt you. Besides, he was killed before they brought him here. Look at his skull; it's damn near busted in two."

Something was odd about the crack though.

"Let's get out of here," Kyle said, nervously licking his lips as the second torch began to flicker, throwing shadows that jumped and danced across the walls.

Matt needed no encouragement.

Their campfire led them the last few yards through the dark, and though neither of them said anything, both were glad to be away from the dead medicine man. They stoked up the fire as they made preparations to turn in for the night. But sleep was the farthest thing from their minds.

"Think I'll go out and see what the weather's doing," Kyle said, making the first excuse. "Maybe if it's quit snowing, we can get an early start in the morning."

"Good idea. Check the horses and make sure they're doing all right. Be sure to give 'em some extra feed."

Kyle made no effort to move.

"What's on your mind?" Matt asked in a wary tone.

"I was thinking maybe one of us should keep watch tonight. You know . . . just in case there's something to what we saw back there." He laughed, but his laugh sounded strained.

"What we saw back there was just a few smudges of paint and the rotting bones of some dead Indian." Matt's words were a curious mixture of mocking and concern. "You ain't afraid of that, are you?"

Kyle looked ashamed, yet from his voice, Matt could tell he was still scared. "It's the way you looked when you first saw those paintings. Your face turned pale, like you'd seen your own ghost. Something bad happened back there. I don't claim to know what it was, but it just felt wrong. I think we should get out of here tonight. Right now."

"How far you think we'd get in that storm?" Matt hunkered down and poked at the fire, even though it was burning just fine. "I done told you everything I know about what we saw. Will you quit bending my ear and get some rest?"

Kyle looked closely at Matt, trying to gauge the truth of his words. A look of reluctance crossed his face, but he finally nodded. "Don't forget to wake me up in a few hours."

Mat nodded. "You got it."

As Kyle wrapped up and prepared for sleep, Matt stared into the flames, brooding about what he'd seen earlier. There were gaps in the story on the cave wall, but he was able to fill in most of the missing pieces . . . because he'd heard the story once before. His memories carried him back to when he was young and living with the Sioux, back to a long ago night when he had heard a story he had never forgotten.

There had been a raid on a neighboring tribe and an old warrior had been wounded, a lance in the stomach. Matt had felt pity for the hurt man, and so, amidst the wailing of the women, he had sat and listened to the fevered recounting of stories about battles fought, coups counted, as the man who had been like a father came to grips with dying.

But one story had been different from all the others; one had been about a good man's sacrifice that had led to eternal damnation. From what Matt could make out, there had been a year when the buffalo didn't return, and in an effort to save his people, a medicine man had struck a bargain with the Tena-Ranide, a spirit of the underworld. The tribe was spared starvation, but the forces he had tried to use for good were now using him for their own purposes. Dark purposes. The man who had become the servant of death became more evil as the days passed, and beneath a hungry, staring moon, strange rites were held—rites that soon demanded human sacrifice.

After untold suffering, the tribe managed at last to bind his mortal body, to hide it deep in the earth. They made great magic to seal him in his final resting place, and the fear of his evil was such it was forbidden to even speak his name.

The fire popped, yanking Matt back to the present. A feeling of unease rested like an icicle in his guts as his thoughts turned to the last painting on the cave wall. Painted in blood, it said not to disturb this final prison, that whoever intruded was in great danger because the only way the Tena-Ranide could ever have any form of life beyond this cave was

. . . if it found another body to inhabit.

And it came to Matt what was strange about the crack in the medicine man's skull; it had been split *from the inside out.*

Kyle stirred in his sleep, mumbled something, but after a few seconds his breathing became regular again. Matt stared at the young man's back and thought about his own son, dead at five, taken by the cholera. Sometimes he wondered how the boy would have turned out, if he would have been like Kyle. He shook his head, trying to rid himself of the painful images that seemed to haunt him more and more of late. There was no point in thinking about a past that brought only sadness.

He stretched out and tried to find a position that didn't cause his leg to ache so much.

Outside the wind rose.

It sounded like the wailing of women.

Kyle awoke to find Matt asleep and the fire down to a few embers. Something had pulled him awake. A sound? No, it wasn't a sound. Something else. He started to add some wood to the fire and that was when he first noticed the smell. God, it stank something awful in here, like every rotting buffalo carcass in the world. What could cause such an odor? He was about to ask Matt if he smelled anything when he heard movement—wet, slithering noises, like a snake crawling out of its skin, coming from somewhere back in the darkness.

The sounds grew louder.

He stared deep into the cave, but he couldn't see anything moving in the cold, moist darkness that circled them. Whatever lived back there was getting closer. The stench grew stronger, becoming overpowering, and his hands covered his mouth as he fought to hold down his rising bile.

All thoughts of being sick vanished when he got a look at what was emerging into the feeble light. A patch of blackness on the wall had detached itself from the rest. It was the shadow of a man wearing a tall hat, and yet, when Kyle looked around the cave, he saw they were all alone, that there was nothing to throw such a shadow. His eyes followed the thing as it somehow crept along, possessed of an impossible life.

Kyle backed away as he softly called out Matt's name.

At the sound of Kyle's voice, it darted across the wall with unnatural speed. While he watched, it abandoned the shape of a man altogether and changed into a writhing mass that sent thin, ropelike tendrils shooting down the wall. He was reminded of a spider spinning a web as they gathered about Matt's head and hung there, coiling and uncoiling with a rhythmic pulse that matched the old man's breathing.

Kyle called out again, louder this time.

Why didn't Matt wake up? Couldn't he feel it hovering above him? Couldn't he smell the damned thing? Kyle tried once more to warn his partner, but only small gagging sounds came from his lips. He was frozen, and everything began moving with nightmare slowness while he watched the clinging shadow continue downward until it touched Matt's battered hat. Several tendrils entwined themselves around the old man's throat, and there was something obscene about the way they caressed the flesh. The rest, as though they were a nest of rattlers, struck out at the sleeping face . . . but instead of drawing back afterward . . . they began crawling *into* him.

Matt began twitching like a rabbit in an ever-tightening snare . . .

. . . once again he was standing on that hellish plain while the buffalo thundered by, and he watched as the Indian who now wore his face reached out and drew him close. They embraced. When Matt tried to pull away, he found that he couldn't separate himself from the clinging figure, that the Indian's flesh was still melting, flowing over him in rippling waves, crawling down into his mouth, into his throat, choking him so that he was unable to even cry out in his revulsion and fear. He realized they were merging to-gether—

that soon they would become one.

Blood erupted from every opening in Matt's head . . .

. . . his eyes jerked open and he screamed. He tried to stand, but his bad leg gave way and he pitched forward into the dirt. As he struggled to rise, the sounds that came from him were the high, keening sounds of a man who has gazed upon something he cannot bear to see, something that has driven him over the brink of sanity.

The screams broke the spell that kept Kyle from moving. He scrambled to his feet and the .44 that Matt had given him for his birthday appeared in his hand. The screams grew louder, and he was screaming himself when he emptied the pistol into whatever had hold of Matt. His bullets had no effect. And neither did the smoldering stick of wood he plucked from the fire. He might as well have been striking at the air.

Kyle grabbed Matt, trying to pull him away, when one of the tendrils wrapped around his wrist. It was no longer a shadow. It was real, solid and cold as barbed wire when it cut into him, and for a second, Kyle was able to see into the mind of whatever held him. His whole being recoiled when he got a brief glimpse of what hell must look like. With every once of his strength, he wrenched his arm free, stripping off most of the skin where the tendril touched him. The arm filled with burning needles.

Matt continued to struggle as the thing drew him nearer, his body arching backward, contorting in agony, but the fight seemed to be going out of him. He looked like a broken puppet being tugged across the floor by a careless, impatient child.

Kyle was reaching out with his unhurt arm when Matt raised his eyes and looked at him. The eyes had changed. Something cold and inhuman stared out from Matt's face.

Enraged at his own helplessness, Kyle grabbed Matt and shook him. The old man stiffened, his eyes filming over, and for a moment, the Matt he knew was looking at him. But he seemed to be dwindling away, as though he were being dragged downward to some terrible, distant place. His eyes held the pleading look of a drowning man each time he struggled to say something.

At last, in a strangled whisper, "For God's sake, shoot me. Don't let it have me. Promise . . . don't let it . . . promise—"

Kyle nodded and the taste of ashes was in his mouth.

The old man's struggles were growing much weaker. The thing was almost totally inside him now, and whatever made Matt Thomas human was just about gone. The eyes glittered like chips of winter ice when they locked with Kyle's.

The farm boy from Marion, Ohio, knew what he had to do, and he knew nothing he'd ever done would be as hard. Reaching down, he picked the Sharps off the floor, raised it to his shoulder . . . and slowly pointed it at Matt. His finger inched forward like a blind worm until it wrapped around the trigger. He gradually increased the pressure, trying to hold steady while the blood thundered in his head. His teeth were bared like those of an animal in pain as he tried to pull the trigger.

"I can't do it," Kyle pleaded in a grainy whisper, "don't make me. *Please don't make me.*"

His finger loosened its grip and he let the huge rifle drop to his side. And then the screams started; in their pain and rage, they were the most awful sounds he had ever heard. It was impossible such cries could be coming from a human throat. Kyle knew he could no longer stand by and let his friend endure such agony. He raised the rifle and centered the sights on Matt's forehead.

When he gently squeezed the trigger . . . just the way Matt had taught him . . . a part of Kyle McCreedy died too.

He started to turn away. Movement caught his eye, stopping him dead in his tracks. Matt, in a pool of his own blood, was moving in broken, wet circles the way a bug will after being stepped on. Fear flooded Kyle's insides with a warm liquid rush. He jammed a hand into his coat pocket and found more shells for his .44. Working quickly, he reloaded with hands that shook so much he could barely hold the revolver.

This time he didn't hesitate. The pistol jumped in his fist and a foot-long tongue of blue flame erupted from the barrel. For an instant, everything became bright as day, letting him see his shot was a good one, catching the thing that had once been Matt Thomas high on the chest. The impact of the slug lifted the creature from the floor and flung it backward against the cave wall.

Kyle's ears were ringing, but he heard its labored efforts to rise, and fired again. His shot went wide this time. In the flash, he saw the thing smile, showing teeth that were startlingly white in the blood-drenched face. He fired again before it could move, and his next four shots found their mark, pinning it to the wall. Blackness streamed from each bullet hole, and when it hit the floor the blackness began crawling toward him.

With a moan, Kyle flung the pistol. There was no stopping the thing. He wheeled and ran blindly from the cave, paying no heed to the cold that waited outside. His only chance was to get to the horses. He heard the jingling of their harness, but they seemed impossibly distant as he plowed through the drifts. His feet kicked up gouts of snow that hung in the air like shattered faces.

There was no moon. The animals were shadows in the dark and they were spooked, dancing sideways, shying away from the stink of fear on him. Several times he almost edged close enough to grasp the reins that dangled in front of him, but each time they managed to elude him. Around and around they went in a mad dance until his footing betrayed him and a windswept patch of ground frozen hard as iron rushed up to drive the breath from his body. He lay paralyzed, listening to the wind blow softly through the ice-covered branches, causing a tinkling noise that sounded like glass. As he watched the trees sway, he heard steps crunching in the snow. Grunting with the effort, he raised up and scuttled sideways, a crab covered with white.

The horses were mad with fear as Kyle staggered nearer. They must have caught the scent of what was behind him because they bolted. Kyle, gathering his fading strength, flung himself forward. His hand touched a heaving flank, sliding downward, and he felt himself falling. The animal stumbled, and Kyle's fingers wrapped around a piece of the harness, slipped, then grabbed hold. His arm was nearly wrenched from its socket. Ignoring the blackness that danced at the edges of his vision, he held on.

A shot rang out. The horse squealed, a sound nearly human in its agony, and pitched sideways in the snow. The wounded animal floundered, trying hard to rise. Another shot came, and Kyle heard the bullet strike home. The horse let out a final death rattle before going limp. Kyle struggled to free himself from beneath the crushing weight.

"You weren't planning on leaving me here, were you, son?" the familiar voice said, moving closer. "All alone in the cold. I thought we were partners. Remember?" Then came laughter. Obscene laughter.

Kyle noticed that the sickening odor was growing stronger, and he tried with all his might to get loose. But he knew it was too late. Already the tendrils were drifting down toward his face like cold, black snow. He screamed . . .

. . . and his screams floated across a vast dry prairie that had never been touched by rain. In the blinding sun he watched the walking man draw near, and the earth began to tremble with a stain that grew dark on the horizon.

The figure stopped and Kyle saw it was an Indian dressed in ragged gray buckskins and a funny stovepipe hat. The broad copper face regarded him without expression. In the distance, the dark stain had drawn close enough for Kyle to see it was a herd of buffalo, but what a herd it was, an ocean of heaving flesh stretching farther than the eye could see, rippling and swelling as though driven by a storm. On and on they came, and the world became

*filled with distant thunder. Kyle could feel the rumbling deep in his bones.
Soon they were near enough for him to see that every animal was soaked in
blood. It dripped from their straining flanks, it spilled from their gasping
mouths, turning the ground red. He caught their smell, the stench of sweat
and dust and blood, and worst of all—the smell of fear.*

*Kyle fell to his knees, unable to stand upon the trembling ground.
"What does all this mean?" His voice was drowned by the growing thunder. "Why have you brought me here?"*

*The skeletal figure said nothing, and the buffalo kept on spilling across
the prairie, drawing nearer, and the dust they kicked up blotted out the sun.
Kyle waited in the gathering darkness.*

*Just when it seemed they would be crushed in the stampede, the Indian
doffed his hat and everything changed. The charging herd disappeared in
the wink of an eye and Kyle saw desolation beyond knowing: buffalo carcasses by the hundreds of thousands glistening naked beneath the sun,
skinned and left to rot, and wandering among the rotting flesh, Kyle saw
entire tribes. They moved through the carnage, their gaunt faces bearing the
specter of hunger. Their sorrow was a great cry that rose like a bird on the
wind and then was swept away.*

*Kyle looked across the plains and saw things that defied understanding.
He saw warriors sitting by darkened fires, heard the lament of the women as
they tried to console hungry children. They prayed to the old gods, called
upon them to stop the slaughter, but their prayers fell upon deaf ears. The
old gods were powerless before the advance of the white man who rode
upon the iron horse, sweeping everything before him.*

*Some things he witnessed he didn't understand at all. He saw Indians
dressed in white-man clothes living in white-man houses. There was no
pride in their faces. Many were lying drunken on the street in the shadow of
buildings so tall they blocked the sun. Others climbed from strange-looking
wagons that moved without horses and went into places that colored the
night with all manner of bright lights. When they came out, the smell of
whiskey was upon them, their steps were drunken.*

*Stranger sights awaited. He saw many of them cross great oceans to die
in battles in places he had never seen, using weapons that cut men down
like wheat in the field, fighting the white man's wars, and their names were
not spoken with honor, even though their blood was spilled just as often.
Their numbers, like the buffalo, dwindled to a few and they no longer
prayed to the old gods. They now lifted their voices to the white god.*

*All this he witnessed and more. How long he stood there watching, Kyle
had no way of knowing. One by one the strange sights disappeared, until*

only he and the medicine man were left on the plain. The wind blew and it was a high keening that sounded as lonely as dying.

The medicine man began to chant, and somehow, without ever being told, Kyle knew it was a death chant he heard; there were no words, only an anguished cry mourning a people who wandered a world that no longer held a place for them, speaking a farewell to a way of life lost forever, lamenting a people who had even forsaken their gods. The sad, wavering voice rose and fell for a moment longer. Then turning his back to Kyle, he placed his hat back upon his head and began walking away, each step covering an incredible distance until, finally, he was gone from sight. At that instant, the buffalo returned; and when the first horn pierced Kyle McCreedy through, he learned that a god, even a dying god, can still thirst for vengeance.

A Cold Way Home

ARDATH MAYHAR

Ardath Mayhar is the author of more than twenty novels (some of them written under a pen name) and somewhere near two hundred short stories. She is best known as a science fiction and fantasy author, but she has successfully written mainstream stories about her native East Texas, Westerns, young-adult novels, and poetry. Her story in the previous volume of this series, "Night of the Cougar," was a Spur nominee. Here, her ironic tone and feeling for East Texas comes through beautifully.

The norther gusted through the big pines, carrying with it a spatter of sleet. A strand of auburn hair flipped against Callie's cheek, and she tucked it under her head scarf with an icy finger. Behind her, in the wagon, she could hear Jason's small feet thunk-thunking against the pine box on which he sat.

She turned to look back at the small, cold figure. "Don't do that, son. It's not respectful to Papa."

The boy's cheeks were mottled with cold, his eyes full of tears. Some probably were from the chill, but she suspected the others might be for his father, beneath him in the rude coffin. She reached back one-handed, tucked the red scarf more tightly about his neck and checked the buttons of his outgrown coat.

"Is it very far, Mama?" he asked, his thin piping almost inaudible in the roar of the wind among the pines.

She turned back to look ahead, at the flanks of the shivering horse, head-down against the cold, the sky still barely touched with a scarlet sunset. "Not very long now, son. Grandpa will have a good fire, and Luke will probably have something good fixed to eat. Be patient. We'll get there."

He huddled into his coat, red hands in its skimpy pockets, and said no more. She sighed and fumbled out the lantern and a sulfur match. It was dark now along the tunnel-like road through the forest.

It grew darker, even colder. She was shivering, there on the high seat of the wagon. She hoped that her body and that small barrier of the seat sheltered Jason a bit from the blast out of the northwest. The horse was grunting with each step. The light wagon and its small burden couldn't work him that hard; she suspected that he, too, was suffering from the chill.

The sky went entirely dark. Only their tiny circle of lantern light bobbed through a world of rushing blackness. She was wishing so desperately to see the lights of home that when they did twinkle into view, she half doubted her vision. But it was . . . They rounded a bend, and the square of a window glowed steadily with warm lamplight.

She stood and shouted into the wind. "Papa! Luke! Papa!"

She sat to flick the horse with the end of a rein. Her voice, she knew, had been carried away by the wind. How could her father and his old servant have heard her amid the uproar of the night?

Now only a scant half mile separated her from her home. She shouted again, her throat raw with chill and stress. And this time something changed at the house ahead. After a short while, a lantern bobbed into view on the back porch. She gave a sound that was as much a sob as a laugh.

"We're home, Jason! We're home!"

The boy made no sound. She could hear his teeth chattering like castanets behind her. She whipped up the horse, and the beast, no less ready than she for shelter, stepped out at a trot, the wagon banging and jouncing behind him.

Waiting in the small yard behind the house was an ancient black man holding high his light. "Miss Callie?" His voice was quavery.

He caught the horse's head as she pulled to a halt. The old man was staring into the dimness of the wagon. He nodded when he saw the child, but he was looking for someone else. "Where Marse Will?" he asked.

A tall old man had come onto the porch wrapped in a blanket and scarf. She jumped down from the wagon and reached for the child. Then she answered the servant.

"He's in the wagon. In the box. He'll keep. Thank God, it turned cold. We'll tend to him tomorrow, Luke."

The old man had staggered down the steps to meet her. "Callie, girl! Come in . . . come in. We've got a good fire. Luke can fix some ham and biscuits real fast. Here, bring the boy inside out of the cold. You both look frozen."

She carried her son in and set him down before the huge fireplace, where hickory logs crackled, emitting fragrant smoke. She peeled away the layers of coat and scarf and sweater as the child shivered under her hands.

Her father was staring at her. "Callie . . . what has happened? Where's Will? Why are you home . . . alone?"

She glanced up, her amber eyes crackling a command. "Not now. Later, when Jason is asleep!"

The old man sank painfully into a rocking chair and kept looking from his daughter to his grandson. His puzzled eyes followed every move, but when Luke had the food warmed on the iron cookstove, he knew it at once.

"Come and eat," he said.

Jason looked up. "Grampa Anderson!" he said with pleased recognition. "I 'member you!"

The old man reached down to take his hand. "You come on and eat Luke's good grub now. Then you can sleep. All right?"

Callie fed the boy, who was too weary to manage his own meal. He nodded off against her shoulder before he was quite finished, but she lifted him and took him to the trundle bed Luke had pulled from beneath the big four-poster. He didn't stir as she tucked the bright patchwork quilt about him.

Her father waited while she ate her own supper. Then he drew her over to the fire and sat again in his rocker. "What has happened, Callie? And where's Will?"

She sighed, backing up to the flames and lifting her skirt in back to warm her chilled legs. "I loved Will Lightwood, Pa. You know that. I'd have followed him to Hell if he'd asked me to." She laughed harshly. "I never thought he would ask me to though.

"When he wanted to go down and live on the coast, I hated it. You know that . . . I love the woods and this farm and everything about home. But I went. I bundled up Jason, and we followed Will to Galveston. Lived in hotels. The only thing down there worth seeing is the Gulf of Mexico, and we saw too much of that."

She drew up a small splint chair and sat facing her father. "Will took to gambling. After he saw everything there was to see, he seemed to change. He got in with people . . . not the sort of people my son's father should associate with, Pa.

"The Lightwoods have always been respectable people. Not just because they had land and money . . . because they were good, decent people. But Will took in and lost all the money. Sold the woods his Pa left him, and lost that money. He lost and he lost, and it changed him more."

Her father reached to pat her hand. "Surely it wasn't that bad," he said.

"It was worse. It got so he'd come home drunk and hit me. Worse than that, he'd hit Jason! The more money he lost, the meaner he got. That last night . . . he came in wanting me to sign away this place, Pa. That was left to me by my mother's folks! I wouldn't, and he threatened to rent me out to the drummers at the hotel so he'd have money to gamble with. And he beat me, though I fought him the best I could. So I decided that it couldn't go on.

"I took Grampa Lightwood's pistol out of the drawer, and I shot him dead."

Anderson sat up straight, his face slack with shock. "Callie . . . but how . . . is the law . . . ?"

She shook her head. "The people in the hotel heard him, what he threatened to do. The sheriff asked me if he could help me get home, but I'd already bought a horse and wagon and hid it out, knowing that I might have to head home alone."

She unbraided her long auburn hair and began to comb out the curling strands. It crackled in the firelight, clinging to her fingers as the comb moved.

She looked up again at her father. "I wanted Jason to be proud of his papa. Looked as if the only way to do that was if Will was dead. All the land's gone. Only thing left was Grandpa Lightwood's pistol and my own place here."

She smiled then, her face suddenly radiant in the firelight. "But Jason will be proud of his papa. No matter what, Jason will be proud."

Hell's Substation

ROY LEE FISH

Roy Lee Fish has written a number of short stories for horror publications and is currently working on a novel. He has been an oil field roughneck, pulled cotton, dug ditches, and is a retired bricklayer. Knowledge of this fails to prepare you in any way for what follows. This is a delightful surrealistic piece that is to the Western field what the stories in Judith Merril's and Harlan Ellison's groundbreaking anthologies were to the science fiction field. It not only knocks down boundaries, it then goes on to mistreat them.
I love it.

Dog pounds in Clear Lake, Iowa; McPherson, Kansas; Guthrie, Oklahoma; Denton, Texas; Fort Smith, Arkansas; Carthage, Missouri; and Mason City, Iowa, were, in that order, demolished and strewn with the remains of their inhabitants.

A wall of a museum at the Fort Worth stockyards was knocked down and a Studebaker wagon and a Confederate uniform stolen. Two graves in Dallas yawned empty. A lone resting place immediately east of Oklahoma's Eufaula Dam surrendered its occupant. Another gaping hole was left in a cemetery at Dewey, Oklahoma.

In Fort Smith, another Studebaker was stolen; several blocks west, thieves broke into the boarded-up Green Pea bawdy house and took the piano. An auto collector reported that a 1934 Ford sedan had been taken from his warehouse. Among other burglaries were those of an auto body shop, an auto parts store, and a distillery. Linking all of those depredations were oversize bear tracks that began in southern Minnesota and returned.

An old barn near Dundas, Minnesota, glowed like a jack-o'-lantern. Inside, five men wearing only western hats and boots, leather aprons, and pistols stirred the coals of a pit. Cow chips browned on a grill—a Stutz Bearcat radiator. An attractive woman dressed like the men used a Bar X Bar branding iron to flip the patties. A middle-aged man missing an earlobe drew a piece of charcoal across a canvas in a corner.

"Mon Dieu! I would give the rest of my ear and a palette of guilders for some paint!"

The woman said, "Tell me again what you call that drawing."

"Night Cafe."

She flipped a chip. "Well, it looks like a place that might serve this stuff."

"It is a low place, but that is blasphemy!"

"Tough titty. I call 'em like I see 'em."

"Mon Dieu! You insult—"

"Vince! Eugenia! Quiet!" said Bob. "Can't hear myself thunder!"

"Oh," the artist moaned, "I should have stayed with the ministry!"

Bill said, "Cole should have become a preacher like his Grandma Fristoe wanted; it might have saved him twenty-five years in prison, and"—he looked about—"I might not be here."

Vincent studied his work and shook his head. "Got to have colors. Yellow, green, and red would permit me to resurrect the *Cafe,* and with orange, I could paint an autumn landscape."

"Preachin', drawin', cookin'," a big fellow drawled, spitting on the grill. "I wouldn't swap a drink of whiskey for all of that!"

The chef shoved a pattie onto the sizzling phlegm. "One mucus tamale coming up for you, Grat."

"Just serve it with whiskey."

Eugenia skewered him with "And just where am I to get it?"

Vincent's eyes had never left his drawing. "Curses, it is drab!"

"Of course it's drab," said Clell, jabbing his poker into the embers. "Everything is drab and dry. You want colors, Grat wants good whiskey."

"It don't have to be good," Grat corrected.

"Well," Sam offered, "maybe the boss will bring some Indian-trade rotgut."

"Can't be too soon."

Eugenia's spatula sprang to attention. "Listen!"

Snorts. Growls. A dog's high-pitched yelp. A piano tinkled.

With the charcoal, the artist nudged his beret and scratched his head. Charcoal peppered his smock. "Let me see, now—a little more shadow over there . . ." He delicately stroked the canvas.

Curses from outside.

"Sounds like the boss is back!" Bob said. He and Grat flung open the door.

Breaking into the glow was a grizzly bear pulling two wagons. The foremost vehicle hauled a piano, the other a 1934 Ford sedan. Miscellaneous items filled odd pockets of space.

A horse-faced woman wearing a plumed hat and a low-cut velvet dress sat on a stack of buckets of paint at the piano. Her fingers moved across the keys.

A handsome Cherokee in suit and tie sat with the driver. A nervous Chihuahua shuffled between them.

A Confederate officer's hat was impaled on the teamster's horns; a shredded right-foot cavalry boot clad his left hoof; suspenders had merely been passed through his crotch and knotted. He held a writhing rattlesnake by its tail.

The artist said, "Shades of Hades!" threw away the charcoal and joined his associates in the doorway.

"Well, I'll be damned!" Bill said. "Lucifer was a Yankee when he left here!"

"Must have suckered General Lee or somebody into a bout of strip poker," Bob reckoned.

Clell said, "Naw, had to be General Hood; he just had one leg, sent the shot one to friends in Texas."

"Well, then," Bob deduced, "either he found that Texas leg, or—"

"Say, Bob!" Grat said. "Ain't that Henry?"

"Damn sure looks like him!"

The piano player broke off the tune and looked up.

"And that's Belle!" Bob added.

"Howdy, boys!" Belle called.

Henry said, "Good to see y'all again!"

Satan whipped the snake across the bear's back. "Get up there, old Mose!" The animal grunted and pulled the wagons inside. All eyes dwelled upon the cargo in the last vehicle.

"What in hell is that?" Sam asked. "And who shot it to hell?"

A couple rose from the Ford's front seat—a petite blonde with a red beret and a dimpled man wearing a snap-brim hat.

"And who are they?" asked Grat.

Lucifer leaned back and smiled. "I told y'all I'd bring new talent. That's Bonnie Parker and Clyde Barrow and their, er, motor wagon, you might call it."

Grat snorted. "Never heard of them or it. You bring whiskey?"

"Yep, but you ain't gettin' any till we're geared up for the big job."

"Aw, hell, Luci—"

"From now on, I'm General Lucifer, y'all, since I liberated this boot, galluses, and this hat from Texas." He turned and told the couple to get down from the car.

"Meet Bonnie and Clyde, and Henry Starr and his Aunt Belle. Them folks out there are"—each nodded and smiled upon being named— "Grattan and Bob Dalton, Clell Miller, Sam Wells, Eugenia Moore, Bill Stiles, and Vincent van Gogh."

Sam said, "Bob and Grat told me a lot about you, Belle."

"They tell you that they made so many free runs through my daughter's whorehouse that she went broke?"

Bob grinned. "Heck, Belle, we wasn't that steady."

"No?" Belle played a chord. "This piano was the only thing Pearl had left. Couldn't take it with her, couldn't find a buyer; so, she left it in the Green Pea. The general and I thought it a fine idea to bring it. Came in handy too, because I played for some weddings, revivals, funerals, and dances, and sold whiskey every time."

Grat gulped. "Whiskey is made to drink, not to sell!"

"Don't worry," Satan said, "we got here with most of it."

Grattan relaxed. "Good! This is sort of like old home week—would be if you'd spring that alcohol."

Vincent spied the paint and froze.

Eugenia asked, "General, when are you going to tell us about the job?"

"When I'm damned good and ready. You'll do well to tend to your present business." He sniffed and went on, "Don't I smell somethin' burnin'?"

"Feces!" Eugenia ran to the grill.

Van Gogh eased toward the paint wagon.

"Now, y'all, unhitch Old Mose and unload this stuff. Had a devil of a time loadin' it by myself."

"Hallelujah!" Vincent snatched a bucket of paint from beneath Belle. She tumbled to the ground, cursing.

"Damn you!" Lucifer yelled. "That's no way to unload!"

Van Gogh ran, holding the container before his eyes. "Excellent! *Magnifique!* I may even paint sunflowers!"

Bonnie helped Belle to her feet. Belle dusted herself off and asked, "Did you say that yokel's name is Rembrandt?"

"Wouldn't make a pimple on Rem's butt," Satan allowed. "He's a failed preacher, half-assed artist, and a suicide."

"Well, I'll be damned!"

The Daltons removed the harness and stepped back. Lucifer hurled the Chihuahua and said, "That's the last one." Old Mose's jaws caught the dog in mid-air. "Get out, but don't go too far; I may need you again, hear?" The bear grunted around his supper. "Git, y'all!" Satan popped the snake against the beast's rump. Old Mose lumbered into the night. Yelping faded with his footfalls.

"Poor Old Mose," the devil sighed. "Doin' all that work on an improper diet. Dogs are all right for side dishes, but he needs a fat heifer."

Old Rattler whipped and sank its fangs into its master's hand. "Damn, can't even trust my old servant nowadays!" he said, flinging the reptile into the flames. He held his hand over the fire and watched the wound sear shut.

The small items were unloaded: new innertubes, paint, cans of Bondo, a paint gun and hose, twenty-two cases of Valvoline aviation oil, a keg of whiskey and one of gasoline.

Grat warned, "Keep that whiskey away from the fire; let's put it beside the fuel."

Lucifer ran to Vincent, who was trying to pry the lid from the bucket of paint, and stomped his fingers.

"*Mon Dieu!*"

"You were in France too long! Have you forgotten English?"

"My God! I must continue my work!"

"Right now, you'll help the others." He turned and called, "Belle, Bonnie, let's have some music to work by."

"I think," said the woman with the hatchet face, "I'd rather be in the Oklahoma Territory."

"And I," added the cute gal, "had just as soon be in Dallas."

The horns came to attention so abruptly that the hat slid up three inches. "The very idea! Y'all ought to appreciate Hell after livin' in them places!"

Belle conceded, "Well, there *are* certain things I don't have to put up with since I was ambushed."

"Me neither. Clyde is the only one who pinches my fanny nowadays." Bonnie and Belle climbed to the piano.

The sideboards were layered into a ramp and the Ford rolled, on flat tires, to the ground.

"Henry, install them innertubes! And you, Clyde, show Vince how to use that nozzle, then mix the Bondo!"

Bonnie lay on her side on top of the piano, head propped in hand. Belle stood at the keyboard. They launched "He's a Devil in His Own Hometown."

"Ah," Lucifer smiled, "you make me proud! I remember Bonnie singin' that in Sunday school. Damned fine job, too!"

The Daltons and Stiles stirred the coals. Lucifer speared his tail through the bullet holes and rasped away the rust. Vincent pressed the compound into the holes with his palette knife. When the plastic hardened, Satan sanded it with the backs of his hands.

"General," Clyde said, "you forgot a compressor for the paint gun."

"And," Henry put in, "that means we can't inflate the tires, either."

"Ah, I forgot nothin'!" Satan squatted on a valve stem and broke wind. The tire ballooned.

"Hell's bells!" Eugenia screeched.

Bonnie fainted and fell to the ground. Clyde ran to her and fanned her with his hat.

The devil stood, bent his hat brim back, thumbed his suspenders, and drawled like John Wayne, "Aw, she's all right, pard; just pee in her face."

"And you go to hell!"

"Heh, heh. I do miss the old homeplace. When we've finished our project, we'll all go there."

Vincent wandered up.

Clyde continued to stare at Lucifer.

Vincent gawked at Bonnie. "Nice." He exchanged berets with her and mumbled that Henry VIII was unfair.

Satan shrugged, then aired another tire.

"The job," said Bob, "I keep wondering what it is and what's in it for us."

The devil grinned. "Might get y'all a shade tree at the homeplace, if y'all don't mess up."

Sam's left eye questioned hard. "Not an apple tree?"

"How'd you guess?"

Sam flinched.

"And apple cider?" Grat wanted to know.

"Depends."

"You're a butt, you know that?" Grat smashed an ember into a myriad of sparks.

Satan chuckled.

Henry bounced a tire, declared it firm, then tested the second one. "Too tight."

The devil leered. "Let some out."

"Damned if I will!"

Lucifer hee-hawed, then inflated two more tires.

Bonnie stirred, without benefit of a urine facial, and said, "Clyde, I didn't get to go home before they buried us; please take me to Mama's."

"In time, dear. Right now, we've got to get the car ready."

The one with the red, raspy hide said, "We'll paint before puttin' on the tires. Vince, get ready; we'll see whether you can paint worth a poot." Then Lucifer sat on the last tire and filled it.

"B-but, General Lucifer," Vincent stammered, taking the nozzle, "how—"

"Same way I pumped the tires."

"Mon Dieu!"

"Will you quit sayin' that?" Lucifer tugged a gallus aside and scratched his crotch.

"But the impurities—"

"Will affect the quality of the paint, huh?"

"I fear that is true. Perhaps with my brush—"

"Never mind." Satan fitted fingers to his lips and a whistle pierced the night. Old Mose rambled in. Lucifer jammed the hose end into the bear's mouth and told him, "Seal your lips around that, big Bubba." Then he zinged the tip of his tail into the creature's rump. The animal whooshed. A bubble of air shot through the hose like an egg being propelled by mineral water through a snake. The nozzle twitched in Vince's hand, and paint showered his canvas.

"Mon Dieu! My *Cafe* is ruined!"

Satan crowed, "Beautimous hue of baby feces!"

"But, Luci— General, my masterpiece!"

"To hell with it! Aim that thing at the motor wagon!"

"But—"

The barbed tail pricked the artist's rear end. He hollered and squeezed the trigger. Another stinger to Old Mose's posterior assured a fresh volume of air. Paint sprayed onto the Ford's roof and streamed down the windows.

Bonnie gasped; Clyde grabbed her and begged her to not faint again.

"Pretty! A few more squirts like that, Old Mose, and you can go back to your calf-killin'!" Three more gushes.

Bonnie's breath returned. "Clyde, we can't drive that thing to Dallas!"

Clyde patted her hand. "We'll pick up another one."

Clell's ears perked. "Dallas? Why the hell are we going there?"

"Y'all ain't!" Satan said.

Bonnie moaned, "Oh, I wish I were back in Sunday school."

"General," Sam prodded, "tell us about the damned job."

Satan rubbed his hands together and said, "All right. You, Clell, and Bill are goin' to get another crack at that bank in Northfield."

Clell's jaw dropped.

"Crazy!" said Bill.

"Not if you want that tree. It's too bad that the Youngers, Frank James, and Emmett Dalton deserted me, but Clyde and Bonnie's motor wagon will make it easier this time. All of you together can suction that bank and shuck it like last week's drawers; if you do that and murder, say, five people, I'll give y'all a chance to undo the Dalton fiasco at Coffeeville. Then if you don't louse up that, we'll give Henry another shot at that Harrisonville bank."

Bonnie sighed, "All of that for a tree."

"But," Grat protested, "you said *a* job, not—"

"Tell y'all what I'll do," Satan hooked thumbs under his galluses and stretched them to the point of breaking. "Do all three capers, and I'll give you a really big tree. Even furnish a gallon of cold cider for everyone every week."

"Well, now!" Grat grinned. "That's somethin' worth considerin'! And as far as I'm concerned, it don't have to be cold!"

The tone of the rumble disagreed with the whole proposal; nevertheless, the Evil One declared it a contract.

Belle asked, "What do you want Bonnie and me to do, engage the sheriff and his deputy in hanky-pank while the fellows do the job?"

"Certainly not! Nothin' immoral! Just be the pep squad. Give the boys a rousin' send-off and keep the—heh, heh—hearth warm."

"That ain't funny," said Belle.

"No offense meant; it's just one of my damned old jokes. Heh, heh."

Vincent asked, "What about me?"

"Seein' as to how you did a fine job on the motor wagon, I want you to paint portraits of Belle and Bonnie."

"Thank you! A pleasure! Now for a title—"

"Simply call it *Belle and Bonnie,*" Satan suggested.

"No, no, dear fellow! Too unimaginative!"

Grat got an idea: "How about *The Beast and the Beauty*?"

Belle leaped from the wagon and kicked his shin.

Lucifer cackled. "I'd say she don't cotton to that!"

Grat hopped about, moaning, "Oh my, oh my! Every time I get a lick on the leg, my throat gets dry!"

"Well," Satan said, "put the tires on and we'll celebrate y'all's second chance at success."

"Hot damn!" Grat miraculously recovered and raced for the lug wrench.

Before Old Mose could twitch his tail five times, the tires were on; the one that was too full was mounted for the spare.

"Good!" Lucifer was pleased. The point of his tail zapped the lids from the whiskey and gasoline containers. "Ladies first."

"I don't drink," said Bonnie, "but I could use a cigarette."

"The boys will bring you a pack of Chesterfield from Northfield. Heh, heh. Get it 'Chesterfield from Northfield'?" He offered a joint of grapevine from his boot.

"I'm afraid I do get it, and no, thanks."

Belle dipped a slipper into the whiskey and drank it without fluttering a lash. "Raunchy!"

Grat scooped up a hatful, tasted, and agreed. "Deliciously so!"

Clyde said that some hot chocolate would be nice.

With bare hands, Eugenia put bear droppings on the grill; then she returned to the keg and Bob. He put an arm about her and said, "Kind of like old times in the Oklahoma Territory, ain't it, sweetie?" She answered him with a hug and a kiss.

Lucifer dipped the paint bucket into the booze and took it to the bear. Old Mose put his snout in, then bellowed and knocked over the pail.

"Old Mose is a damned sissy!" Clell hiccuped. "Nibbles Chihuahuas!"

Bonnie and Belle went back to the piano and started "There'll Be a Hot Time in the Old Town Tonight."

Lucifer coiled his tail and sat on it. His laughter echoed throughout the barn. "You sons of bitches are a credit to the old general! I'm damned proud to have you in my outfit!"

Vincent van Gogh evaluated the scene: Cowboys, nude except for leather aprons and boots, drinking whiskey from their hats. Belle supping from a shoe and playing the piano with her free hand. Bonnie singing. Clyde murmuring that he would like hot chocolate. Eugenia, naked but for her apron, boots, and hat, sat on Bob's lap, guzzling liquor from his Stetson. Old Mose stomping about, trying to cough the liquid fire from his mouth.

"Mon Dieu!" Vincent cried. "I must get this on canvas!" He dashed to his corner and snatched open the bucket of paint.

"General," said Sam Wells, "you ain't goin' to drink with us?"

"It's against my religion, my boy. Get your belly full, but I expect y'all to be as sober as Judge Parker at a triple hangin' when you go into Northfield this time. Drinkin' is what screwed y'all up in '76."

"Yep, I reckon so."

"I hate it awful that Jesse is the only one of that old gang besides you, Bill, and Clell, whose soul belongs to me. I didn't bring Jesse into this deal, because his temper is too hot. Got to play it cool."

Henry asked, "Anybody check out that bank?"

Satan put a finger to the rowel and spun it. "Yep. I posed as a preacher and opened an account with thirty pieces of silver. Anyway, Sam remembers the layout."

Eugenia went to the grill, wrapped the vittles in corn shucks from a Pony Express pouch, and called, "Come and get it while it's hot, or I'll throw it to Old Mose!"

Old Mose ambled up, sniffing.

Bonnie arrived first. "I'm famished!" she said, accepting a tamale. "Thank you!" She put it to her lips, hesitated, then said, "Old Mose can have mine." Clyde cottoned to her hint. The others tossed their grub into the pit and ate the husks, rinsing them down with whiskey.

An overly cooked chip landed on Old Rattler's head; he sprang from the pit and bit the first thing available—which happened to be Old Mose's butt. The bear snarled and rampaged, trying to get his jaws on the snake.

Sam, Grat, Bob, Clell, Bill, and Eugenia dived under the first Studebaker. Bonnie and Belle clamored onto the piano top. Clyde rolled beneath the Ford.

Satan hollered, "Mose! Simmer down, sir!"

The animal bumped the scrambling Henry, knocking him against the spare tire; it exploded, fouling the barn.

"Fix that tire!" Lucifer ordered.

"To hell with that tire!" Sam was on his stomach, lapping up the rotgut that remained in his hat during the dive.

Satan jumped up and down with rage.

Henry got up, dusted his pants, and calmly said, "Filthy talk. Drinking. Farting. I'm going back to Oklahoma."

"Enough of that! Your souls belong to me! Put that gasoline in the car and check the oil! As soon as y'all dry out, we're goin' to Northfield!"

Old Mose circled the pit, still trying to dislodge the hitchhiker. He caromed into the piano wagon. Belle and Bonnie fell off the instrument and into the wagon bed.

The Bad One yelled again at Old Mose, "Stop, damn your ornery tail!" Old Mose answered with a belch and sped past.

Bonnie turned onto her back and cradled her head in her hands.

Belle struggled to her knees and tested the piano. She looked at Bonnie and said, "I was afraid of that; the brute jarred it out of tune!"

"Borrow Clyde's Jew's harp."

Henry and Clyde emptied the keg into the gas tank.

Old Mose was completing another lap. Lucifer coiled his tail, jabbed the end into the ground, sat on the coil, then leveraged himself through the air. He landed backward astride the bear, grabbed a handful of hair, and snatched at the flapping reptile. "Goddamn you, Mose, I said hold up! Whoa!"

Old Mose bucked through two circles, sending the buckets of paint flying; then he streaked around the pit again.

Vincent repeatedly leaped up and waved his brush. "I say, fellows, will you slow a bit? My arm is not a windmill, you know!" Then he went back to dipping into the spilled paint and splashing it onto the canvas.

Grat said, "I'll bet the Bar X Bar would hire ol' Luci to bust broncs."

Bob drew himself against a wagon wheel and pulled Eugenia to him. "Gal, you never were a hot cook." She slapped him. He tweaked her breasts and reckoned that he hadn't had as much fun since Blackface Charley Bryant sat around groaning with gonorrhea.

Lucifer finally plucked Old Rattler loose, then spun about. Mount and rider shot from the barn.

Clyde hollered, "Now's our chance! Get in the car!" Everyone jammed inside. Clyde started the engine.

Then Grattan Dalton panicked. "The whiskey!"

"Hell with it!" Henry responded.

"There ain't room for it, anyway!" Sam added.

Clyde revved the engine.

Grat baled out.

"Crazy bastard!" Eugenia said.

Clell concurred with Grat: "Well, it's a long way to Texas. Might as well fetch it." He followed Grat.

"Hurry!" Clyde urged.

Somehow Clell and Grat were back in the car, the keg on Grat's lap.

Clyde floored the accelerator and let out the clutch. Vincent's arms were out a window, dragging the canvas and flourishing a brush. "Mr. Barrow, will you be a little more gentle—you are jeopardizing my work."

"Damn it, do it from memory!" Clyde yelled above the roar. The auto sped from the barn, its lights cutting the night.

Bonnie snuggled to Clyde and recited her poem:

You've read the story of Jesse James—
Of how he lived and died;
If you're still in need
Of something to read
Here's the story of Bonnie and Clyde.
    Now Bonnie and Clyde are the Barrow gang.
    I'm sure you all have—

"Phew!" Clell spewed liquid. "Old Mose must have breathed on this!"

Vincent had gotten his canvas inside and was trying to spread it. "Mr. Barrow, old chap, we must return for paint; my brush is rather dry."

"That keg—" Clyde sniffed. "We must have put the whiskey in the tank!"

Grat sighed. "Shucks. Looks like we'll have to make the best of it." He gulped a draught and said, "It ain't too bad."

Vince asked Bonnie, "This Texas—is it a good place for artists?"

"Reckon so. I'll arrange for you to paint in a corner of Marco's cafe. Used to work there; it's just a hop and a skip from the Dallas County Courthouse."

"Magnifique!" He flung his arms. The brush swabbed Clell's nostrils; a thumb reamed Bill's ear. Oblivious to the cursing, Vincent went on, "Marco's is a place of culture like the restaurant on Montmartre, no?"

"No. Not unless that place serves hamburgers, chili, and freewheeling waitresses. Mostly bums, pimps, and law dogs hang out at Marco's."

"Hamburgers? Chili? Free-whatchamacallit waitresses?"

"Yep," Bob answered. "Eugenia knows all about that."

Eugenia would have slapped him, had she room to swing.

Vincent winced. "Er, Grattan, can you spare a sip?"

"Look!" Belle said.

Satan had Old Mose under control; they drew alongside, forcing the Ford to the right. Clyde hit the brakes and cut left behind the bear. Gasoline sloshed right then left. Curses flew left and right.

Lucifer lashed his mount ahead and again caused Clyde to swerve. "You can't escape!" Satan called. "We're goin' to Northfield while we've got a good head of steam! We can make it by the time the bank opens! Follow me!" He whipped the serpent across the front flanks and dug in his spur. The red rider spurted ahead of the Ford. Wind kept the hat brim against the crown.

Clyde sighed and allowed, "Well, looks like that shade tree is the only game in Hell; might as well go for it."

"I reckon," said Bob. The others—except for Vincent—agreed.

Vincent burped and said, "I have been commissioned only to paint portraits of the ladies. Besides, I have an aversion to violence. Would you be so good as to let me out in London? I had a lady friend there—"

"Tough hockey," said Eugenia. "Bob and I want that tree to cuddle under."

Bob squeezed Eugenia and hollered, "Clyde, cock open the boiler!"

"Whoopee!" was Clell's contribution.

Sam said, "Let 'er rip!"

Belle's hand emerged from the compress of bodies, knocked a corner of the painting into the gasoline, and tapped the driver's shoulder. "Clyde, lend me your Jew's harp?"

Vincent wrung the fuel from the canvas and into his mouth.

They were so close behind Old Mose that slobbers splattered the windshield and his breath polluted the car's interior. *"Mon Dieu!* That wretched beast is a scourge to art!" Vincent tossed out the painting and the brush, and buried his face in the gasoline.

Old Mose, Old Rattler, Lucifer, and the Ford full of phantoms sped through the night. Accompanied by the Jew's harp, a chorus of voices repeated after Bonnie:

> Now Bonnie and Clyde are the Barrow gang.
> I'm sure you all have read
> How they rob and steal
> And those who squeal
> Are usually found dying or dead.

The Ballad of Sweeney's Last Ride

LEE SCHULTZ

Lee Schultz writes both poetry and short stories, most of it appearing in literary magazines. He is a lover of horses and Western literature and procrastination. But when he finally stops procrastinating and sits down to write, it's worth the wait.

The long and the short of a very good horse
is the will of his rider to try.
The grease in the hub of fate's wagon of blood
is the texture of leather and hide.
And so it had rained on the low canyon trail
on the morning of Pat Sweeney's ride.

Through the mist of gray clouds from the sky right on down
the zippers of lightning shown white.
Bunched up doggies he saw at the foaming red draw
where their mamas decided to fight.

Now old Sweeney was made of a leather well aged;
he had seen such refusals back home.
But his partners had taken the high canyon trail,
leaving Pat and his problem alone.

First he whipped off his rope, then he slid down the slope,
spurred his solid red roan to the draw.
Though he'd never been scared, he wasn't prepared
for the torrent of trouble he saw.

In the muddy red flow, the cutbank would grow
till the river would wash out the trail.
He hadn't much choice but to use gun and voice.
He'd have ninety head dead should he fail.

So swinging his rope he spurred to a lope
and aimed his old iron in the air.
Through the thunderous sounds, hard white hail came to pound
his pistols reports into flares.

He hadn't a choice; the chill took his voice
when he pushed the big roan out to lead.
Though the old horse was quick, the footing was slick
Pat would live or be damned by his deed.

As the roan stumbled through, Sweeney certainly knew
that he'd paid a high price for his cause.

For one wrangler alone should keep his soul home
on a morning of muddy red draws.

As he swam through the swill, Sweeney's heart took a chill
when he felt his old girth groan and snap.
First he cussed, then he prayed as he grabbed old Red's mane.
But the river would have the last laugh.

The dogies, of course, they followed the horse.
All the mamas came wading in too.
The big roan had tried, but the cowboy astride
knew as he fell he was through.

Though they saved ninety head, fate's red draw had been fed.
The soul of old Sweeney can't swim!
Muddy trail to the foam was his last solid home,
a tale that no witness would spin.

So when dry draws run high, never ask the black sky
if the wrangler for whom tolls the bell
rides his roan in the clouds when the thunder sings loud
that old Sweeney is swimming in hell.

The long and the short of a very good horse
is the will of his rider to try.
The grease in the hub of fate's wagon of blood
is the texture of leather and hide.
And so it had rained on the low canyon trail
on the morning of Sweeney's last ride.

Hell on the Draw

LOREN D. ESTLEMAN

Loren D. Estleman is considered one of the Western field's brightest stars. He's no slouch in the crime category, either. His story in the last volume, "The Bandit," won the Spur Award for best Western short story of the year in 1987. It was in the traditional vein. This one isn't. It's a type of story Loren says he's been wanting to write for a long, long time.

In the weeks to come there would be considerable debate and some brandishing of weapons over who had been the first to lay eyes on Mr. Nicholas Pitt of Providence; but the fact of the matter is the honor belonged to Ekron Fast, Persephone's only blacksmith. It was he, after all, who replaced the shoe the stranger's great black hammerhead had thrown just outside town, and as everyone who lived there knew, a traveler's first thought upon reaching water or civilization in that dry Huachuca country was his horse. Nor was Pitt's a horse for a former cow man like Ekron to forget.

"Red eyes," he declared to the gang at the Fallen Shaft that Wednesday night in July. "Eighteen—hell, *twenty* hands if he was one, that stud, with nary a speck of any color but black on him except for them eyes. Like burning pipe-plugs they was. Feature that."

"Oklahoma Blood Eye." Gordy Wolf, bartender at the Shaft, refilled Ekron's glass from a measured bottle, collected his coin, and made a note of the transaction in the ledger with a gnawed stub of pencil. As a half-breed Crow he couldn't drink, and so the owner required him to keep track of what came out of stock. "I seen it in McAlester. Thisyer dun mare just up and rolled over on the cavalry sergeant that was riding her, snapped his neck like dry rot. Your Mr. Pip better watch that don't happen to him."

"Fermented mash, more'n likely, both cases." This last came courtesy of Dick Wagner, who for the past eleven years had stopped off at the Shaft precisely at 6:45 for one beer on his way home from the emporium.

He chewed sen-sen in prodigious amounts to keep his wife Lucy from detecting it on his breath.

"Pitt, not Pip," said Ekron. "Mr. Nicholas Pitt of Providence. Where's that?"

"East a-ways," Wagner said. "Kansas, I think."

"He didn't talk like no Jayhawker I ever heard. 'There's a good fellow,' says he, and gives me that there ten-cent piece."

"This ain't no ten-cent piece." Gordy Wolf was staring at the coin Ekron had given him for the drink. It had a wavy edge and had been stamped crooked with the likeness of nobody he recognized. He bit it.

"Might I see it?"

Gordy Wolf now focused his good eye on Professor the Doctor Webster Bennett, late of the New York University classical studies department, more lately of the Brimstone Saloon across the street. The bartender's hesitation did not mean he suspected that the coin would not be returned; he was just unaccustomed to having the good educator conscious at that hour. Professor the Doctor Bennett's white linen and carefully brushed broadcloth had long since failed to conceal from anyone in Persephone that beneath it, at any hour past noon, was a sizable bag.

Handed the piece, Professor the Doctor Bennett stroked the edge with his thumb, then raised his chin from the bar and studied the coin on both sides, at one point holding it so close to his pinkish right eye he seemed about to screw it in like a monocle. Finally he returned it.

"Roman. Issued, I would say, sometime after the birth of Christ, and not very long after. The profile belongs to Tiberius."

"It cover Ekron's drink?"

"I rather think it will." He looked at Ekron. "I would hear more of your Mr. Pitt."

"He ain't *my* Mr. Pitt. Anyway I don't much look at folks, just the animals they ride in on. Seen his clothes; fine city ones they was, and a duster. Hogleg tied down on his hip like you read in the nickel novels. And there's something else."

"Gunfighter?" Wagner sat up straight. His greatest regret, aside from having chosen Lucy for his helpmeet, was that he had come West from Louisiana too late to see a real gunfight. The great pistoleers were all dead or gone East to act on the stage. All except one, of course, and he had proved frustrating.

"Or a dude," said Gordy Wolf. "Tenderfoot comes out here, wants everyone to think he's Wild Bill."

Ekron spat, missing the cuspidor by his standard margin. "Forget the damn gun, it don't count. Leastwise not till it goes off. Gordy, you're injun. Man comes in off that desert country up North. Babocomari's dry till September, Tucson's a week's ride, gila and roadrunner's the only game twixt here and Iron Springs. What you figure he's got to have in provisions and truck?"

"Rifle, box of cartridges. Grain for the horse. Bacon for himself and maybe some tinned goods. Two canteens or a skin. That's if he's white. Apache'd do with the rifle and water."

"Well, Mr. Nicholas Pitt of Providence didn't have none of that."

"What you mean, just water?"

"I mean nothing. Not water nor food nor rifle nor even a blanket roll to keep the chill off his *cojones* in the desert at night. Man rides in with just his hip gun and saddle and nary a bead of sweat on man nor mount, and him with nothing behind him but a hunnert miles of sand and alkali." He jerked down his whiskey and looked around at his listeners. "Now, what would you call a man like that, if not the Devil his own self?"

Thus, in addition to having been first to spot the stranger who would mean so much to the town's fortunes, Ekron Fast settled upon him the appelation by which he would be commonly known when not directly addressed. From that time forward, His Own Self, uttered in silent but generally agreed-upon capitals, meant none other and required no illumination.

At the very moment that this unconscious christening was taking place, Guy Dante, manager at the Belial Hotel, was in the throes of a similar demonstration, albeit with somewhat less theater, for his wife. Angel Dante had come in perturbed to have found Dick Wagner gone and the emporium closed and therefore a trip wasted to purchase red ink with which to keep the books. As was his custom, Guy had been bleating on while she unpinned her hat and removed her gloves, and so went unheeded for the crucial first minute of his speech.

". . . registered with no mark like I ever saw, and him from his clothes and deportment a city gentleman who should certainly have enjoyed a considerable education," he finished.

"What mark? What gentleman? Oh, Mr. Dante, sometimes I believe you talk sideways just to increase my burden." She tugged on green velvet pen-wipers for another go at the books.

"Room six. He registered while you were out. I just sent Milton up with water for his bath. Weren't you listening?"

She didn't acknowledge the question. In truth she was slightly hard of hearing and preferred to have people think she was rude rather than advertise the fact that she was seven years older than her husband; a piece of enlightenment that would have surprised many of the town's citizens, who assumed that the difference was much greater. "I don't smell the stove," she said.

"He said cold water would be more than satisfactory. Here's his mark that I was telling you about." He shoved the registration book at her.

She seated her spectacles in the dents alongside her nose and examined the two-pronged device scratched deeply into the creamy paper. She ran a finger over it. "It looks like some kind of brand. He must be a cattleman."

"He didn't look like one. What would a cattleman be doing in this country?"

"Perhaps he knows something. Perhaps the railroad is coming and he's here to check out the prospects for shipping beef. Oh, Mr. Dante, why did you give him six? Nine's the presidential."

"He asked for six."

"Land. I hope you had the presence to have Milton carry up his traps."

"He didn't have any. And he didn't talk like any cattleman either. He asked about the Brimstone. Wanted to know if it's for sale."

"An entrepreneur, in Persephone?" She cast a glance up the stairs, removing her spectacles as if the portly, diamond-stickpinned figure she associated with an entrepreneur might appear on the landing and see them. "Land. He must know something."

"If he does, this town sure isn't it. Nor Ned Harpy. He'd sell his sister before he'd let that saloon go. And for a smaller price to boot."

"Nevertheless we must make him comfortable. Prosperity may be involved."

Dante made that braying noise his wife found distressing. "I hope he tells us when it's fixed to start. Wait till you see what he gave me for the room."

Only the manager's familiar bray rose above the first floor, where Milton heard it on his way to room six. Inside he hung up the fine striped suit he had finished brushing and asked the man splashing behind the screen if he wanted his boots blacked as well. Milton made beds, served meals, and banished dirt and dust from the Belial with an industry that came naturally to the son of a stablehand.

"If you would, lad." The man's whispery voice barely rose above the lapping in the tub. It reminded Milton of a big old rattler shucking its skin. "There's something on the bureau for you. Much obliged." Then he laughed, which was worse than when he spoke.

Milton picked up the boots, handsome black ones with butter-soft tops that flopped over and a curious two-pointed design on each toe that looked like a cow's hoofprint. They were made of a wonderful kind of leather he had never seen or felt before, as dark as his father's skin. His skin was much lighter than his father's. He knew that some mean folks around town said he wasn't Virgil's son at all, sired as like as not by some unparticular plantation owner—disregarding that Milton was only thirteen and born well after Mr. Lincoln did his duty. Such folks could go to hell.

He got a chill then, in that close room in July in Arizona, and took his mind off it by examining the strange coin he had picked up from the dresser. Confederate pewter, most like. No wonder Mr. Pitt had laughed.

Only he didn't think that was the reason. Damn little about strangers made sense—those few that found their way here after the last of the big silver interests had hauled its wagon east—but this one less than most. Where were his possibles? Why weren't his clothes caked and stinking of man and horse, instead of just dusty? And how was it, after Milton had filled the bathtub himself with buckets of water ice-cold from the pump, that steam was rolling out under the screen where the stranger was bathing?

Josh Marlowe rode up from Mexico in the middle of a September rainstorm with water funneling off his hat brim fore and aft and shining on his black oilskin. Charon's hoofs splashed mud up over his boots and made sucking sounds when they pulled clear. The gray snorted its misery.

Josh concurred. In times past he had preferred entering a town in weather that kept folks indoors. There were some short fuses then who'd throw down on him the second they recognized him but wouldn't later when they had a chance to think about it, making arrivals the most dangerous time in a gunman's experience. But that was before he'd given up the road. Persephone was home, and now that there was no danger he discovered he hated riding in the rain.

Peaceable though he was these days, he clung to his old custom of coming in the back way. He dismounted behind the livery, found the back door locked, stepped back, and kicked it until Virgil opened it from inside. He stood there like always with coal-oil light at his back and his old Colt's Dragoon gleaming in his big black fist.

"Virgil, how many times I tell you to snuff that lantern when a stranger comes?"

The stablehand's barn-door grin shone in the bad light. He stuck the big pistol under his belt. "Balls, Mr. Josh. You ain't no stranger."

Josh left the point short of argument and handed him the reins. "How's Milton?"

"Gettin' uppity. Hotel work's got him thinking he's town folks." He led the gray inside.

The barrel stove was glowing. Josh slung his saddle and pouches over an empty stall and warmed his hands. When he turned to put heat on his backside he spotted the black standing in its stall. He whistled. Reflection from the fire made its eyes look red.

"That there's Mr. Pitt's horse." Virgil began rubbing down Charon with burlap. "You stand clear of that animal, Mr. Josh. He's just plain evil."

"Who might Mr. Pitt be?"

"That's right, you been gone."

"Two months trailing grandee beef to Mexico City. This Pitt with the railroad? Credit won't acquire a mount like that."

"If he is, the railroad done bought the Brimstone. Mr. Pitt he runs the place now."

"Horseshit. Ned Harpy told me he'd die before he sold out."

"I reckon he wasn't pulling your leg."

Josh saw the stablehand wasn't smiling. "The hell you say."

The black horse reared, screamed, plunged, and kicked its stall. The hammering mingled with a long loud peal of thunder. Even Charon shied from it.

"You see what I mean about that animal," Virgil said when it had calmed down. "It happened real quick, Mr. Josh. Mr. Ned he got mad when that Mr. Pitt wouldn't take no as an answer and pulled on him right there in the gameroom. Only Mr. Pitt filled his hand first and just drilled that man full of holes. He was dead when he hit the floor. Mrs. Harpy she sold out and went back East."

"Ned was fast."

"Near as fast as you." Virgil was grave. "You stay out of the Brimstone, Mr. Josh."

He grinned. "Save that talk for your boy. I gave all that up years ago."

"I hopes so, Mr. Josh. I surely does. You can't beat that man. Nobody can."

From there Josh went to the Fallen Shaft, where he closed the door against the wind and rain and piano music clattering out of the Brimstone. Gordy Wolf was alone. He took his elbows off the bar.

"Josh Marlowe. Gouge out my eyes and pour vinegar in the holes if it ain't. What can I draw you, Josh?"

"Tanglefoot. Where is everybody?" He slapped water off his hat and hooked a heel over the rail.

Gordy Wolf shook his head, poured, and made a mark in the ledger. "You could touch off a Hotchkiss in here since they put the piano in across the street. Nobody'd mind."

"What about Professor the Doctor Webster Bennett? He'd never desert the Shaft."

"He's give up the Creature. Says it don't fit with teaching school."

"That's what the council said when they booted him for falling on his face during sums. Then they closed down the schoolhouse."

"Mr. Pitt bought it and opened it back up. Professor the Doctor ain't got but six pupils and one of them's near as old as him. Way he struts and fluffs his feathers you'd think he's still learning Eyetalian and Greek to them rich men's sons back home."

"This the same Pitt killed Ned Harpy?"

"If there's two I'd hear about it."

"From what Virgil said I didn't take him to be one for the community."

"Before the school he bought the Belial Hotel from Old Man Merry and deeded it to Guy and Angel Dante and then he bought the emporium from Dick Wagner and made him manager at the Brimstone."

"I can't feature Lucy Wagner sitting still for that."

"Lucy went back to New Orleans. She got on worse with Mr. Pitt than she did with Dick. You wouldn't know Dick now. He's got him a red vest and spats."

"What's Pitt's purpose? When the mines played out I gave Persephone five years."

"He told Ekron Fast there's future here. Then he bought him a new forge and an autymobile."

"Ain't no autymobiles twixt here and Phoenix."

"There's one now. 'Thisyer's the future I been telling you about,' he says to Ekron. 'Master it.' Ekron run it straight into an arroyo. But he fixed it with his new forge."

"I reckon he's one stranger who's made himself popular," Josh said.

"He's got him an eye for what every man he meets wants more'n anything, plus a pocket deep enough to get it for him."

"Except Ned Harpy."

"Nobody much liked Ned anyway. If Mr. Pitt was to run for mayor tomorrow I reckon he'd get everybody's vote but two."

"How is it he ain't throwed his loop over you and Virgil?"

The half-breed put an elbow on the bar and leaned in close enough for Josh to discover that his ledger-keeping had not prevented him from sampling the Shaft's stock. "On account of Virgil's a Christian man," he said. "And on account of I ain't. Mr. Pitt he gets what falls between."

"That's heathen talk."

"It ain't neither. Just because they throwed me out of the mission school after a week don't mean I didn't hear what they had to teach."

Josh drank whiskey. "I got to meet this fellow."

"How long's it been since you wore a pistol?" Gordy Wolf kept his good eye on him.

"Three years."

"You'd best not."

"Talking's all I'm after."

"When your kind meets his kind it don't stop at talking."

"What kind's mine, Christian or Ain't?"

"I seen you struggling with both."

He stopped grinning and drained his glass. "It's a damn shame the mission school didn't keep you, Gordy. You'd of made a right smart preacher."

"Call me what you like. I'm just saying you'd best climb on that gray horse and ride out and forget all about Persephone. That Mr. Pitt is hell on the draw."

Thunder cracked.

Two months was hardly long enough for the Brimstone to change as much as it had since Josh's last visit. It was one thing to cover the knotty walls with scarlet cloth and take down the prizefighter prints behind the bar to make room for a gilt-framed painting of a reclining naked fat lady holding an apple and laughing; quite another to rip out the old pine bar and replace it with one made from gnarled black oak with what looked like horned evil children carved into the corners. Such items, like the enormous chandelier that now swung from the center rafter, its thousand candles filling the room with oppressive heat, required more time than that to order and deliver. Let alone make, for what catalogue house stocked statuary representing serpents amorously entwined with more naked femininity like the two Amazons thus engaged on either side of the batwing doors?

Mr. Pitt's tastes were apparently not excessive for Persephone's nightlife, however. The main room was packed. Under an awning of lazily turning smoke the drinkers' voices rose above the noise from the piano,

where a thickish man in a striped suit and derby was playing something fit
to raise blisters on a stump. The strange fast melody was unknown to Josh,
who decided he had been below the border a mite too long.

"Look what the wind blew up from Mexico!"

Gordy Wolf hadn't lied about the spats and red vest. They were accompanied by green silk sleeve garters, a platinum watch chain with a dyed
rabbit's-foot fob, and an Eastern straw hat tipped forward at such a steep
angle the former merchant had to slant his head back to see in front of
him.

"Howdy, Dick." Josh sentenced his hand to serious pumping by one
heavy with rings.

"What you think of the old place?" Dick Wagner asked. His eyes
looked wild and he was grinning to his molars.

"Talks up for itself, don't it?"

"Loud and proud. Lucy'd hate it to death." He roared and clapped a
hand on Josh's shoulder. "Keep! Draw one on the house for my gunsling-
ing friend here."

"After I talk to the owner. He around?"

"That's him banging the pianny."

Josh stared at the derbied piano player. He was built like a nailkeg and
very fair—a fact that surprised Josh, though he could not own why—and
wore jaunty reddish chin-whiskers that put the former gunman in mind of
an elf he had seen carved on the door of Irish Mike's hospitable house in
St. Louis. As Josh approached him he turned glass-blue eyes on the new-
comer. "I'll warrant you're Marlowe." He went on playing the bizarre
tune.

"I reckon news don't grow much grass in a town this size."

"Nor does your reputation. I am Nicholas Pitt, originally of Providence.
You'll excuse me for not clasping hands."

"It sounds a difficult piece."

"A little composition of my own. But it's not the reason. I only touch
flesh with someone when we've reached accord."

Something in Pitt's harsh whisper made Josh grateful for this eccentric-
ity. "I admired your horse earlier this evening."

"Beelzebub? I've had him forever. Ah, thank you, Margaret. Can I
interest you in a libation, Marlowe?" He quit playing and accepted a tall
glass from a plump girl in a spangled corset. She looked to Josh like one of
old Harry Bosch's daughters. He shook his head. Pitt shrugged and drank.
A thread of steam rose from the liquid when he lowered it. "I watched you
as you came in. You don't approve of the renovations." It was a statement.

"I ain't used to seeing the place so gussy."

"The gameroom is unoccupied. I'll show it to you if you'll mosey in there with me." Laughing oddly, he rose. His coat-frock swayed, exposing briefly the shiny black handle of a Colt's Peacemaker strapped to his hip.

The side room was similarly appointed, with the addition of faro and billiard tables covered in red felt. Milton, the black stablehand's son, sat in the dealer's chair polishing a cuspidor.

"That will be all, lad." Pitt tossed him a silver dollar.

Josh laid a hand on Milton's shoulder as he was headed for the door. "Your pa know you're here?"

"Nosir. I get a whuppin'. But Mr. Pitt he pays better than the hotel." He lowered his voice. " 'Specially since he started paying real money." He left.

"Good lad. But I have hopes for him." Pitt took another sip and set his glass on the billiard table, where it boiled over.

"Who are you?" Josh asked.

"I am a speculator."

"Persephone's past speculating."

"That's where you're wrong, Marlowe. My commodity is most plentiful here."

"What's your commodity?"

"Something that is valued by only three in town at present. Milton's father Virgil, because he understands it. The half-breed Gordy Wolf, because he does not possess it. And I."

"What about me?"

"You have been a signal disappointment. When you came to this territory, that item which you are pleased to call yours was more than half mine. Since then you have begun to reclaim it."

"You came to take it back?"

Pitt laughed. It sounded like scales dragging over stone. "You exalt yourself. What is your soul against the soul of an entire town?"

"Then Virge and Gordy was right. You're him."

"Succinctly put. Gary Cooper would be proud."

"Who?"

"Perhaps I should explain myself. But where to start? Aha. Has it ever occurred to you in your wanderings that the people you meet are a tad too colorful, their behavior insufferably eccentric, their language over-folksy? That they themselves are rather—well, *broad?* Half-breed Crows tending bar, drunken college professors, henpecked merchants, gossipy black-

smiths, Negro liverymen who talk as if they just stepped off the plantation
—really, where does one encounter these types outside of entertainment?"

"Keep cranking, Mr. Pitt. You ain't drawed a drop yet."

"There. That's just what I mean. Why can't you say simply that you
don't follow? I don't suppose you'd understand the concept of alternate
earths."

Josh said nothing.

"There is, if you will, a Master Earth, against which all the lesser
alternate earths must be measured. Each earth has an equal number of
time frames, and it's my privilege to move in and out of these frames
among the Master and alternate earths. Now, on Master Earth, the American West within this frame is quite different from the one in which you
and I find ourselves. *This* West, with its larger-than-life characters and
chivalric codes of conduct, is but a mythology designed for escapist entertainment on Master Earth. That earth's West is a much drearier place.
Are you still with me?"

"Sounds like clabber."

"How to put it." Pitt worried a whiskered lip between small ivory teeth.
"You were a gunfighter. Were you ever struck by the absurdity of this
notion that the faster man in a duel is the moral victor, when the smart
way to settle a fatal difference would be to ambush your opponent or shoot
him before he's ready?"

"We don't do things that way here."

"Of course not. But on Master Earth they do. Or did. I get my tenses
tangled jumping between time frames. In any case, being who and what I
am, I thought it would be fine sport to do my speculating in this alternate
West. The fact that I am mortal here lends a nice edge to those splendid
fast-draw contests like the one I enjoyed with Ned Harpy. His soul was
already mine when I came here, but I couldn't resist the challenge." He
sighed heavily; Josh felt the heat. "I'm aggrieved to say I've found none to
compare with it. I'd expected more opposition."

"You talk like you got the town sewed up."

"I bagged the entire council this very afternoon when I promised them
they'd find oil if they drilled north of Cornelius Street. The rest is sweep-
ings."

"What do you need with Milton?"

"The souls of children hold no interest for me. But his father's would
be a prize. I'm certain a trade can be arranged. Virgil will make an excellent pair of boots when these wear out." He held up a glossy black toe and
laughed. Wind and rain lashed the windows, howling like demons.

"You trade often?"

Pitt cocked an eyebrow under the derby. "When the bargain is sufficient. What are you proposing?"

"I hear you're fast against saloonkeepers. How are you with a genuine gunman?"

"Don't be ludicrous. You haven't been in a fight in years."

"You yellowing out?"

Pitt didn't draw; the Peacemaker was just in his hand. Lightning flashed, thunder roared, a windowpane blew in and rain and wind extinguished the lamps in the room. All at once they re-ignited. The Peacemaker was in its holster. Pitt smiled. "What will you use for a gun?"

"I'll get one."

"That won't be necessary." He opened a drawer in the faro table and took out a glistening gray leather gun belt with a slate-handled converted Navy Colt's in the holster. "I think you'll find this will fit your hand."

Josh accepted the rig and drew out the pistol. The cylinder was full. "I sold this set in Tucson. How'd you come by it?"

"I keep track of such things. What are the spoils?"

"Me and the town if you win. If I win you ride out on that red-eyed horse and don't come back. Leave the town and everybody in it the way you found them."

"That won't be necessary. In the latter event I'd be as dead as you in the former. In this world, anyway. What is hell for a gunfighter, Marlowe? Eternity on a dusty street where you take on all challengers, your gun hand growing swollen and bloody, never knowing which man you face is your last? I'll see you're kept interested."

"Stop jawing and go to fighting."

Smiling, Pitt backed up several paces, spread his feet, and swept his coat-frock behind the black-handled pistol, setting himself. Josh shot him.

The storm wailed. Pitt staggered back against the billiard table and slid to the floor. Black blood stained his striped vest. The glass-blue eyes were wide. "Your gun was already out! You didn't give me a chance!"

Josh shrugged. "Did you think you were the only one who could travel between worlds?"

Hansel's Finger

LEIF ENGER

Leif Enger's story is not a Western. I admit it up front. There are some mentions of Western things (boots, etc.) herein, but it isn't a Western and it isn't playing with the Western myth. I wanted it anyway because it's good.

So sue me.

I felt that if I didn't take it, it wouldn't find a home, as it's such a nongenre story, and I feared that, worse, it might end up in some stuffy literary magazine.

So, Western or not, here it is. My love is for good fiction first, then the Western.

And this guy knows what he's doing. And he's young. And this is his first story!

Personally, I hate him.

In a painted plastic boat, the silver safety rail snug against your lap, you begin the little voyage: a cave is where it all starts, cement stalactites fingering the artificial river, which still manages to trick you with its salamander smell. Outside it is midafternoon, hot as bird screams, and heavy with the cumulative breath of exhausted tourists; here in the cave, bumping through the water, it is ten at night and twelve is just visible if you lean forward. There's a small skidding sound now as your shell accelerates. You scrape the bottom once more, tilt several degrees to the right and *floom*, into the dark and down a drop that makes your arms float up in front of you. Celia wouldn't have liked this, but you've left her back in Paradise Valley to eat onion rings until your return, which is tomorrow. Actually you could have gone back yesterday; the conference ended early when two vice presidents forsook their places at the table for a day of charter deep-sea fishing. But your reservations were already made, and here you are, waiting to be amazed in a cave, and the first of the celebrated pirates is now ahead, on your left.

It's a skeleton pirate, actually, the fake remains upright, pinned contrapposto by a cutlass. Disney *invented* pirates, Celia would have said; in your mind she walks the plank, leaving you alone, in danger, happy. The skeleton turns its head to watch as you scoot slowly past, and now you enter larger waters. The sea, apparently. It's nighttime on the coast of some homely Caribbean point of land, and offshore a ragged galleon is pouring a hell of ball and grapeshot into the streets of an honest village. This is long-distance battle; some of the cannon just don't have the range, and shipside ammo keeps pounding the water near your fragile craft. You're on the pirates' side, of course. If the villagers had wanted to avoid fire and pillage and all the rest of it, why didn't they set up shop further inland? But there they are, under siege, and evidently indignant about it. Landlubbers. They shout angrily, waving brooms.

You regret having to leave the invasion before it's finished—one of the fist-raising village viragoes, certain to get hers eventually, looks a little like Celia—but your boat's leaving now, and you have to go with it. Under a bridge, two loutish mannequins (my word, they even have hair on their *legs*) grin at you as you pass, offering the brown bottle. It's nearly done, so short a ride—and now, as the tunnel narrows down again and that midday heat shines from a hole in the distance, a final attraction. You cruise past so slowly, so close, you could reach out and brush a finger against his cheek. He is a strong, old pirate. He is the veteran of a million days on the water, a thousand years of breathing salt and gold. In the crow's-feet of his eyes are the weight of doubloons, the kisses of stolen women, the corpses of his mates. There are pistols braced in his belt, a huge throw of ale in one fist, and a cutlass in the other, which he pounds, in slow motion, upon a stump. The stump, you notice as you slip away, is the pirate's table: it holds a lump of cheese, black bread, and a bottle. The cutlass jerks firmly up and down, a robotic exercise, missing the cheese by an inch.

And after that it's over. You're in the last run now, surfacing, coming awake. The subterranean humidity begins baking away with the first breath of afternoon that reaches you, and you twist in your seat, checking the wallet, the keys. As you do so the butt of someone's old cigar rolls away from you and bumps into the corner of the car. Disgusting. You pick it up to toss it away, now while you're still in the water, and it surprises you and makes you stare. It isn't a cigar. It's someone's finger.

On September 24th, 1984, at approximately 2:30 in the afternoon, within the steaming confines of Disney World, Florida, Howard Arvis became the only person he knew ever to find a finger outside its normal scope of human involvement. Although his first impulse was to throw it away, he was unable to do it. He held it out in front of him, both of his hands gripping part of someone else's, the finger as black and vertical as an exclamation mark: *Look at me!* Howard Arvis looked, reaffirmed the rare digit for what it was, and remembered to close a fist around it before the ride dry-docked and was boarded by a bright new crew.

"When you're trapped with a finger in a crowded amusement park," Howard Arvis would later write to his brother in Iowa, "there are no conventional escapes." This was a truth he discovered as he was looking for a fitting dismissal of his new secret; when he tried dumping the finger into one of Disney's frequent trash bins, a corner of his conscience wouldn't let him. This wasn't a corn dog he was tossing away unfinished, or a chocolate-covered banana; this was someone's trusted finger, a once versatile index which had point at sunsets and rubbed the chins of chuckling babies. "With five fingers and a thumb in your right-hand pocket, there's very little else you can keep your mind on," Howard wrote.

He also found he couldn't leave the park. He hadn't intended to stay all day, under pre-trip admonitions from Celia that more than six hours of that bloated Florida sun was bad for one's body thermostat, but when he neared the outgate, still one finger richer than natural man, the thought of leaving and riding for an hour and then arriving back in his clean, white hotel room with that blackened holy object still on his person was too much for his honest mind. He'd parked the rented Skylark in the Goofy lane, row thirty-eight, at 9:05 that morning. Twenty minutes later, goosed into the park by shuttle and monorail, he had breakfasted on Mickey ice cream, vanilla-faced with two chocolate ears. Then he did all the rides he could find, sweating out the ice cream under the sun and a sport coat, ignoring his hollow stomach as the day got hotter and hotter because *Boy* there's so much to see here, and then he'd found that famous pirate ride. It was the one he'd seen film of on a Sunday-night TV show years before, when the Disney thing was just beginning. And the cave sure looked cool, and *was* cool, and he had gone into it thinking of Celia and come out with a sorry old finger which demanded proper disposal. He stepped out of the sidewalk crush and into a vast rest room, where he was able to examine the finger in the private blue light of a stall. Taking it from his pocket (it was rubbing against a load of change, he realized with disgust—he remembered putting pennies in his mouth as a child, and understood his mother's consternation to a degree *she* never had) he held it at eye level. It quelled his whining stomach. The finger had apparently been owned by a Caucasian male of medium size, and the amputation hadn't been clean. Howard closed his eyes. The finger, clasped between his own index and thumb, felt very dry and wrinkled and slightly rubbery, like a carrot forgotten over the summer in the refrigerator. Howard dropped it into a jacket pocket—no change there—and aimed his mind at a juniper bush he'd planted with Celia last spring. So wonderfully fragrant. So green and romantic and promising. Howard Arvis stepped from the stall with the dead stem in his pocket. He knew he would never eat again.

Howard had been just nine years old when his neighbor Hans Harrickson had dismembered a hand with a lawn mower. Hans' father owned a tired Minneapolis Moline tractor under which was wired a wide-swath grass-cutter, an arrangement which predated the Cub Cadet by decades. The Moline was fired up a couple of times a month to return a sense of domicile to the sage-grown Harrickson yard; one Saturday, only hours after Mr. Harrickson had sharpened the scary blades and lubed the rotor, Hans got off the tractor to snag a wayward garter snake, and as he fumbled in the grass a blade spun free and flicked off the leading edge of his right hand. It was pretty weird, he'd told Howard two days later while showing off the bandages. The ring finger and pinky, took right off. *Zippo,* he said, just like that. The snake got away. And long after the scar tissue had set and turned the color of regular skin and Hans had become used to giving less than he got in a handshake, the wound remained a sort of barometer. It predicted autumn, Hans said, a good six weeks before the last mowing of every summer. "Got to keep it in my pocket," he told Howard. "Or my armpit. Always July in there." No one had ever found Hans's fingers. "Didn't think to look," Hans said.

"When you find a finger in Disney World," Howard wrote to his brother in Iowa, "you quickly realize there's no Lost and Found." Actually Howard had walked right past the Lost and Found, but was preoccupied enough to miss it; if he had seen it, he probably would have passed it anyway, not wanting to approach the clear-faced girl behind the counter: "Here, found this on one of the rides. Has anyone been looking for it?" Howard Arvis was not a seeker of that sort of attention. Instead, he found he was gazing at the hands of men he passed on the walk—full, four-finger-and-a-thumb men without exception, the hands swinging at their sides mostly, though some were tucked into pockets. These he viewed with more care, looking at their faces, seeking concealed agony. He saw many smiles, many empty expressions, many squints from tired parents. It was too late anyway; the finger was beyond resuscitation, and its former owner was probably home from the hospital already, whiskeying down in preparation for the novocaine's fade-out. Howard thought, *Probably a college student, who was well watered when it happened and is going to be*

awfully surprised when he wakes up. Howard imagined a new freshman on
his first weekend home: "How was Hell Week?" his parents would ask.
"Did you make the fraternity?" "Sure did," the kid would say. "Shake."

By dinnertime Howard Arvis had covered most of the Disney park on
foot and needed to sit down. He headed on instinct for a neat quick-
seafood shop with blue colonial siding and white Shaker chairs, but got a
peek of someone's shrimp before he reached the counter and recommitted
himself to starvation. The shrimp were curled, pinkylike, their still-at-
tached tails spatulate, like fingertips slammed in a car door. Howard
turned on his groaning soles and aimed for the closest ride.

It turned out to be the Snow White adventure, in which the main
character was not Snow White or the Seven Dwarfs but a wart-ridden
witch that darted out and offered him poisoned apples every time he
turned a corner. Howard was grateful for the rest, but annoyed by the
ride; there were too many witches here, and too few dwarfs. He had never
seen Snow White on TV or read the story in a book, but it was his
understanding there was only one witch in it. Maybe he'd been wrong.
Howard's car bumped forward through a dark cardboard tunnel and, *bam,*
another witch slid out, leering: *Have an apple, sonny.* He wanted to slap
the witch, but instead closed his eyes and leaned back in his seat. Why
didn't they build a story-ride you could understand? Something straight-
forward like Hansel and Gretel: it had a witch, just one, and there was
even something about a finger in it. Yes. The blind old witch was fattening
Hansel for a stew and was feeling his finger every day to check his rate of
weight gain. Only he was tricking her, poking a bone through the bars:
Sorry, lady, fast metabolism. It was pretty clever of Hansel, really, staving
her off like that day after day, staying out of the pot by displaying a
surrogate. Probably his real fingers were like link sausage. It worked
though, and in the end he and Gretel had followed a trail of bread crumbs
back to their quaint little woodcutter's hut in the forest. Helped by a
substitute finger, they had turned the corner from the witch's nasty shop
to the ultimate place of warmth and safety: an oven that presumably
baked bread instead of children, and a father within yelling distance,
whose job it was to carry an ax. Howard wondered if Hansel had then
carried around his lucky finger bone, which had, after all, served him
better than a plump rabbit's foot would have, or if he'd given it a decent
burial. Probably neither, Howard decided; probably he just threw it at a
tree stump or a sparrow on his walk home through the woods with Gretel.
Just, *zing,* threw it away.

It would never work that way in Disney World.

After Snow White, Howard went on the Peter Pan ride, in which his car took off and flew, like Peter, only in slower motion, over the rooftops of a tiny London. He was not fooled, as he had tried to be among the Caribbean pirates, especially when he caught his first look at the Peter Pan pirate, Captain Hook. Even with a detached finger getting old in his pocket, it didn't bother Howard that the Captain was an amputee; the cartoonity of this particular ride was tiring to his mind and suggestive to his stomach. As a boy he had practiced a rigorous exercise of eating during cartoons, especially on Saturday mornings. One favorite show concerned the adventures of a boy, probably a cousin of the Pan family, who could fly, and young Howie Arvis had watched him do it week after week while eating yellow bowls of Cheetos. The taste, which had been hidden in his mouth just where the tongue joins the back of the jaw, came out now and began to tease the salivary glands. *I'm going to eat,* Howard thought. *Something huge and fried and salty,* he thought. *Finger or not.*

He did not eat something huge and fried, though his intention was firm. It was past nine o'clock when he got done with the Pan flight (it had ended with Captain Hook about to be reunited with his lost hand, in the belly of a crocodile which had swallowed it years before), and all visible venders were closing up. Not a taco, not a burger, not a godforsaken foot-long wiener was available, and to head for a sit-down place at this hour was to be a nuisance to the cooks and janitorial staff. Howard had, in the end, to settle for a watery malted which was like vanilla with a misplaced spurt of chocolate. A glass of melted Mickey Bars. *As I began,* Howard thought, *so shall I end. Hungry, and with only my fingers to count on.*

In his freshman year of college Howard Arvis had been taken with a girl, a woman, not Celia, and he had carried her lipstick in the glovebox of his Ford for six years. It was the only item he'd ever owned for which he felt the same solemnity and responsibility as the stale joint in his polyester pocket. Sheila. The "she" at the beginning of her name was perfect, a fitting prefix for a woman so inveterate at squeezing the nectar out of whatever crowd she happened to be with. Sheila wore whipstitched work shirts, a wild white grin, and peg-leg Levis that dove into sharkskin boots. The boots were Sheila: tall-heeled, narrow-toed, and white as the Western sun. Her smile made her invisible to the night guards at the all-male dorm. By herself she could create a mob, then pick out one soul from the condemned and gallop away like a high wind, leaving the rest grabbing at their hats. Howard had been the survivor one night, plucked from a pearl-snap bar and pulled along by Sheila's soft hands, blinking in surprise.

"Where should we go?" Howard had said, love-uncertain, struck by luck.

"To the country," said Sheila, and Howard was amazed at how faint and true her voice was away from people. Warm as new skin.

He angled the Fairlane off the highway and into a piñon stand, black in the high Nevada night. Just before they turned it off, the radio told them forty-nine degrees.

"Would you take off your shirt for me?" said Sheila.

Howard would have taken it off and then eaten it. When his torso was bare and chill as a brick, Sheila touched him with her fingers, then asked him to turn around and face out the window. He did, and heard her hands searching her purse. It clinked softly with combs, compacts, feminine things. She said, "Hold still." He held and in an instant arched high with the waxy tickle of her lipstick running patterns on his back. It dipped and dodged, and he laughed in fear and disbelief, squirming.

"Hold still," she said. "I'm drawing." She said it so quietly he gripped the door handle in one hand and the wheel in the other and let her draw. It was an abstract design, she told him, a series of up-and-down lines raked over by some side-to-side lines, not a real picture of anything at all.

"Like a fishnet?" said Howard, who couldn't see it.

"I suppose, if you've got to put a name on it," Sheila said.

He kept her lipstick after that, sliding the tube into the pocket of his on-again flannel shirt and later placing it gently into the corner of the Fairlane's glovebox. The fishnet attracted the envy of his roommate and came off during his next three showers. Sheila saved another soul the next week, and then another, leaving Howard as dry as a slow south breeze.

"To depart from a finger one is just beginning to know," Howard wrote to his brother in Iowa, torturing his brain to form the thought, "might be similar to divorce. There must be a good deal of grace present, and when it's over you just stand there by yourself."

With the light gone and the temperature down to sixty degrees in the Magic Kingdom, Howard cupped the finger in his pocket and made a glazed walk toward the exit gates. The alien felt cool as Sheila's lipstick in his palm and ticklish to his skin. It also felt bigger, heavier, important, a growing child to be responsible for. He did not want it, could not leave the park with it. He leaned forward against its tug.

In the flannel glow of blue-white Disney light, the cobblestones lead you over a bridge. The exit is ahead, an impossibility for you: your little passenger won't have it. The bridge arches more dramatically than it needs to, and at its peak you look down and see the swan. It's a Disney swan, but living; it shakes droplets from its beak like mercury and splays its feathers. The swan sways its neck and looks at you the way Sheila did. It is a good sign. The last of the tourists are at the exit now, boarding trams. The swan is waiting. With the mind of Hansel and the grip of a Barbary corsair, you pull the finger free and hold it high. You stretch back, whip forward, and release. The throw is better than you ever thought you could be, high and spinning, better than all the cucumbers you tossed growing up. The twig comes down, deflated now, black against the water. The swan lunges, its neck wand-white, and you look back toward the exit. Your plane leaves tomorrow, for Celia.

First Dawning

ROBERT EASTON

Robert Easton, who, along with William F. Nolan, helped locate and supply the Max Brand piece in this volume, is the author of three novels, a trilogy dealing with California from 1769 to the present day, and he has also written a number of short stories and nonfiction works. Among the latter is Max Brand: The Big Westerner, *a biography of his father-in-law. It has been called "the standard work on Max Brand." It is that, indeed.*

And the following piece by Mr. Easton is part of a novel in progress. It is beautiful and poetic and haunting.

That night Francisco was unable to sleep. The new way he'd determined to follow did not appear easy. But he resolved to pursue it with all the stubbornness of his obstinate nature.

His mother's repudiation of him followed by his humiliation at the hands of Buck Jenkins in the oak grove had changed something in him irrevocably. Beneath his rage and shame, a nearly dead ember from his youth had begun to glow: that desire to be united with a cause larger than himself, something great and worthwhile such as he'd once dreamed of and sought.

As a first step he decided to go in search of old Tilhini, the aged Indian wise man, friend and counselor of his youth, set aside and neglected all these years.

Lighting his bedside candle he rose and went to his clothes cabinet. Rummaging through it he found the garments and equipment he'd used as a young man. Here was the ancient waist net of milkweed fiber for carrying personal articles. Here were the moccasins beautifully beaded by his mother's hand. Here also was the bow of polished juniper reinforced with deer sinew which old Tilhini with his parents' encouragement—they wanting their son to embody both white and Indian ways—had taught him to use.

Putting on waist net and moccasins, tying his coarse dark hair into a knot at the top of his head and thrusting the bone-handled flint knife through it, Francisco picked up his bow and took down the quiver made of a mountain lion's tail which hung on the wall with the red-shafted arrows in it, and was about to leave the room when he remembered something.

Rummaging again in the cabinet he came across a bowl containing powdered red ochre. Carrying the bowl to his dressing table he moistened the ocher with water from the pitcher, mixing in tallow fat from the candle. Then, using his fingers he smeared his body with red paint to protect it from sunburn.

Glancing scornfully at the costly silk shirt, fashionable velvet jacket and trousers, and the fancy shoes and tasseled leggings he'd discarded onto a chair the night before, he suddenly changed his mind and bent and stuffed them into his waist net.

Then taking bow and quiver again he slipped quietly out of the dark house and made his way under the stars to the Indianada, that collection of huts by the river his parents had established decades ago as an alternative to mission Indian life. There old ways had been practiced all these years.

Finding Tilhini's hut empty, Francisco thought he might be in the sweathouse nearby at the edge of the stream, its mounded surface clearly visible in the starlight, where men sometimes spent the night.

Descending into the interior of the mound by its pole ladder, he scented smoke, glimpsed coals, heard a quavery voice he recognized as coming from old Ramon, the crippled caretaker, who though bent nearly double from rheumatism brought wood for the daily fires and kept the sweathouse clean so that others might enjoy meditation and conversation there.

"He is not here. He has gone into the hills!" Ramon explained, staring in silent astonishment at Francisco's garb, and instantly Francisco remembered this was the time of the summer solstice and that Tilhini had very likely gone into the backcountry to worship at a special shrine.

This rejoiced him because it seemed exactly in keeping with his new determination.

"Give me a handful of food, old man, for I travel a long trail!" Without a word Ramon took a handful of seed meal from his pouch and handed it to him.

Leaving the sweathouse Francisco proceeded into the wild interior, moving at a steady jog along the familiar river trail, the water singing beside him, the night air exhilarating. Soon he was among steep-sided mountains where dense chaparral came down with its fragrant odors and the loneliness and embracing silence opened his mind to thoughts almost forgotten since youth.

He recalled setting out along this path to find his uncle Asuskwa, his mother's brother, the famous leader of resistance against the invading white men—remembered finding Asuskwa in his hideaway deep in the fastness of the interior, and how their meeting ended for Francisco in bitter disillusion when he decided against embracing a cause which seemed doomed however admirable. "Am I then out of my mind now?" he asked himself. For word had reached him of the terrible slaughters of Indians of the interior mountains and valleys by white settlers and soldiers. He was taking his life in his hands as he journeyed in that direction with what he had in mind, yet his thoughts encouraged him too. Because the killing had not all been one-sided. The wild hinterland was a center of valiant resistance. White men's blood had stained Indian arrows, knives and bullets. A struggle was taking place which had begun in the time of his father the conquistador, in those days of first contact between native Californians and white-skinned invaders, and continued to this moment.

At midday he stopped in the shade of a giant sycamore by a deep pool where he'd fished and swum as a boy, and took a refreshing dip, ate a handful of Ramon's seed meal and jogged on, feeling more at peace with himself than in years. With night came weariness and he scooped a hollow for his body in a dry sandbar and covered himself with the sun-warmed sand, and the earth seemed to envelop him like a blessing.

Toward midafternoon next day he recognized familiar landmarks, looked up and saw the outcropping of brown-gray rock which contained the Cave of the Condors, the shrine to which Tilhini had once conducted him and where he guessed the old man might now have retired.

As he climbed the steep path amongst fragrant sage and prickly yucca, he saw the short paunchy figure standing at the mouth of the huge scallop-shaped opening. Instead of the coarse woolen shirt and trousers of a ranch hand which he usually wore, Tilhini was naked and painted red like himself, and wore the sacred ceremonial skirt of long dark condor feathers and the headdress of tall upright owl and magpie plumes surrounded at the base by sacred white down signifying clouds and sky power. Tilhini was painting the rock. His brush of badger tail hairs moved steadily from the tiny pigment containers at his belt to the wall of the cave and back.

Francisco remembered that the solstice activities of astrologer-priests like Tilhini were directed at placating supernatural forces, particularly those of the Sun, the Great Ruler, and the Moon, the other great eye which watches the earth, and thus were aimed at keeping the universe in balance and enabling human life to continue despite drought and pestilence and flood. Ordinary people were not supposed to approach at these times but Francisco relied on his special relationship with his former mentor and advanced slowly in respectful silence.

He was surprised to see that Tilhini was painting not a sun disk or a moon crescent or a sacred condor, but a long black line of settlers' wagons like those of the Jenkins family with white hoods drawn by black mules following one another over a cliff into oblivion.

Tilhini was painting to exorcise the white invader and Francisco's excitement rose because it made his arrival at this moment seem especially propitious.

The old man turned as if he'd been expecting him and said simply, "You have come!"

Francisco was filled with joy by the intimate affection of this welcome and burst out: "Old Father, I have come back! I wish to be admitted again into the Indian way! I wish to receive again from you my Indian name, Helek the Hawk, which you gave me in my infancy and which I'd almost forgotten!" He was surprised how true and strong these words sounded. They came from deep down, like the gush of water from a spring.

"Very well, my son. I paint to preserve that way from those who would obliterate it." He pointed to his work. "The rock speaks my meaning. The Sky People may hear. But I have prepared myself for this moment over long hours and years, so that I am sure of what I say. What about you? Are you sure? I see you have brought your clothes with you."

"For special reasons, Old Father, that I may not disclose even to you.

Yes, I am sure. Look at me. Do you not see someone new? I wish to take once more and for the rest of my life the Indian way."

Tilhini smiled with pleasure but also with thoughtfulness. "My son, I celebrate this moment. But let me speak truth. One does not easily reenter the ancient path. First you must prepare yourself. Are you ready for the vision in which you may see the dream helper who will guide you into the future? It is after that vision that I may name you again and start you on your new course."

"I am ready!"

But Tilhini was not to be hurried.

"Have you lain with a woman during the past three days?"

"No!" Francisco declared, since indeed it had been four since he'd stopped in San Luis at the home of a certain young widow.

"Have you recently eaten meat or grassy or salted foods? Such things are hostile to the blood of the dream seeker."

"Old Father, my hunger lies elsewhere! Except for a handful of meal from Ramon, I've not eaten for two days!"

Still Tilhini would not be hurried. "Suppose you spend the night in contemplation of the stars who are the immortal First People and are also the Great Ones from among our own ancestors? Ask them for guidance while your eyes remain open like theirs! And tomorrow if you still are sure, I will prepare the dance. Afterward you may have your dream."

All night Francisco lay watching the stars. They seemed closer in the clear backcountry air. Some moved while he watched. Some were fixed in their wisdom. And when he prayed to the unwavering North Star, or Sky Coyote, benefactor of mankind, for steady guidance into the future, it was the first heartfelt prayer he had uttered in longer than he could remember.

Suddenly he felt transformed, renewed. And at that moment he heard the call of an actual coyote from the dark mountain side above—wild, uncanny, as if in answer to his prayer.

His heart raced. He could hardly believe what was happening. Old Tilhini on his bed of soft earth at the mouth of the cave stirred as if he sensed it too. When day came Francisco told him all.

"Then you are sure you wish to embrace the Indian way?" the old man asked.

"I am."

"Very well." Tilhini took from his waist net his magical cocoon rattle. "Sit here beside me on the Earth Mother. Close your eyes. Listen while I prepare the path."

Moving slowly around him in a circle, lifting and pressing each naked foot deliberately against the earth, Tilhini began to shake his rattle rhythmically. The rattle was made of the dried cocoons of spirit moths. Each contained a pebble that rasped against its inner surface with a peculiar penetrating sound. Gradually the rhythmic insistence of this sound enveloped Francisco's consciousness, as he sat with eyes closed, until it seemed to represent all reality.

At last he heard Tilhini asking, "Are you ready for your vision?"

"I welcome it!" Francisco replied, opening his eyes dreamily as the rattling ceased.

He watched Tilhini take six tiny white waferlike seeds of the jimson weed from the medicine bundle at his waist, place them in a small bowl of green serpentine, steep them in water from his gourd, mash them with the charm-stone which hung by a thong from his neck. After tasting the mixture Tilhini added three drops of water, nodded gravely, handed the bowl to Francisco. "This is Momoy, Mother Truth. She enables us to see past, present and future clearly. But she is also death and must be treated with utmost respect. Drink, my son. Drink, then stretch yourself on the earth. And remember carefully everything you see in your dream vision."

At first Francisco saw nothing but those luminous shapes of many colors which appear when you shut your eyes tightly. Then gradually he seemed to rise and float through the air. He realized he was descending a long dark tunnel which was very dangerous though he could not quite tell why. After what seemed an interminable journey he emerged into a sunlit world which appeared strangely familiar, and he realized it was that long lost world of his youth and of his heroic Uncle Asuskwa. Once again he'd arrived at the secret stronghold deep in the labyrinthine heart of the interior where Indians came from all over the land for refuge and trade and exchange of news and plans of resistance; and there he saw the stocky brown figure of his uncle, like his own, conferring earnestly with a group of chieftains, exhorting them to forget their differences, to unite and resist the invading white man. But one by one the chieftains' eyes glazed with inattention and soon they drifted away toward the places where trade was in progress or games were being played or food eaten, until Francisco alone remained. He stepped forward and his uncle embraced him joyfully.

"At last you have come! The quail have scattered, as you saw!" Asuskwa indicated the departing chieftains. "Soon we shall know if you are indeed Helek the Hawk, as you say!"

But Francisco had said nothing. Because suddenly he felt damned by his white blood. And as he endeavored to explain this important point he saw his uncle's smiling figure begin to fade into nothingness till he himself was left alone in the midst of that vast wilderness. All the great camp vanished. All the chieftains gone. He alone remaining. Until by desperate effort he managed to shout into the emptiness: "Yes, I am Helek, the Hawk!" And as if by magic he saw the figure of Asuskwa reappear and moved toward him joyfully.

When he waked he felt dizzy and nauseated. It seemed he'd been unconscious only a moment. Actually all day and all night had passed and dawn was breaking. Tilhini, seated cross-legged nearby, was bending toward him solicitously. "Gently, my son. One returns slowly from a long journey."

Francisco smelled the smoke of a campfire. He sat up and shook his head to clear it. "Drink this!" Tilhini held out a steaming bowl. As he sipped the broth, Francisco felt normalcy return. Yet he remained strangely elated, wonderfully transformed.

"Tell me of your dream vision!" Tilhini's voice was gentle but insistent. The old man seemed larger than life, enhanced by supernatural power.

Francisco told all that had happened in his dream. "What does it mean?"

Tilhini nodded sagely as if a guess had been confirmed. "It means you are the true follower of your uncle. It means the blood that flowed in him flows in you, the spirit which guided him guides you!" Tilhini's voice rose with conviction. "Like your uncle in the days of his greatness, you too will lead your people!"

Francisco's thoughts raced wildly. Could this be believed? Could he actually reincarnate the spirit of the legendary hero who led the long bloody struggle against the white men, rallied the wayward tribes, planned the massive uprising which threatened to drive the invaders into the sea?

But before he could think further, Tilhini's voice was saying, "The Sun our Father is rising. Let us proceed!"

Francisco straightened himself, the sun's rays full upon him. The seer was taking from his medicine bundle a white cord made of down from the breasts of condors and eagles.

First holding it gravely up to the sunrise, Tilhini lowered it and placed it in a circle on the earth surrounding Francisco. "My son," he pronounced solemnly, "again you are Helek the Hawk, the far-flyer, the peerless hunter," and Tilhini added in a different voice, one charged with powerful intensity, "the leader your people have awaited so long!"

Francisco was appalled by the enormity of what Tilhini said. In apprehension he gasped out: "Show me the way, O wise old man!"

Tilhini smiled enigmatically. "He who holds the secret of the world holds the power of becoming. And so, my son, I leave you to find your own path."

"But where am I to go? What am I to do?" Francisco cried, still bewildered.

But like the figure in his dream vision Tilhini seemed to be receding. "That is up to you. I can go no farther."

And even as he spoke, Francisco's eyes rested with astonishment on a faint trail, imperceptible before, which led on up the mountain above them.

Jimmy and Me and the Nigger Man

SCOTT A. CUPP

Scott Cupp is a new writer. He has been a book reviewer and has had one story published in Hardboiled, *a magazine devoted to, as you might have guessed, hardboiled crime fiction. This story is an odd mixture of Twain, the Tar Baby, Frankenstein's monster, Lovecraft, and Disney's* Fantasia. *In other words, you won't be reading two just like it.*

It was really dark out that night when Jimmy and me made the Nigger Man. It was dark as a black hole in Hell where the fire don't blaze nor glow, but burns just the same. The thunder crashed over the hills, but the lightnin' never come nor did it rain. Heaven was not pleased. Within a day, neither was we.

It begun as simple as anything. Jimmy and me had had to read about Huck Finn and Nigger Jim for Miss Johnson, she being the English teacher around here. I thought as it was a good enough story but Jimmy seemed to go kinda weird on it. When he read it his eyes would start to glaze over and you could hear his mind cogs clinkin' all the way over to Raymond's Blacksmith Shop. I should have known then that it was trouble. It durn near always is when he gets that look.

He looked at me with that shit-eatin' grin on his face. "Bob," he says. "We got to get us a good nigger just like ole Jim from the story, so's we can go raftin' down the mighty Mississip and fight pirates and be heroes and the like. I can be the Captain and you can be the First Mate. We'll keel-haul anyone who don't agree with us, and"—there was this hesitation in his voice and the gleam in his eye begun to sparkle—"there won't be no more school!"

Well, I got to say, I weren't quite sure how Jimmy was gonna pull this one off. I mean, he has had some of the most consarndest schemes ever to lay rest in a mortal mind. There was that time that we was gonna make wings out of bird feathers and fly away to Araby to be sheiks and have us a harem and genies. I durn near broke my neck when I fell out of that tree. And, I had to work for old Farmer Harris for two months on account of them chickens we plucked for their feathers. And there was the time that we was gonna dam up the river and charge all the people for their water. We both got good and soaked over that one.

"Now," I thought, "how's he gonna get a nigger?" Lincoln done freed 'em all and lots of people around here are still sore about that mess. Jimmy's unk done died in that war. His mama never would talk about it. When she died, we finally found out that he'd fought for the Blue. Most folks round here took to the Gray, so I guessed as how I could see why she didn't want to talk much about it. She were only three when he went and left. The note tellin' the family that he was dead come just a week afore her sixth birthday. He weren't but seventeen at the time. I forget the place he died but I'd never heard it before and I ain't heard it since. Jimmy found the cap that they sent as part of his stuff and took to wearin' it around town until Bully Bentley and six others took it off his head and burnt it. Three of them boys ain't been the same since and Bully still cain't hear out of that one ear.

Anyways, Jimmy says, "We gotta get us a good nigger. That means we got to make our own. That way, he'll be owin' to us and'll do whatever it is that we wants him to do. If I was to say, 'Nigger, jump in the water and go get us that big catfish,' why, he'd do that very thing. He'll be our personal slave and friend."

Now, I may not be the smartest thing that ever walked the streets of Fairfield, but I knowed that you didn't just up and make a nigger and I told Jimmy so. He just stared there looking at me with that grin never movin' and he says, "You remember Raoul the Magnificent?"

How could I ever forget Raoul? We'd just seen the Amazing Traveling Magic Man the week before. He'd amazed us with pullin' rabbits out of his top hat and makin' fire appear at his fingertips and such. Me and Jimmy had waited days to get the chance to see his show. One of these days I'm going to take the time to learn the magic arts and travel the world just like he done. I'll be Robert the Wonderful and I'll entertain kings and queens in Europe and walk through the walls.

"Yeah," I said. "I remember the show."

"Well, Raoul the Magnificent is over to Waterton on Saturday. I figure that you and me need to go over and see him."

I was beginnin' to get lost. "Why does we need to go see Raoul the Magnificent?"

"We need to see him on account of his magic wand. You remember the one with the big star on the top that he used to put the lady he'd done sawed in half back together with. I figure that we can use that to help build us our nigger."

I turned for the house. I didn't hold no truck with stealin' no magic wands from magicians who might saw you in half and leave you that way wheres you could still talk and breathe but you couldn't walk or who might turn you into a toad so's you'd have to eat flies. No sir, I didn't want nothin' to do with that.

Jimmy was callin' to me as I was walkin', but I weren't listenin'. I'd done that too many times in the past.

Saturday, we was standin' in Waterton, Jimmy starin' like he ain't never been in the city before and me tryin' to avoid steppin' in the cow shit, there havin' been a trail drive through there two days before.

We found the saloon where Raoul was to perform. Jimmy snucked around back to see if he could get in. That boy has got a way with locks that ain't mortal. He can just ask one to open and, clunk!, it falls at his feet.

He weren't gone five minutes when he come hotfootin' it up the street, wavin' at me to follow and fast. When dealin' with magicmen, I make it my business to get the Hell out when someone says it needs to be got out.

I hit one of them cow turds full speed and slid into another. There'd be Hell to pay when my Ma smelled my pants. But, that was tomorrow and I was tryin' to avoid a mad magicman today.

When Jimmy finally stopped runnin', we was a good mile from Waterton. He was kinda laughin', kinda gaspin' for air. But, from under his shirt, he pulled the wand and he begun to wave it over his head and dance. This was the beginning of the end.

For a while, I'd done forgot about the magicman. I guess I thought that he had so many magic wands that he might not miss one. I hoped I was right. Anyways, if we got the nigger made before he found us, I woulda give him the wand back just fine.

It was Monday at school that Jimmy give me the plan for makin' our nigger. I was to meet him that night at the cave. "And," he said, "be sure to brung a freshly dead cat. *One that's got blood on its paws!*"

I found Mrs. Riley's cat under the front stoop. It were a Siamese and I hated that egg-sucker almost as much as he hated me. We'd had us a disagreement sometime back over who owned this dead mouse I'd found near his bed. I wanted it so as to make a potion to ward off swamp demons and I reckon as how he'd wanted it for lunch. We'd both ended up with somethin' less than half, there bein' this other cat that et the head whiles we was fightin over the whole mess. My potion didn't work with only half a mouse so I'd left it with him and the hopes of stomach cramps leading him on up to Kitty Heaven.

He weren't hard to catch. I brung a dead fish and purty soon he was shinin' up to me like it was money, just a purrin' and tryin' to go for that fish. I dropped the fish down to the ground and, as he went for it, I grubbed him by the tail and lifted him high 'bove my head. "You gonna die now, you bastid!" I screamed as I swungged him by the tail over my head. He'd done forgot the fish and was hangin' on to me with them claws, a-yowlin' like the Saints comin' on in. When I could feel the blood starts to flow down my wrist, I swungged him hard against the side of the buildin', never lettin' go of that tail. He let out one more yelp and then sorta collapsed. He was fresh dead with my blood on his paws. I hoped he would do.

I was to meet Jimmy at the regular hideout down by the caves near the river. We usually met behind this dead tree and had some of our secret potions and spells hid down among the ruts. It was there that we dreamed about pirates and knights in armor and damsels in distress. It was Jimmy's favorite spot in the whole damned world. It was there that we was gonna make our nigger.

When I got there, Jimmy had done been at work for a while. I could see that he'd made a man out of river mud clay for his head and legs and this old tree trunk for his chest with long tree limbs for his arms. As I got there, he added two berries to the face, for eyes I guess.

It was dark out, but Jimmy didn't have no trouble at all recognizin' the cat. "That's Mrs. Riley's cat, Herkyles, ain't it?" he said, knowin' right well that I hated to acknowledge that damned cat's name. It seemed sinful to name such a cat after a god of strength and valor and golden fleeces.

I just held it out to him. "It's freshly dead and it's got my blood on its paws." The damn thing had done started to go stiff on me. Just like it to start trouble even when it was done dead. I shoulda just burned it and found me another one to kill.

"Put him here," Jimmy says, pointin' to the tree trunk that was the chest. "Stuff him in there real deep. It'll give the nigger cunnin' and the ability to see in the dark more'n me and you."

I put the cat in there deep. He was so stiff that I kinda had to force him a little, but I reckon he didn't mind too much.

I reckon it must have been around midnight then. Jimmy said that these things were always best done at midnight. Neither of us had a watch, so we had to guess. I bet that that's where things went wrong.

Somewhere Jimmy had found this jacket of bright red and there he stood, with that grin on his face, with that jacket hangin' loose on his back (it were too big, but he didn't seem to notice), and that wand in his hand. He was wavin' the wand all around. Or, maybe it was wavin' him. I couldn't tell.

All of a sudden, he jumps around, that coat a-swirlin' behind him with a mind of its own. The star on the wand begun to glow, just a little at first and then it got brighter. Jimmy, he starts to howlin' like a dog and sayin' words that weren't never part of the secret ceremonies we'd had before. They wasn't English and I couldn't recognize hardly any of them. They sure didn't sound like none of the made-up words that he'd used before. They was words like *Yuck Succotash* and *Shubby Niggerath* and *Cruel Loose*. I didn't like the sound of them words and I sure didn't like the way that wand's star was shinin'. It was a white star on the wand, but then it begun to glow in lots of colors—red, then green and blue. Finally, it shone in black. I passed out then. You cain't imagine the horror of seein' your best friend traipsin' around like a crazed gypsy with a magic wand that was glowin' *black* as a dark night in Hell.

When I come to, there was thunder rollin' through the hills, but I couldn't see no clouds.

Jimmy let out a scream that made me want to go join old Herkyles. And then he fell over. The wand continued to glow.

I run over to Jimmy. Just as I got there, there was a flash of black light from the wand to the nigger.

Then, the berries begun to move on that black mud face. They looked like eyes. Jimmy rose up, took the wand, and slammed it into the black mud head. "LIVE!" he screamed.

The wand stuck in the mud and the berries was gone. In their place was eyes. Black, evil-lookin' eyes that didn't have no whites around them and that seemed to stare into your very soul.

Jimmy had hung onto the wand and wouldn't let go. I tried to pull it out of the Nigger Man's head, but I couldn't get it to come. Jimmy finally let go.

The Nigger Man started to rise. He used them tree limb arms to push hisself up. Parts of him were still mud and tree then. But, as I watched, they seemed to get real smoky and, suddenly, they wasn't mud nor tree. They wasn't quite flesh neither. What they was I didn't want to know. Dreams of raftin' down the Mississippi no longer bothered me. We had made our Nigger Man and all I wanted to do was be shut of it.

Jimmy started to become hisself about then. The Nigger Man was startin' to stand. He weren't quite sure on his feet, seein' as how they was two pieces of not-quite-wood that didn't really match. He fell down once, maybe twice before he seemed to get the hang of it.

Jimmy just stared and kept sayin', "We done it! We just damn well done it!" like there was ever a doubt in his mind. He stood up and raised his body to his full height. "Nigger," he said, "I am your Master and Creator. This here is Bob, your Co-Master and Co-Creator."

The Nigger Man didn't seem to hear. Then, as I looked at his not-quite-mud face, I noticed that Jimmy hadn't made him no ears. I don't know how he expected the Nigger Man to be followin' orders when he couldn't hear 'em none.

But, the Nigger Man turned kinda slow-like and begun to walk over to Jimmy. He still didn't have the walkin' down so good, but I figured he'd get better as it got along. He just stood there, not movin', not talkin', not doin' nothin'. Jimmy reached up and grabbed one of them tree limbs that was sort of a hand and begun to lead the Nigger Man away.

"What you doin'?" I asked.

"I'm gonna put him into the cave until we can come out and work on teachin' him the things that he's got to know. How to talk, how to fetch. He's a big one, ain't he? And, he's *our* nigger."

We packed the Nigger Man into the cave. He didn't fight us none. I was tired and ready for sleep when I got to home. This week had already been more than a Saint could bear and I weren't no Saint.

I don't know how I slept that night. If I'da known what was comin' . . . well, I don't know as I would have done nothin' different. I like to think I would, but sometimes, you just don't know. And with Jimmy, it was hard to do things any way 'cept the way he wanted 'em done.

Anyways, the things that was done was done and nothin' I can say or do now is ever gonna change that one bit. It went like this:

The next mornin' when Jimmy and me got to the cave, we was astonished to find that the Nigger Man weren't there. You could tell that he'd been there cause everythin' inside were all scuffed up and the like and you could see where he'd uprutted some bushes when he'd left the cave. So, at least, there was a trail to follow.

It seemed funny trackin' someone through the woods without callin' for them. Jimmy had started to, but since he didn't have no name other than the Nigger Man, and we hadn't even called him that, Jimmy didn't figure it would do no good to yell it. I pointed out to him that he hadn't give our slave and friend no ears, so it weren't no wonder that he didn't stay put like he ought, but were out wanderin' around.

The Nigger Man had just crawled out of the cave and had went wherever he wanted to. Sometimes it were in circles, over and over again. Sometimes it were through bushes that didn't want nothin' to go through them. He were persistent, though, and often as not, them bushes weren't planted no more when we found them.

It took a while, but finally we caught up to him, settin' by the river, throwin' flowers in it like he had some good sense. Jimmy went up and pulled him on his arm, him not havin' a sleeve (nor any clothes, as it was) to tug on. The Nigger Man turned around and looked at us with them dark berry-eyes.

Jimmy started in on the lecture I knowed he'd been rehearsin' all durin' our hunt. All about the Nigger Man's responsibilities to his Masters and Creators and why was he runnin' off like that, didn't he have the sense that God give a crawdad?

I'd done heard most of it durin' the hunt, so I was starin' into space, watchin' the birds fly by. The Nigger Man weren't doin' much of nothin'. I still don't think he could hear nor think.

He finally stood up and I spied a piece of cloth on the ground under him. It weren't much, just a piece of blue gingham, just like all the girls wear. It weren't even much of a scrap, but it also weren't supposed to be there. A glance to the right brought my eyes to the river. I found the rest of the gingham.

Out there in the current, there was something hooked onto a limb of a fallen tree. It were a blue gingham dress, filled with Mandy Spencer. I remembered as how she liked to come down to the river and throw flowers into it. I guess she found the Nigger Man and musta started to scream, she being noted for that. I remember once she screamed for thirty minutes when Harry Allison shoved a garter snake up in her face. And . . . I guess . . . the Nigger Man done went out and killed her.

My eyes was suddenly filled with tears and I was lookin' for somethin' heavy. I found a rock and begun to beat on the Nigger Man with it. For a while, he didn't even seem to notice. The rock kept makin' a kind of boomin' noise on the tree trunk chest.

Finally, he turned. I dropped the rock, sorry that I had ever seed it. There was hate in them berries, and on the left side of his face, there was a small white ear with a pierced earring in it, just like Mandy always wore.

The Nigger Man stretched his arms out towards me. The tree limbs that was his arms started to move. They was growin' and headin' towards me. I tried to run, but them arms growed fast. First thing I knowed, I was on the ground, wrapped in the arms of the Nigger Man. Then the limbs started to shrink, drawin' me back towards him.

I didn't even think about Jimmy whilst this was goin' on. I guess I forgot he was even there. Suddenly, he's standin behind the Nigger Man with the rock I dropped and he's smashin' it into the head as hard as he could.

The tree limbs finally released me after what seemed like forever. My ankles was red and sore as Hell. I began to rub them.

Jimmy was yellin' at me, but I wasn't listenin'. He finally dropped the rock and grabbed me, half carryin', half draggin' me with him. The Nigger Man's head was a mess, all kinda squished up. It didn't quite look like flesh all messed up. Then, the muck started to ooze back together and his head was reformin' right before my eyes.

We ran around in the woods. I'm sure we must have run in circles. There was one rock I'm sure we passed three times. But it was hard to notice where we was goin' when the Nigger Man was a-chasin' us, his head reformin' as he run, that magic wand still stickin' out the side. As his head was fixin' itself, the wand was glowin', this time it was a green color.

We run like bats out of Hell. The Nigger Man never was far behind. He didn't move fast, but he didn't dodge much neither. If somethin' got in his way and was smaller than he was, it got runned over. Jimmy and me occasionally had to run around things like trees.

Sometimes Jimmy was in the lead, sometimes it was me. Neither of us had a plan. I don't guess that we'd have made one if the Nigger Man hadn't chunked a boulder at us. Big thing just come crashin' through the air and made a path through some mesquite where there hadn't been none before. Jimmy decided we'd better hole up somewhere.

"Make for the cave!" he shouted, not carin' if the Nigger Man heard us or not. "We'll hide in there until someone can find us."

"All right," I said, "but, remember, if someone finds us, they also gonna find him and that may not do us no good."

But, we run for the cave. And barely made it. There was another boulder come swishin' through the air. That one nearly took off Jimmy's head. Tree limbs may be good for holdin' ankles, but they cain't pitch rocks for shit. Thank God!

Then, I saw it.

The mouth of the cave was glowin' blue! I didn't want to go into no shiny blue light, but fear of the Nigger Man drove me into the unknown.

Jimmy hadn't even noticed the glow. He was still lookin' glassy-eyed from seein' the ear and dodgin' the boulders. He was also twitchin' and jerkin' from side to side, like a dog that's been partial run over by a wagon.

"SO!" boomed the voice. "THE THIEVES RETURN AT LAST TO MEET THEIR FATE!"

I died. This was for sure the voice of *DOOM* and it was right here in the cave. It was the voice of Raoul the Magnificent, wizard to kings and emperors. Jimmy just sorta twitched. I think one of them boulders must a grazed his scalp a little 'cause I could see some blood on his ear. His blood. His ear.

Raoul increased the glow. I saw it was comin' from another of his fabulous wands. "So, my boys, let's us talk about Magic and thieves." Jimmy moaned.

"Did you know that in the court of Charlemagne, thieves had their thumbs cut off and had to serve to the Queen's lap dog, which licked the stump if it was thirsty? Or that, in Argo, thieves had flaming embers placed inside their stomachs and were used as ovens to roast potatoes in? Now, what do you suppose I have planned for you?" The glow begun to change from blue to a dark red or purple. Raoul seemed to glow. His long mustache begun to writhe like snakes that was attached to his face. Then they grew heads and was snakes, strikin' at my eyes. Lightnin' flashed from Raoul's eyes and hit the walls of the cave. "WHERE'S MY WAND?"

"Well, sir, Mr. Raoul, it's outside stuck in the head of the Nigger Man that's done got Mandy's ear and killed her and now wants to kill me and Jimmy and please don't turn us into toads. I don't like flies and couldn't eat a one and then I'd die. We didn't mean no harm!" There was tears in my eyes and my mouth was runnin' faster than my mind coulda ever thought. I told him everything, from readin' Huck Finn and Nigger Jim and stealin' the wand (his eyes glowed fire red at that) and the killin' of Herkyles and the buildin' of the Nigger Man and Mandy and the tree limbs. I think I told him everything, maybe not quite in the order that it happened, but he got the idea that things wasn't goin' the way that Jimmy had seed it.

All the time we was talkin', the Nigger Man was still comin'. He'd found the cave and begun to come in, them tree limbs growin' fast and explorin' the walls of the cave, lookin' for us. Finally, the limbs crawled into the part where we was. I didn't see them as I was still runnin' off talkin' to Raoul. He'd lost most of his fearsomeness and seemed to be interested in just exactly what it was that we had done. I was tellin' him what I could of the stuff Jimmy said at midnight, but the words didn't make much sense to me then and it's real hard to remember nonsense words. But Raoul knew what they was all about.

He got a funny look on his face when them tree limbs circled round his ankles, like it didn't quite hurt, but he sure didn't want to do it again. Then the limbs tried to pull him outside. They should never had tried that. He rose up to his full height (around ten or twelve feet, I think) and begun to mumble some funny-soundin' words, like Jimmy had done. The wand was movin' around like it had a mind of its own. Suddenly, there was this blaze of light and a scream of tortured agony. The tree limbs was on fire and the Nigger Man was fryin' away. Raoul sent another ball of fire down the cave mouth. There was another scream.

Raoul run to the mouth of the cave. The Nigger Man was burnin' just like he was in Hell. His arms and chest was blazin'. The clay mud of his face was beginnin' to harden. The berries oozed out juices. It was horrid and I watched ever second of it. Finally, I could smell the fur on Herkyles begin to burn. I knowed it was over then. The Nigger Man just fell over into some heaps. The head stayed in one piece, Raoul's wand still there, not even fazed by all of the fire and stuff.

Raoul waved to me. "Get the wand, boy! You two put it in, it has to be you that takes it out. Smash the head and bring me that wand!"

I grabbed the head. It was hot to the touch. Raoul had fired the clay mud head into a pot. I raised it over my head and flung it into the ground. "Take that, you bastid!" I screamed. "Breakin's too good for you!" The head broke into a zillion pieces. Only two parts was whole—the wand and Mandy's ear.

The wand weren't glowin' no more. It was cool to the touch. "Do you surrender this wand to me of your own free will and renounce all claims to it?" he asked, lookin' at me first, then back at the wand.

Somethin' struck me. "What if I doesn't?"

That weren't the thing to say to Raoul just then.

"Why, I'll raise the Nigger Man up right where he lies and have him eat you like you was a squash." The mustache started movin' again.

"You can have the wand on three conditions," I says.

"Conditions! You are hardly in the place to be making conditions!"

"Still, I has three. The first two is for Jimmy and me. I wants you to fix up Jimmy so's he don't moan and twitch like he's been doin'."

"Well, I guess that can be accomplished. What is it that you desire for yourself?"

"Let's talk about the second condition first. I wants you to bring back Mandy and fix her ear so's it's right and she ain't dead." I figured I owed it to her, since Jimmy and me had made her dead.

Raoul looked at me and shooked his head. "It can't be done, my boy. There are rules to all of this. That's why you have to surrender the wand. I can't take it from you. You could take it from me, because you didn't know the rules. Me, I know them and, at times, they are very constricting. With the wand, I can make things that weren't ever alive appear to live. But, I can't make something live that has died. I wish that I could. There are a great many people besides Mandy that I would bring back." Tears began to form in his eyes as I could see him rememberin' someone who was now gone.

"Now, again I ask, what is it that you want for the return of the wand?"

My voice caught in my throat. Here goes. "I want to travel with you and learn Magic and entertain kings and queens and learn to walk through walls. I always wanted to, so I'm askin' now. Take me with you."

Raoul looked at me with his eyes beginnin' to glow again. "So, you want to learn Magic and walk through walls?" He stared at me some more. "Give me the wand and it's done."

"And, you'll take care of Jimmy, too?" Makin' sure that he didn't get out of that part.

"Done!" he said. I gived him the wand. He went to Jimmy and laid the wand upside of his head and whispered stuff into his ear. Jimmy's eyes begun to unglaze and he started to smile.

Raoul lifted out his hand to me. "Now, my friend, let us go."

And we walked out through the walls of the cave.

Calamity

MELISSA MIA HALL

Melissa Mia Hall lives in Fort Worth and is known, though not as well known as she should be, for a number of quiet horror stories that have appeared in magazines such as Twilight Zone *and anthologies like Charles Grant's award-winning* Shadows *series. She has a degree in journalism, a background in film (one of her films was shown at a film festival), and she's had photographs and poetry published. She has also been a gift wrapper at a men's store and says, "Believe me, it takes real guts to gift wrap four-piece suits!"*

The following story has nothing to do with four-piece suits. It is a chunk out of an ongoing work of historical fiction of the same name, and from Melissa's comments, it may well be ongoing for some time. Meanwhile, she still writes short stories and has two novels circulating among the publishing houses.

My papa was a gunfighter. He rode a white horse with silver spurs on his black boots he bought in San Antonio. He killed many men, bad men, men that deserved to die. He was real tall. My papa had blues eyes the color of the sky at noon, on a clear day, of course, with nary a cloud in sight east or west, north or south. My papa was smart, good and upstanding. He liked guns. His guns were so clean they sparkled. He twirled his pistols like a magician. He impressed people with his antics and could tell stories that made you laugh so hard your belly would start to aching. I wish I had known him before he went out west and got killed by some lousy government man. I'm always pressing my mama to tell me more about him, him being so fine and all, but she won't say much except "I don't want to talk about Clifford." I have never thought he went by that name professionally. Seems to me I heard Patience say he went by the name Doc Smiley because he had bright white teeth and he smiled all the time, especially right before he went for the draw. Patience is the colored maid that works for mama. She is fourteen.

"What you doing, girl, mooning around when you ought to be in bed. Go on, now."

Patience thinks she's twenty years old, bossing me about every time she gets a chance. I'm nine years old and very intelligent. I'm going to the Ursuline Academy next school term. I don't want to but mama's making me. She thinks I need to be brought up a lady instead of a snippety tomboy. I'm not a tomboy just because I don't like dolls and like to climb trees and run around with the boys in the neighborhood when they'll let me. But she has decided I'm not being brought up proper by the public school. Atlanta says I'm too smart for my own good. She's Patience's mother and our cook.

"I said get in that bed." I'd like to pinch Patience's head off. It's not even dark outside and they expect me to sleep. As soon as she leaves I'm crawling out the window and going to see the man in the carriage house. Mama doesn't even know he's there. I'm so smart. Patience might suspect, I reckon, but she doesn't care one way or another, long as it don't get her in trouble. I take him food. He's extremely thin and rickety, like a door half off its hinges.

I sit still and wait for the house to fall quiet, then I reach under the bed for the pillowcase I got stuffed with cornbread and ham. Atlanta never bats an eye when I ask for food or slip some out of the pantry. I tell her it's for picnics and she just says, "uh-huh." and I know if I don't take too much she won't tell on me. Mama's so absentminded about household procedure I sure enough don't think it would matter if she did notice too much food disappearing each week. Mama doesn't much care about anything. Mrs. Beadle Brown from the Ladies' Aid Society of Trinity Episcopal told Mrs. Rose Hawkins, who lives down the street, that it was a crying shame how someone from such a fine family, as my mama, had to be brought to such low standards by a fool man. I know she was talking about Doc Smiley. Tin Type Gods. Yes, Mrs. Beadle Brown said one must never be fooled by Tin Type Gods. My papa probably had many photographs made of him but I've never seen any. That is unfortunate.

I love crawling out of the window in the summertime. It is purely wonderful. I've put on my modeling pinafore that mama had made for me when I'm sculpting clay. I am going to be an artist in Paris one day. After I go to San Francisco to make sure my papa's dead. That's where he was shot down by the unscrupulous character with the evil eye and the mustache that hangs down off his chin like two horse tails, thick, bushy and ugly as homemade sin. I call him Red Nevada but I've never rightly known his real name.

We don't have horses or carriages out here anymore. We just rent from Mr. Jack Swanson, a cousin of Mama's. I guess that means he's a relative of mine, but I don't particularly like him. He spits tobaccy juice constantly. One time he got some on my boot. He also stinks like he sleeps with the horses instead of going home to his wife, Mirabelle. There is one broke down carriage, a two seater and lots of ancient hay that a cat had kittens in a couple of weeks ago. Patience says there's rats out there, too, but I don't go looking for them.

Nobody sees me slip around to the back. I play-like there are Indians hiding in the vegetable garden and I shoot me a few before I squeeze in through the opening in the back of the carriage house, or the barn, as I prefer to call it. It's my barn. I play-like there are horses and cows in here. Mr. Leroy, that's Atlanta's man—that's precisely what she calls him, "My man," he does handywork around here, keeps his tools in here. He don't come around everyday because mama has to pinch pennies and can not afford a full staff seven days a week. Especially since Grampa died and did not leave all of his estate to her, but split it with her brother, Uncle Joel, and her sister, Aunt Hester. Mama was mortified when that happened. What with my papa, Doc Smiley dead out west, she'd come to depend on the money Grampa sent to us monthly, to help us keep up appearances. Grampa believed profoundly that appearances matter. We're a fine family because we look fine. The house—Grampa gave us this house in Galveston; it was his vacation estate—after my papa was gunned down by the notorious Red Nevada—well, it's a mighty fine house, gleaming white and surrounded by oleanders and other lovely plants. But the oleanders are poisonous and mama's told me time and time again not to eat them. As if one would want to!

"Missy?"

That's the man in the barn, expecting me.

"Hey, Arizona, how's the bunkhouse tonight?" It's dark in here and a little cool. It feels good. "You going to light the lantern?" He never lights the lantern for fear he'll catch the barn on fire. I don't much mind the darkness 'cause I can see him plain enough, hunched down, studying his callused hands. He's so old, but wiry, strong enough to go out and work on the docks during the day. I don't know why he don't go to some cheap boardinghouse on Winnie. I think it's because he likes me. He's lonesome. I throw him the pillowcase and he pulls the food out.

"You don't have to do this. I ate well at noon. I'm not much hungry tonight." He says that but he plows right into the food.

"I truly wish you would call me Calamity, Arizona."

"But your name is Miss Camellia."

"A disgusting, sissy name if'n I've ever heard one."

"I think it's might pretty."

"Sissy." Twilight's dropped down and the barn's thick with smoky shadows. I light the lantern with Arizona's matches. The light reveals his lined but kindly face. He smiles, revealing that gap in his bottom teeth. He sees me flinch at that awful gap and he closes his mouth tight. I don't mean to be disrespectful, but Arizona's teeth are not at all like my papa's. It's not his fault, though. "Work go good today?"

"Tolerable." He's finished gulping his dinner. Now he folds the case carefully and then folds his big hands in his lap. "See here, now, Missy—Miss Calamity, I've been here going on a week and I've finally got the means to get me my own place. I want you to know I've been grateful for all the niceties you've shown me, the kindness of you all allowing me to bunk here while I get to me feet. But it's time to fly the coop."

"Aw, do you have to?"

"Yes, I surely do." He can see I'm not feigning my disappointment. He reaches out and touches my hand. "But I can come here and check on you sometimes, that I could. What do you think about that?"

"In secret?" That would be divinely grand. I love secrets. "Like on a special, pre-arranged night, say, Thursdays?"

"Sounds possible to me."

"And you'll keep telling me about life out west?"

"I promise." Arizona was a gunfighter, too. He tells me stories of some of his adventures. He told me once he met Buffalo Bill and he's killed so many men he's lost count, but found God last year and resolved to never again take another human life. That's why he came here to Galveston, to start a new life unsullied by sin. I asked him a few days ago, right after he showed up here in the barn, about whether he might have heard about my papa, Doc Smiley, also known as Clifford Shepard. He said he had not but that didn't mean anything. He said though, he thought he would've remembered meeting anyone related to me. He was just being nice. It bothered me. I wish he had heard of Doc Smiley.

"Arizona, did you sell your gun?"

He gives me a shocked glance. I guess you hadn't ought to switch subjects so fast-like but since he's planning to up and leave, I may as well get another story out of him tonight. "Your gun."

He reaches behind him for the battered valise he brought with him, like a doctor's bag, bulging with all his worldly possessions. He opens it and fishes around inside. My heart leaps to my throat. Lord Almighty, he still has his gun. He produces it with a grand flourish. He says it's a Colt something and it's clean as a whistle. He waves it around proudly then puts it back into the bag. He won't let me touch it but I respect that. I don't imagine any self-respecting sharpshooter would let a kid get her hands on his gun. It doesn't figure. "Golly." I am impressed as all get-out and he knows it.

"Yep, I still own a gun but it no longer owns me."

"I should say so."

"Not so long ago this here gun could shoot a man down without looking twice. Lord knows I didn't. Comes a time, though, when you have to look, you have to look long and hard or a body loses his soul. You might say I almost lost my soul."

"When was that?" I hug my knees through my pinafore and shiver, although I know it's summertime and the air in the carriage house is close.

"The last time I killed me a man. I think it was just one too many."

"But why do you keep that gun if you feel so bad about it and all?" He cradles the bag. We can both see the gun even though it's hidden in the depths of that bag. It's glow radiates through the worn leather and takes my breath away.

"Old habits die hard," Arizona says mysteriously, smiling crookedly.

I hear Atlanta calling for me. They've discovered I'm missing. I'm liable to get a hiding for this escapade. I say goodbye to Arizona as quick as I can, making him promise to rendezvous next Thursday. But I might not get to meet him. They'll be watching me like a hawk from now on. My palms sweat and I hurry outside, careful-like and fast. I'll think of something to tell them. They're slow. I'm good at pulling the wool over they eyes, especially mother. She never pays attention. That's why it takes her an eternity to finish a piece of needlework. She stares a lot. But Atlanta's not so dreamy. Atlanta's sharp as a tack. I don't want Atlanta mad at me. She won't let me help bake them molasses cookies tomorrow and she promised I could. I got to stand on the good side of Atlanta. She moves slow because she's such a big woman but her mind's not so slow.

"I been mindful of how you've been carrying on with that no-account man sleeping out in the barn."

"Yes ma'am."

"I'm a good Christian woman and I allow as to how you've got to take care of the poor, so I've been looking the other way while you've been taking food out of the pantry, taking it out to that beggar. Yes, ma'am, I've been sure enough mindful, little missy."

"Yes ma'am."

"Yes ma'am, that's surely right. But I've had my man tell him its time for him to look elsewhere for a hand-out. You've spent entirely too much time hanging around that stranger. I don't want you to do that nomore. Say yes ma'am, Atlanta."

"Yes ma'am, Atlanta." I see Patience peeking around the corner. I stick out my tongue and Atlanta tells Patience to get back to her dusting. Atlanta's brown arms are sprinkled with flour from the day's baking. I stare at the loaves of bread waiting to rise. They better rise or Atlanta will spank them.

"Tell Atlanta you're sorry."

"I'm sorry, Atlanta."

"Just think what pain your doings-on would give your mama if she knew. Why her weak heart might give way and then what would you do?"

That's a perfectly awful thing to say. I didn't know my mother had a weak heart. Atlanta notes my sudden ashen pallour. I do feel like I might faint away at any moment, causing me to reflect upon the state of my own heart. "I'd be sad," I whisper.

Atlanta looks stricken with remorse, as well she should be. She wipes her hands and bends down, with much effort, to hug me. "Don't worry little darlin', it's not that weak. I just have to put the fear of the good Lord Almighty into you because my man done told him to leave last night and I don't suspect he'll ever be back and you got to understand why."

"He was nice to me. He didn't mean no harm; he was just an old man. I liked him. He was a gunfighter, Atlanta, a real, honest-to-God gunfighter from the West. He met Buffalo Bill—"

"Don't you be taking the Lord's name in vain, now Miss Camellia and Buffalo Bill was no gunfighter and anyone toting up the price of admission could see Buffalo Bill right here in Galveston, why my man seen him. You understand me, child?"

"Don't call me that awful name. I'm *Calamity*."

Atlanta heaves one of her enormous sighs and fans her damp face. "Yes, Miss Calamity. Go on with you, now, I've got work to do that's not getting done talking to you."

"Ain't I going to bake cookies with you today? You promised!"

"Merciful heavens, I suppose so, but you mind me and keep quiet. Your mama's already had one sinking spell this morning trying to get over your little adventure last night and if'n you go clattering around dropping pans you're liable to give her another."

I think of mama lying up on her chaise lounge staring out the window.

"Maybe when your Aunt Hester comes to visit she'll take you to the beach. You know your mother can't abide too much sunlight."

I've been playing with that girl who lives down on Avenue I. I thought she was a prissy-tail and that all she'd ever want to do is play dolls or dress-up, but we got to talking today and she said she liked playing cowboys and indians but her mama was always fretting about her clothes and if we played careful-like, so as not to soil anything dreadfully, she'd just adore playing cowboys and indians, so we played all day. Her name is Daisy Anne Thornbush and I have decided she's not a sissy. I am certainly tired. I'm supposed to go meet Arizona and I'm trying to keep my eyes awake but it's extremely difficult.

Night falls down and the sheets smell good. I drift away. I'm a jellyfish floating in the ocean. I sting people. I am big and mighty. The giggling bathing beauties scream as I approach the shore. The screams wake me. The house is still, my room in darkness. Guiltily I jump out of bed and go to the window. Has Arizona come and gone? I don't take time to dress and escape across the windowsill into the night. The 'squitos are biting my legs and my heart's in my throat jumping like a leap frog. I hope he's not mad at me.

I pull the door open slowly, afraid to see nothing. But there's a lantern light bobbing in the corner, someone almost swinging it, the rays of light bouncing around the barn. Two people are there, talking hoarsely, but clearly, a man and a woman. I'm afraid it's Atlanta come to tell Arizona how the cow ate the cabbage and for him to leave and never come back. But as my eyes see clearer, I see it's my own poor mother. She's standing tall and strong, hovering over an Arizona sitting on a wobbly stool, head in his hands. I pull back. They haven't heard me. She's telling him he has no right to someone. She says that she's her child and he's never to bother them again. She's saying he's deader than dead to her and that she never loved him. She's telling him to go away and never come back, Clifford. And he's coughing, certainly not crying. He has a bad cold. He wipes his nose with the back of a sleeve and looks up at my mama. I leave quickly, absolutely embarrassed. She couldn't have been talking about me being his child. That couldn't be Doc Smiley. I know that sure enough can't be. The Fates would not allow it. Atlanta believes in the Fates. I picture them as tall women wearing white curtains and gold ivy in their hair. I feel horrible. I'll go back to bed. I am probably dreaming.

Today is hot and fair but there's a steady breeze. Mother says perhaps we will go down to the Midway, but I know it's just talk. Or is it? Mama moves briskly about the house, like a bird wanting to fly out of a cage. She has two pink spots blazing on her cheeks and she smiles at me several times. I don't like that. My tongue's dry and I keep swallowing, trying to get enough spit. I'd like to spit at her; she's so happy. She says she's glad Aunt Hester's coming. That's not all it is. Atlanta looks like she's worried too. Atlanta has her hands full with wash day and tells me to look after my mother. What am I supposed to do? Atlanta expects too much from me.

"Why don't you go out and play?" My mother says. I shouldn't call her mama anymore. "Mama" is childish. She stares out the window at the sun-dappled street.

"I don't want to."

"That surprises me, sweetheart; my girl's always out playing." She swishes her morning glory skirt and I stare at the blueness of her waist. She is a flower. I duck my head, devastated at the awareness of my own revolting ugliness. I'll never be as lovely as her. Lovely and cruel, mean as an outlaw, telling me my father was dead; 'cept he is dead, deader than a doornail. Arizona's teeth are crooked and dirty and there's that awful gap. I reckon I hate my mother.

"Did you have a bad dream last night?" I say suddenly, picking at a scab on my knee.

"Don't sit like that; it's not lady-like," she scolds.

"I heard a scream," I say.

"Well, I didn't. I don't dream."

"I do."

"Well, there you are. I think I shall go shopping this morning."

"I thought we were going to the Midway."

"Maybe when Aunt Hester comes," she says, smiling airily, dismissing me.

Atlanta has been having trouble with Patience. Patience hasn't been working at the house of late. Atlanta is afraid she's going to run off with Alfred Pickens. Alfred is a wild boy that Patience told me hung out the moon and brought it in again. I asked Patience why would anyone want a moon in the house. She pinched me. Atlanta is so worked up over Patience that she doesn't seem to mind what I do. I've been doing some interesting things. I stole some money out of the collection box at church and no one noticed. I've ridden on the cars several times without paying. I've gone all the way down to the Midway by myself lots of times and met some boys and girls that do the grandest things. One girl surf bathes with her clothes on, very daring-like and smart. One girl, about my age, fishes off a jetty. I never done that; she showed me how. But I got a sunburn the other day and Atlanta caught on to what I'd been doing. She told mother and she spanked me with the back of her ivory hairbrush. I spat at her like a hysterical cat and she spanked me some more. That's when I told her I knew about papa not being dead and she sent me to my room without supper. Atlanta's mad at me, too; she won't speak to me. I wish Patience was here. Patience is too young to get hitched. I wish I was dead.

Aunt Hester came the other day and mother has been occupied with showing her about town, introducing her socially, seeing she's not been here since she was a child. It's very helpful to me that they're out calling on people. Atlanta is preoccupied and doesn't much care what I do as long as I stay out of her way. Patience did run off with Alfred Pickens and she's breaking in her sister's girl, Francine, a bug-eyed thing who never talks. It about drives me crazy.

I'm going down to the docks to confront my "father." I figure he works for the Galveston Wharf Company. I can't see him as a dock worker but I have to find him. I want to run away and maybe I can convince him to go with me. I've found some money in the bottom of mother's wardrobe and I think it's enough to get to Dallas—Houston at least. Then I figure we can get on a train and go even further. I just know I don't want to live with mother anymore.

I ride the streetcar as far as I can; then I walk on down to where the ships come in. The men watch me with curiosity or indifference, like I'm invisible. Children aren't that uncommon a sight around here, but a little girl dressed nice is a tad strange, I reckon. I've got the money with me, wrapped up in a silk handkerchief and tied with blue ribbon. I don't know where to start looking for Arizona. He's not Doc Smiley. There never was a Doc Smiley, and Patience must've been joshing me. I ask around for Clifford Shepard and after a while it seems like he must not work around here, everybody just shrugs or ignores me. Adults are bad about ignoring kids. Sweating like a stuck pig, I come to this swarthy man with a curly black beard, what Atlanta calls an Eye-talian. He grins at me and I ask him about Arizona, describing him as best as I can and he points down the dock to a restaurant where you don't do much eating. A watering hole. I thank him and go on down. The doorway is thick with flies and arguing workers. I sidle past them and wait for my eyes to adjust to the dim room cluttered with diners and drinkers.

The bartender sees me and shakes his head. I'm breathing heavy, scared he's going to thow me out before I can find him. I start to looking as fast as I can and finally see him sitting at a table with three other men, playing cards, poker, I bet. He looks clean, in a suit with a vest. It's not a new suit, but it's clean. He sees me, looks away, pretending not to know me. I say, "Papa?" The other men are watching me going to the table. The noise in the restaurant seems to get worse.

"Hey, papa, it's me, Calamity Shepard, remember me?" My voice is squeaky and sissy sounding but I can't help it.

"This your girl, Doc?" One of the men with him, a balding sort with a squashed-in nose nudges the guy next to him, a gray-haired fat man. "Old Doc's girl, ain't she a looker?" He's making fun of my looks. I feel for my bow and sure enough, it's slipped to the side. And I know I've got circles under my armpits and I stink.

Doc?

"What you doing here, girl? Oughtn't you better off to home? Does your mother know you're here? This ain't no place for a young girl."

"I wanted to see you, papa."

He won't look at me. His eyes are blue, though, bluer than the sky at noon. "You've seen me, now, go on with you."

He is my father. It feels like bugs are crawling down my neck. I hold out the money. "I got money for us; we can run away. I don't want to live with mother anymore. She don't love me and I don't love her. Anyway, Aunt Hester's come and she won't miss me." The men look at the dirty silken wad with greedy eyes. They'd take it, that's for sure. Papa's hand uncurls from its fist. "Where'd you get that, little missy?"

"In mother's wardrobe."

"Take it back home where it belongs."

"Don't you want me?" He doesn't answer me. The restaurant sounds quiet. Lots of folk are watching me and I'm embarrassed. The bartender has come out from around the bar and is headed for papa's table. He wants me out of here. Just like papa.

"I'll take your money little girlie, considering your pa owes me more than usual today."

"Forget it, Paulsel."

"Just joking," mutters the balding man, fingering his pocket watch.

"Go on home, Calamity." At least he called me by my rightful name. I put the money in his hand, my palms dripping. I wipe them on my dumb dress and then cross my arms across my chest. The bartender stops about a foot from the table, his mouth pursing with some admonishment. I like that word, admonishment. It sounds so solemn, real. I want to give papa an admonishment. I stand tall, fixing my hair bow and then crossing my arms again.

"Arizona, you are a yellow bellied coward."

"Well, ain't she a little sassbox," the fat man laughs.

"That I am," he says.

"Pardon me, Mr. Shepard, but this establishment can not condone the attendance of children, especially female children. I'd be obliged if you'd see the little girl out—" The bartender pats his mustache, and my father gets up, clutching the money. He touches my shoulder and we move outdoors into the hot sunshine. For a minute I think he means us to go off together, after all. We're walking to the nearest streetcar. He holds my hand.

"Did you kill an awful lot of men, papa? Was you—I mean, were you really a gun for hire?"

He squeezes my hand.

"I'd like to go out west, I would, with you. Galveston is boring."

"I came back to be near you," he says. We get on the streetcar.

"Ain't you going back to your friends?" I feel breathless and light-headed.

"Later, maybe, but for now I want to get you safely back home. I ought to give you a tongue-lashing but I can't. I love you little missy; I know I ain't been a good father but better late than never." He put the money in his coat. I wonder if he's going to keep it.

"You want to run away with me?"

"You're staying with your mother and that's an end to it."

"I want to go out west and meet an indian."

"You're staying here and don't tell your mother you saw me."

"What about the money?"

"I'll give it back to you once you get home."

"The reason you've been gone is because you were a gunfighter, right?"

Papa decides that we have to get off several blocks from home. He never answers me; we just walk towards home, him holding my hand like I'm some sort of baby. We pass Mrs. Beadle Brown's house and I feel her watching us, even though no curtains seem to be stirring. I hope mother's not home. He seems to hear my fear. He stops about a block away. "You go on without me."

"No!" I want to cry but tears won't do any good.

"I'll be seeing you."

"Papa!" He turns and starts to walk away without another word. I run to him, hold out my arms and he picks me up and kisses me hard on the cheek and the tears come tumbling out despite my best efforts to stop them. He puts me down and hits my bottom. "Run on," he whispers.

I'm all the way to the porch when I realize that he's forgotten to give me mother's money. I turn around to call after him, but he's gone. I smell the oleanders and I sink down on the porch step, truly dispirited. I do not think I will ever see Doc Shepard again. I am heartbroken.

Mother is much taken with Aunt Hester and her concerns. It appears that her sister has gone and fallen for some disreputable man. Atlanta says this disposition to love the wrong man might run in the family. She did not say this around mother. I hope this is not true. It would be terribly tragical. I told Atlanta about my father. We blamed that silly niece of hers of stealing the money so mother let her go and Patience came back to work, an old married girl of fifteen. Atlanta says she is with child but her stomach doesn't look any bigger to me.

My papa has not returned to see me. Atlanta says it's just as well but he does have a semi-respectable job with the wharf company. My birthday is next week and I'm thinking maybe he will remember. I will be ten years old.

Mother says I'll have an ice cream social out in the back yard with paper lanterns. Aunt Hester has a present for me she says she brought all the way from Boston. I've no idea what she was doing in Boston, up there in Yankee land. Atlanta says Aunt Hester has a Past. I think this Past has something to do with the disreputable man.

My father did not forget me. I hold the present in my lap. The postman I thought brought it, but it was on the front doorstep all done up in white paper before the mail came. Atlanta thought Daisy Anne had left it for me, but Daisy's coming to the party later.

Mother and Aunt Hester was up in her boudoir. They're still there, laughing and talking. Atlanta does not know this present is from my father. She's back in the kitchen working on my birthday cake. She told me to wait to open this till later, at the party. I did not wait. The minute she was gone, I opened it.

His gun. He's given me a most wonderful gift. His sparkling gun and a note. The note said: "My dearest child: herewith my best wishes and the gun I used to shoot one man. It's not a grand thing, as you may think, to take a human life. It takes a life just to get over it. You will note I took the bullets out. With Sincerest regards and abiding love, your father, Doc Smiley."

I'm going to hide it in my room. Someday, if I have to, I bet I can buy some bullets for it.

Maybe.

Chief Wooden Teeth

LEE SULLENGER

I couldn't pass up this wild little piece by Lee Sullenger, who uses the images of Western literature and the illogical logic of dreams. I heard him read it at a writer's workshop and got a big kick out of it, and knew then and there that I had to have it. Lee Sullenger, the son of a cowboy, grew up on ranches in West Texas and graduated from Texas Tech in Lubbock and the University of Texas in Austin. He has written a number of historical articles on Western subjects. "Chief Wooden Teeth" is his first published fiction.

It's the Old West, see, and I'm riding shotgun on this stagecoach that's being attacked by Indians. The coach is racing down the dry road, raising a huge cloud of dust behind it. The six horses are running all out, wet with sweat, wild-eyed, nostrils flaring, having the time of their lives. To the left, the right, and the rear as far as you can see there are wild Indians racing on their horses and screaming their lungs out. The sky is dark with arrows. Some of the Indians' horses are not running on the ground, but up in the air, some of them hundreds of feet up. The stagecoach has five passengers; three men, a woman, and a little baby. All five are screaming and all five have pistols in both hands, and they are shooting at the Indians as fast as they can pull the triggers. They sound like a whole platoon of infantry. The sound of hoofbeats is a deafening roar. Oncoming automobiles swerve by us in a flash of honking horns and screams.

The driver is bellowing at the horses and popping his long whip above their heads. He has an idiotic wild grin as he shouts "Hee-yah! Hee-yah! Giddyup!"

I'm really scared. The arrows go *whoof* as they zip past my ear. I'm shooting the shotgun once per second, sometimes at point-blank range, but I never hit anybody. Don't know what's wrong; too scared to shoot straight, I guess. Come to think of it, nobody seems to get hit. We must be holding them off, because they're not getting any closer.

Then all of a sudden I'm aware of this giant Indian riding down out of the sky. He's half a mile up, riding down at a hard run on the biggest, whitest horse you ever saw. I sense he's the chief.

When he gets close enough, he lets fly with a five-foot arrow, and it zips right past my ear with a *whoof* that I hear for two seconds after it passes. I take dead aim at his three-foot-wide chest and fire the shotgun. I miss.

He's riding alongside the coach laughing his head off, white-skinned, white-haired, looking just like his picture. All of a sudden I recognize him. "My god!" I hear myself saying. "You're not an Indian! You're George Washington!"

He throws back his head and bellows out a big laugh, wooden teeth shining. "Surprised, are you?" he says. "Well, my fellow American, this is nothing compared to some of the things that have been lost to history!"

He rides alongside the coach for a few seconds, and then he lets out a loud whoop. Quick as a wink he yanks out another long arrow, bows it up and lets fly straight at me. I duck, and the arrow zips right by my ear with a loud *whoof.* I let him have both barrels of the shotgun point-blank. I don't see how I miss, but I do.

Then George reascends. The big white stallion tears off in a steep climb and in a minute they're out of sight up in the sky. I turn my attention back to the Indians. I shoot at a big buck and miss. I think to myself, this has been a strange day.

The Wild One

MAX EVANS

Max Evans is one of the best writers this field has seen, and though he hasn't been completely ignored, he certainly hasn't gotten the attention he deserves. He is best known for The Rounders, *which was also made into a successful movie with Glenn Ford and Henry Fonda.* The Rounders *is a funny story with a tragic underpinning and should be on any reader's list of*

novels to read and reread. He is also the author of the Spur Award winner,
The Orange County Cowboys, The Hi Lo Country *and* Bobby Jack
Smith, *as well as a number of fine short stories, "Candles in the Bottom of
the Pool" being one of the best. He is a painter of some repute and has
acted in Western films. Some enterprising publisher out there needs to
encourage him to do a new novel. I'll be first in line to buy it.*

It was the most fantastic story Forest Ranger Joe Healy had ever heard.
"It just can't be," he said in stunned disbelief. "Don't you realize if she's
over thirty years old, that would make her almost a hundred and twenty in
human terms?"

"Yeah, something like that," Randy Lindsey answered. "She does truly
exist. I first spotted her tracks about three years ago, and I felt just like you
until I finally saw her for real a couple of months back. Yeah, she's up
there alright."

Randy was a young cowboy who worked for Jimmy Bason's F Cross
Ranch. Bason leased out most of the grassland on his hundred thousand
acres, so he needed only his son, Brent, and one extra cowboy to help take
care of his small herd. Jimmy was lucky . . . Randy was a "throw back"
of the Old West. He liked living by himself in a line-shack, and preferred
to work with horses instead of a pickup truck. He wanted to carry on the
old-time traditions.

The two men were sitting at a table in the one-bar, two-church town of
Hillsboro in southwestern New Mexico. The bar also had the only restaurant available for thirty miles.

Ranger Healy knew that Randy would never lie to him about a thing
like this, but he found it almost impossible to believe that a horse could
have survived, totally alone, for all those years. He leaned forward across
the plate of red chile burritos and the bottle of beer, saying softly, "Does
anyone else know about this?"

The young cowboy said, "Only Jimmy Bason . . . and he don't want
anybody to know. He says the do-gooders and the do-badders will both try
to capitalize on her." He paused. "In fact, he'll probably fire me if he finds
out I slipped up and told someone."

Joe laughed softly, "You don't have to worry, Randy, I won't tell anybody except my daughter. She's crazy nuts about animals, you know.
That's why she's definitely decided to become a vet. And, by dogies, she'll
never have another chance to see anything like this. That mare has to be
some kind of miracle. My God, even gentle horses, that are pampered and
cared for, don't live that long. I'd say this is about the rarest dang thing I

ever heard of. It's like being first in line at the Second Coming. Yeah," Healy said as if to himself, "Pauline's got to see this horse."

Randy reluctantly agreed to describe the area the mare currently habituated. He was unaware that their conversation was being overheard by a vacationing young reporter for an El Paso, Texas, newspaper, who was sitting at the next table with his wife and two children. The young man hurriedly grabbed a pen and pad from his pocket and, with noticeable excitement, started scribbling.

Joe Healy drove the pickup, pulling a trailer containing two good saddle horses, as near as the rough terrain would allow, to the designated wilderness area. He and his fifteen-year-old daughter, Pauline, quickly set up camp. They had enough supplies to last over a month if that's what it took to find the wild mare. They had come prepared and totally dedicated.

They rode the piñon-and-cedar-covered foothills. Then made their way up to the edge of the tall pines on the mountain. They roamed for five days looking at the ground, hoping to find a sign of the horse. Even in their anticipation of the latter, they still enjoyed the markings of the other wild creatures. They actually saw twenty or thirty deer, ten elk, a coyote, many kinds of birds, and even glimpsed a black bear disappearing into a patch of heavy timber.

On the sixth day they found her hoofprints. The tracks were at least a week old, but to the Healys, they were as new as first frost. The excitement of discovery surged through all the tissues, nerves and thoughts of their bodies, but nevertheless, on the seventh day they rested themselves and their horses.

Pauline said, "Daddy, if she's never had a colt, she's still a filly no matter what her age, right?"

"Now don't get technical on me, Pauline. As old as she is, we're gonna call her a mare."

Pauline pushed her long, blond hair back from her face, and said in a soft voice filled with wonder, "She's really out there. We've found her unshod hoofprints. Poor thing . . . all alone. Just think of all the bad weather, and the predators, and the loneliness she has endured, and now she's *so* old. Wonder how she's done it?" Her blue eyes widened in astonishment at the frightening images.

Joe Healy searched for a special answer for this question, but he could only come up with "It does seem impossible. She must be blessed. That's the answer, Pauline. She's blessed."

Father and daughter rode out of camp at dawn the next day. The two had spent a restless night, but now they were keyed up and tuned in to the whole world. It was midafternoon when they found some more recent tracks—these were only a couple of days old. Joe recalled Randy saying, "I was ridin' old Birdie, when I cut my first sign of her. I just knew she had to be the last of the wild ones. I never had a feelin' like it before. It was sorta like I'd just invented the first saddle." Healy was having some of the same feelings now. A sense of the primordial permeated his being. He couldn't have been more in awe if he'd just come face-to-face with a living dinosaur or the Loch Ness monster.

Pauline almost cried aloud, but instead, she let the tears rivulet silently down her cheeks. To her it was a sacred moment and she looked up to the heavens. In the distance, she saw several buzzards circling. She lifted her wide, blue eyes above the birds to a patch of sky and then on above that she saw something that caused her to cry out, "Daddy, look! Look way up there!"

He looked in the direction of her pointing, but his vision missed what she had so briefly seen. His eyes moved, by nature and training, back down to the tracks they had been following. Pauline reined her horse in line. Now her eyes were focused on a movement nearing a huge cumulus cloud. She stared in wonder.

The mare was born in the spring of the year the Space Age dawned. In October 1957 the Russians fired *Sputnik 1* into the heavens. It circled the globe at altitudes ranging from 141 to 588 miles above Moscow and Washington, D.C. It traveled at 14,700 miles per hour. The people of the Soviet Union rejoiced and justifiably felt enormous pride. The Americans were embarrassed and scared. There was an outcry for more defense spending and the whole educational system of the free world altered. The emphasis was placed on science. Literature, all the arts and old-time basic schooling was greatly neglected. The Space Age and the mare had been born.

Far below on the solid rocks of the Black Range, the colt frolicked, nursed and grew stronger daily. She did not know, or care, about this monumental change in the world. From the beginning, she was more agile and faster than the other colts in one of the dozen or so scattered bands of wild horses. Her chestnut coat glistened in the sun and her large, dark eyes were full of adventure and mischief.

Her first winter was an easy one with little snow. The horses fared well in the rolling hills between the private ranches and the national forest area, but the springtime came dry and the grass was short.

The ranchers moved their cattle into the wild horses' domain under individual leases with the government. There was competition for the shriveling grass between the wildlife, the mustangs and the domestic cattle. The ranchers and Forest Service joined forces to get rid of the wild horses.

They built log-pole traps around waterholes in an attempt to capture them alive. They tried roping the young, the old or the lame. This effort only delivered ten head of the wily bunch, and in the process they crippled three cowboys, one ranger and twenty-two of their tame horses.

The ranchers and Forest Service executives argued over other means to dispose of this threat to the welfare of their cattle and consequently their families. During one of their meetings, word came of a forest fire in the area. It had been started by lightning from a small, shower cloud. The flames caused the dry trees and vegetation to snap and pop like infantry machine guns.

One small band of horses was trapped and perished. All living things ran together now, to escape the inferno. Deer, elk and cattle raced alongside coyotes, bears and cougars. Rabbits dashed in and out of the flames until some caught fire and fell in kicking, smoking bundles. Everything attempted to escape in a terrible panic. Most small things like lizards, ants, grasshoppers, spiders, tree worms, squirrels, skunks, and nestlings were cooked as black as the forest floor.

The colt raced beside her mother as the dominant stallion of the band circled, squealing commands, kicking, biting and trying to drive his harem and offspring to safety. The prevailing southwest wind joined in the chaos and whipped the flames in circles and drove it forward with destructive speed. The smoke could be seen one hundred aircraft miles away in El Paso, Texas. Fire fighters tried to organize, but their efforts were futile against the raging force.

Then the winds suddenly quit as if on command from the gods and the fire died out at the banks of the North Percha Creek. It had decimated the five-mile width from the upper Animas drainage to the creek. The existing forage would be much sparser now.

The ranchers moved their cattle back to the home ranches with great effort and much loss of weight. The decision was made—the wild horses had to be destroyed. They organized and came with camping gear, horses and rifles. They rode for weeks driving their prey into the burned areas where they killed them.

Joe Healy's father, John, who was a ranger at the time, led the onslaught. He instructed the Rangers and cowboys to try to "bark" the wild horses. That is, shoot them through the top edge of the neck knocking them unconscious so they could be saved for live capture. It didn't work. The fire, followed by the cracking of rifles, the squeals and groans of dying animals, created a madness of desperation. The stallions lost control of their bands and ran about as erratically as their broods. Over a hundred and thirty horses were slaughtered.

The area became, and looked, like a battlefield. What with the dead horses scattered about through the massive burned area and the buzzards gathering from miles around to join the coyotes, bobcats, bears, lions and other meat-eating predators to feast on the carcasses.

The Rangers and ranchers agreed there were none left to scatter the seed. They were wrong by *one*.

The yearling colt had been barked from a long distance and when she regained consciousness, she raced blindly across the scorched earth through the stench of the rotting bodies and kept on going up and up until the greenness of undefiled timber surrounded her. The sweat had turned to a lather over her entire body and her lungs bellowed in and out in painful gasps.

She kept going until she was deep into the high forest and her legs began to tremble and caused her to fall over and over. Then she stopped. She could move no more. She was sore and weak for several days before she found a spring and enough feed from brush and the scant grass to live. She was totally confused about where she was or what had happened to her world.

Then the late-summer rains came and the earth was soaked, cleansed, revitalized, and so was the colt. The soreness and the gauntness disappeared. She was alone in several hundred thousand acres of wilderness. But she lived.

The rains had made good feeding for the grazers, and the remains of the horses and the other burned animals gave plentiful food to the predators. This one winter, when she needed help so much, the fanged animals had no need of her flesh.

The spring grass and vegetation came again. She was feeding and nourishing her muscles and bones, and rapidly growing into a fine two-year-old equine specimen. She looked better than she felt. The flashes of fire still raced behind her eyes, and over and over she heard the death screams of her mother. Sometimes she would hold her head high, with nostrils straining wide, thinking she smelled the smoke from the scorched forest floor and the rotting flesh of her family and ancestors. After these flashbacks of horror, she would tremble and run about, trying to escape the imagined destruction. Finally, she'd calm and return to her normal watering, feeding and exercising. The fearful images slowly grew dimmer as she grew older.

She was walking to her secret waterhole when the warning chatter of a tassel-eared squirrel became louder and more urgent. It was October the first, 1961. Roger Maris, who played baseball for the New York Yankees, had just hit his sixty-first home run of the season, breaking Babe Ruth's old record. Just as the standing ovation of the crowd drew him out of the dugout for the second tip of his cap, a heavy force hit the filly on the back.

The lion had leapt from a limb above her and dug his foreclaws deep into her neck. His rear claws were locked into her hips. With powerful, open jaws and long, meat-ripping fangs, he reached for the place where the neck bones join the skull. The instant she felt the force of the lion's weight, and the sharp pain of its claws, she bolted straight into a heavy growth of young trees. Before the lion could close his jaws on the death spot, a limb smashed into his forehead and dragged him off her back. In so doing, the claws raked through her hide and into raw flesh plowing permanent lines and eventual scars on both sides of her neck. The claw cuts were painful for a while, with the swelling and draining, but they healed. From then on, her mind was alerted to the warning sounds from other possible victims of predators.

The five-mile-wide and ten-mile-long burnt area had come back lush green. The grass and brush had fought the timber seedlings for space and won. The small surviving trees were scattered widely apart. All the new growth made, for a few years at least, lush summer grazing. For a long time she spent as much of her life here as possible. The trees were so far apart that she could watch for the death drop from above and avoid the tearing claws of the lion. The deer felt as she did, and grazed right along side her. In the fall and early winter she and the other foraging creatures would move high up, out of the healed area, and feast on the oak brush and mountain mahogany pine, putting on fat to hold them through the sometimes hard winters.

She wasn't so lonely anymore. She had the company of wild turkeys, band-tailed pigeons, quail, squirrels and chipmunks, blue jays and mountain grouse, hawks and eagles. Some of the creatures lived at all altitudes, changing locations with the seasons and the food growth, while others were found at only certain heights in special terrain. There were many creatures here she would have to study in order to live out her allotted span of years.

Fortunately, she had found a secluded spring soon after the earlier holocaust. The timber and rocks, while completely encircling it, sat well back from the waterhole. On this special terrain she could drink peacefully, knowing that she wouldn't suffer a sudden attack. She maintained a constant alertness as far as her knowledge at this point allowed.

In late September, she went to the spring and found it frozen over. This was a new surprise . . . another type of warning she must learn to heed. There was much more danger on this mountain than the long-toothed predators, and after this winter she would always remember that early ice and falling leaves, along with higher, more frigid winds, meant heavy storms soon. She didn't have that knowledge frozen into her genes at the time the great snow came.

The dark clouds moved in formation, low, caressing, over the peaks, like Alexander's legions. And underneath them the wind fought with the trees, thrashing them about in agony and sending the flying things coasting up and away on its mad currents. But below, where the wind was less, many of the four-footed animals failed to move out in time.

The snow stuck for a moment on the millions of branches and limbs before being shaken loose by the wind over and over, thousands and thousands of times. The white, frozen crystals were swept and piled into massive drifts higher than the mare's head. She was all right for a few days, pawing the snow down to the little clumps of bunch-grass and oak brush.

She rapidly consumed all edible food in the small radius she was able to control. Soon she had to struggle harder, pawing into the deeper drifts. Her exertions caused rapid weight loss. Her lungs had to pump more warm air which formed ice crystals around her nostrils and eyes restricting her breathing and vision. She was in a white, frozen world and was quickly turning into an immobile ice sculpture.

She could only paw feebly now, and began to lose interest in making any effort at all. She was dozing. Her weakened neck allowed her head to drop down almost to knee level. She felt warm, dry, and totally without concern for food or anything else. Soon one foreleg slid out to the side. She was teetering with her whole body about to fall over, but she felt as if she was running in the summer warmth again with the gray male colt. They were jumping about, dodging and chasing each other with their short tails in the air, and heads up like the Royal British mounts. They were full, free and safe. It was a glorious moment.

Suddenly then, she was certain that she smelled the smoke, envisioned the fire, and heard the squeals and screams again for the first time in months. The fear became so real she began actually running from it. Then she whirled and ran back towards it, craving its imagined warmth. After bursting through drift after drift, she began to feel the cold again, but kept plunging through the forest down, down, always down. Eternity returned. She now fought to reach lower ground as years before she had struggled for the high.

Her lungs pained terribly as she sucked in more and more frozen air, just as she had once breathed the hot ashes and fire-scorched winds. As before, there came a point where her afflicted lungs could not supply enough fuel to keep her body moving. She stood quivering, and made loud gasping sounds as she tried to take in the warmer air of the foothills.

When she could finally see again, she discovered that the drifts were much smaller here. There would be no problem pawing through to the grass and even some of the bushes could be reached with hardly any effort at all. She survived until spring once again. Never, not once, would she be trapped in the high country by the felonious storms.

By spring, she had gained back almost all her weight and strength when she spotted two black-bear cubs climbing over and around a dead log, chasing and cuffing one another about in the purest of fun. One fell, hanging on just a moment before tumbling the short distance to the ground. The mare, feeling good after the grinding winter, eased forward in a friendly gesture to the cub. They had barely touched noses when the little bear whirled and scampered away, and the mare heard the loud "whoof." The sound was followed by a blasting slap to her side and neck. The mama bear had been plunging downhill at such speed that her swipe at the mare was slightly off. The blow to the horse's neck and ribs had not been the solid finishing strike the bear had intended. Even so, it knocked the mare stumbling to the side. Her neck and rib cage were numbed where the mighty paw of the five-hundred-pound beast had struck.

As the bear whirled back to finish the mare off with her teeth and foreclaws, she received an unpleasant surprise. The mare's adrenaline had flushed up ancient resources of genes. An old experience imparted the knowledge to her brain that her numbed body could not outrun the bear. She whirled and started kicking back towards her attacker. The bear stuck her lower jaw right into one of the mare's hooves when it was at its apex of power. The bones cracked like a bull elk stepping on a tiny dry stick. The other hoof caught her on the left eye, chipping the skull around the socket in several places and knocking the bear's remaining vision askew. In a few weeks the coyotes got the cubs and the buzzards discovered the starved body of the mother bear.

The mare's left shoulder had torn tendons that caused her much pain as she traversed the uneven ground trying to feed. Another wide scar undulated with the muscles beneath the skin from the blow of the bear. Since she hadn't fully recovered from the decimation of the winter, it would be late summer before the scar healed and the soreness left her.

By early October, she was well and sufficient winter fat was already on her bones. With this recuperation also came a feeling of longing. Something was missing—something that was a part of her—something that she had every right to be sharing. The vacancy left an aching in her heart, her womb, and her animal soul.

She thought she saw a blur of her own kind, her own blood, in the bushes and trees, but no matter how hard she looked and searched, the images she ached to define would not come clear. This ineluctable feeling pervaded her all during, and past, the twenty-second of October, 1962, when the Cuban missile crisis began. President John F. Kennedy ordered the blockading of Cuba and revealed the discovery of Soviet missile bases on Cuban soil through air reconnaissance photos. The President went on television and gave media interviews in the Oval Office. The two leaders of the superpowers exchanged many accusations and threats. The hearts of the world stood still in dread.

For six days, the mighty powers threatened and blustered. U.S. bombers, loaded with atomic bombs, flew patterns up to the edge of Soviet territory by the hour. The warships were about to pair off for battle. The Russians, vastly outnumbered in the nuclear bomb category at the time, held out six days before they gave in. Never before had the world been so close to destruction in just a few minutes of madness. It has been debated ever since whether Kennedy saved the world by calling the Russians' bluff or gave it away by not taking Cuba while it was in his grasp.

During the six days of worldwide tension, the mare grazed contentedly and enjoyed the cool nights and warm days of autumn in peace. The forest has many eyes and ears, watching, listening, always aware, and now she knew how to use them to her advantage. These animals would voice the movements of danger to her instantly. She only had to listen and act to be safe.

As the other world started breathing again, but as yet looking over their collective shoulders, the mare spent a mild winter with plenty of forage. When spring came, some tiny bit of fat was still left under her long winter hair. She would soon be slick and shiny.

After many years of gaining knowledge through painful experiences and her natural force of observation, she finally chose her favorite spot for repose. About halfway down, between the jagged peaks of the high mountains and the lower meadows, there was a mesa with Mimbres Indian ruins on top. From here she could walk around the edges of the pueblito and observe the far-spreading wilderness in every direction, just as the Indian occupants once had.

Here in her part of southern New Mexico, hundreds of these ruins existed. Some archaeologists dated them back a thousand years, but the exact time period is as much in dispute as how an entire nation of mostly peaceful Indians vanished completely. They did leave behind them, their rock houses, burial grounds, stone and bone tools, arrowheads, and traces of jewelry. However, there were very few implements of actual war. Their main gifts to history were their wonderfully constructed, and uniquely designed pottery.

Here in the ancient ruins, the mare felt a comfort and peace greater than in any other spot in her domain. When the hidden blood-longings and blurred visions came to her, she headed to this spot to share it with the ghosts of its former inhabitants like retreating to a Benedictine monastery. She heard drums and chants and sometimes saw incomplete images in the air, but she didn't know what they were—only that she was comforted.

After the time of the Mimbres and before the time of the satellites, there had been many battles in this part of her range. Geronimo and Chief Victorio had made this area their last hideout from pursuing cavalry. Only half a mile below her, an isolated squad of buffalo soldiers from the 9th Cavalry had encountered a small band of Apaches. It became a running battle. A black sergeant named Williams, realizing two of his wounded soldiers were surrounded, charged back, catching the Apaches by surprise and saving the soldiers' lives. Sergeant Williams was awarded the Congressional Medal of Honor.

In 1963, President John F. Kennedy was assassinated by Lee Harvey Oswald in Dallas, Texas. It shocked a nation and a lot of the world into near paralysis. People will never forget where they were when they heard the news. The mare knew none of this, nor would she have cared, for hers was and had truly been another world. Much more would pass in both dimensions.

The mare was honored in the year of '67 by the weather. The forage was plentiful from the summer rains and the snow of the high country had melted early. She prospered . . . but in the cities of America the flower children came to full bloom, shouting peace and free love, while the rock music cascaded its battering, and often deafening, beat across the land and cheap dope altered minds and history forever. In the Haight-Ashbury district of the lovely city of San Francisco, the children lay about the streets with minds bent and bodies so inert they could barely follow up on the prevalent misguided theory of love being free. They had presumably started out innocent and wound up tasting the refuse of the gutters, seeing visions of such complexity that for many there was nothing left but the accidental and sometimes purposeful ultimate quest—suicide.

That same fateful year ended in near tragedy for the aging mare, even more innocently than it had for the children of the streets. She wanted companionship . . . a direct communication of some kind. During one of those periods of deep loneliness, she was craving something like the image she saw reflected in the water as she drank from her favorite spring. That's when she followed and, in a friendly gesture, stuck her muzzle down to a porcupine. The animal with thirty thousand barbs swung its short tail and imbedded fourteen of them into the left side of the mare's nostrils and face.

In a couple of days one passage was swelled completely shut and the other barely open so that she gasped for breath even while standing still. She started losing weight and strength immediately. The swelling and pain grew so great that she would rub her face against trees, rocks, bushes, the earth itself and sling her head in circles trying to dislodge the darts.

Now the coyotes witnessed this and stalked her. They were far too smart to risk her deadly hooves, if she had been well. Due to their small size, they could only down big game when it was ill or injured. By her erratic actions, the coyotes knew she was both. So they patiently circled and watched, for days. Even with all her pain, the mare watched them too. She turned her rear to them, ready to strike out hard with her hind feet.

Slowly, some of the quills worked their way out, while only a few burst open the swelled spots at her rubbing. She was forced to graze solely on bush leaves. It was slow and painful. She was weakening fast.

Finally one coyote leapt at her nostrils. While she was busy with the first, the other tried to hamstring her. The coyote did manage to get hold of her muzzle just long enough to puncture it. This helped the poison ooze out, and the swelling started down. She kicked the other one in the side and sent it rolling down an embankment with three broken ribs. The wise coyotes left her alone and chose to dine, that day, on game already dead.

She could eat better now and gradually the barbs either worked all the way out or a protective gristle formed around them. She became strong again. It seemed that no matter how long she lived and how much knowledge she acquired, there was still wisdom to be gained that could come only from experience. Just the same, she knew, and had survived, most of the deadly dangers of the wilderness at least once. She had paid a highly inflated price to gain a few years of relative tranquillity.

The last year of the sixties was a good one for her. Most of her scars and injuries were healed. She spotted a bobcat on a rare daylight foray. It crouched in the grass stalking a quail. That same day Armstrong and Aldrin would complete one of mankind's most sought-after dreams. They landed a space ship on the moon. Scores of millions of people worldwide were tied with invisible ropes, to their television sets. The bobcat didn't know any more about this than the mare. It was hungry and the solution to that problem hid motionless in the grass some ten feet ahead.

The cat's ears twitched ever so slightly, trying to catch any sound or movement from the intended victim. The soft, furry belly was actually touching the ground at its lowest point. Its short tail switched once as the cat leaped forward. The quail raised up, took three strides and winged into flight. About four feet off the ground the bobcat's claws hooked into the bird's belly. As they fell back to earth, she locked her jaws on the last flutterings, and crouched, holding it tightly as she looked about for any competition. As soon as the bird was dead, the cat took off towards its den in some rocks out of the mare's sight.

That same day, as the mare wandered, browsing in the brush, a golden eagle dropped from the sky into an opening, hooked its powerful talons into a fat rabbit and flew up to some bluffs to dine. The forest gave sudden voice with squirrels and birds chattering, then became cautiously silent again. This was all so natural in her life that the mare took only a cursory glance at the necessary killing. This golden eagle had landed, and so had the one on the moon. One in an action as old as animal history and the other as new as birth.

A mother elk tried to graze while her bull calf hunched greedily at her bag with switching tail. Three forest moths played in and out of a sunbeam like happy, little angels. The mare, witnessing all of this, would have fed in contentment except the yearning for something more of her own self struck her several times a month now.

She might have felt better about one human endeavor presently occurring if she had known about it. A lady known as Wild Horse Annie from Nevada, had raised so much hell, enlisted so many supporters, and grabbed so much attention from the media, that a federal law was passed protecting wild horses. Of course, it came far too late for the old mare's immediate ancestors. As her life moved in its eternal cycle of daily survival, the world around her was accelerating with a momentum that seemed to gain in speed like a great boulder rolling down a mighty mountain towards a tiny village.

In 1972, the Arabs put an embargo on oil, and while millions of Americans waited in line for hours at gas stations frustrated and unable to move, the mare browsed on luscious foliage and enjoyed an unhurried, uncluttered existence.

Oil prices escalated, and some poor nations became rich and many rich countries poorer. Wealth shifted about like the hearts of young lovers. The Watergate scandal dethroned a president and his men, changing the political attitudes and history of the free world for decades yet to come.

During these outside occurrences, the old mare had, on several occasions, seen a flash of gray in the timber and brush to the east of her Mimbres ruins lookout. She knew somehow that this was a replica of herself. She felt a kinship here at the ruins, and she had the same feeling for the glimpses of gray. She now took excursions trying to get a solid sight or smell of her illusory relation. But none came—no matter how long she wandered about on swiftly tiring legs, or stared with her dimming eyes, or sniffed with her knotted, scarred muzzle. The only place she could conjure up the flashing vision was from the same spot on the east side of the Mimbres ruins. There only. But she kept on searching, season following season. She would return to the magic spot and wait, sometimes hours, sometimes days, until forced to move away for food and water. But the gray thing began to appear more often. She felt warm and elated at each sighting, even if it was blurred and filmy.

Things had been working in her favor for several years now. A chief forester named Aldo Leopold had written an enormously influential essay entitled "The Land Epic." It led to the creation of a huge official wilderness area named after the forester. The mighty Black Range was to the west of the free area. Gerald Lyda's Ladder Ranch, one of the largest and most famous in the Southwest, touched it on many sides. The Cross Triangle joined to the north and Jimmy Bason's to the east. The old mare lived, protected, right in the middle of it all.

Now that no private vehicles could ever enter her area, she sometimes watched the backpackers walking into the Animas Creek area to camp and relish nature. She would watch them through the bushes, standing as motionless as an oft-hunted buck deer. As long as they didn't carry cracking rifles, as did those who hunted yearly in the lower country, they were nothing but a pleasant curiosity to her. Many elk had migrated across the Black Range from the Gila Wilderness to hers. She enjoyed their presence and bugling calls, but it did little to allay the growing sense of an impending personal event.

Friday, September 18, 1987, the two-hundredth anniversary of the Constitution of the United States, the mare spent looking out the canyon from the ruins, hoping her gray companion would show. It was an anxious day for others as well.

The Polish Pope John Paul II arrived in San Francisco toward the end of what would probably be his last junket to the United States, amidst about two thousand picketing AIDS victims and sympathizers. The Pope kept calm.

Headlines around the nation said that the United States and the Soviets had reached an accord on diminishing the number of missiles in the world. When the mare had been born into the Space Age, America had far superior numbers of arms, but now on this day, the Soviets were ahead. Not many people on either side really believed the negotiations were being held for the good of all mankind.

As patriotic parades were held all across the land on this great day, the old mare went on, patiently looking. Then she saw it. Now the gray mist had taken on a little more solidity and form. Her heart beat faster. The figure didn't disappear this time but stayed just inside the bushes as she strained harder than ever before to see and realize what part of her it was.

The year of the celebration of the Constitution passed with many wars in effect. In Lebanon, Afghanistan, all over Africa. The Iranians and the Iraqis went on butchering one another and the ships of the world filled up the Persian Gulf supposedly to protect oil tankers for the Western world market. While the old mare looked for her compatriot there were, in fact, over forty blasting, slashing, mind-numbing wars being fought.

The calendar moved on into the presidential election year, with the candidates made up of preachers and lawyers. The old mare's body was as ravaged as the polluted and war-torn earth. The scars on her neck, ribs and shoulders from the attacks of the lion and the bear looked like little, erratically plowed farms. Her back was swayed, her eyes were dull and clouded over. Her once long, flowing mane and tail had been matted and stuck together with burrs and stickers of all kinds for years. The natural indentions above her eyes were sunken, creating round shadows. Her ribs looked like wagon bows sticking through thin, worn, chestnut-colored cloth. The old gunshot wound in her neck hardly mattered in comparison with all the rest. Her tattered ear bent over like one on a generations-old toy rabbit. She had spent her extended life searching for peace, hurting nothing except those who sought to destroy her breath and blood.

Unbeknownst to her, children of the cities, farms, and ranches ran around playing astronauts and aliens from outer space instead of cowboys and Indians as they had at the time of her birth, and most of their lives as well as those of their parents were hourly directed by computer buttons and little images on various screens. Her natural methods of survival had mostly remained the same through her decades here in the Aldo Leopold Wilderness. These ancient rhythms went back to the forest fire, to the conquistadors, to Spain and Egypt, and throughout history. Since the beginning of man, her ancestors were hunted for meat or used as beasts of burden, as creatures to make war with, and at times for racing, hunting, and even many forms of pure pleasure.

Her genes cried and tugged at her being, taking her back sixty million years to the Eocene epoch, or time of the Dawn Horse, when she would have been the size of a small fox terrier. Now as she strained ever harder to make the gray object clearer, she heard the Indian drums and the accompanying chants become louder. The fuzzed objects were suddenly delineated. Some of the Mimbres Indians were dancing in a circle of spectators. Their brown legs and feet moved faster and faster as the drum's volume increased. Her heart beat in synchronization with them as she looked across the canyon and back to the Mimbres.

She was extremely excited, but a mellowness absorbed her at the same time. The drummer's hands, at their ultimate speed, pounded the hide drums and the moccasined feet thumped the earth with all the skill and power left in them. Intense vibrations filled the air and permeated everything. The sound and movement stopped at its peak—and for just a moment so did the universe, in total quiet and stillness.

Then four elders squatted in a rectangle. Each one took a turn standing and making a gesture with both hands in supplication to all four winds. A medicine man and a medicine woman stood before the mare now, and in contrast to the former solemnity of the ceremonies, radiated smiles of love and compassion towards her.

The medicine man reached into a doeskin pouch and gathered a handful of seeds from all the vegetation of the land. He leaped high in the air and hurled the seeds out over the mare. The seeds turned into uncountable bluebirds. They flew up, up and dissolved the thin mists of clouds across the sky, and moved ever higher, growing into numbers so great they became a solid mass of blue. The birds moved past the sun and the bright land of the sky was reborn.

Just as the medicine man landed back on earth, the medicine woman leapt upwards in a floating jump. She, too, reached into her doeskin bag for seeds, also throwing them above the mare as her compatriot had done. These turned into multitudes of white doves fluttering skyward forming a great flat-bottomed, castle-domed cumulus cloud. She drifted back to earth standing next to the man. Both lifted their arms above their heads and yelled with all the force of their throats and lungs. Their cries were a mixture of all living things of the mountains—the lions and the insects, the bears and the bobcats, the hawks and the hares. All.

The mighty crescendo of sound moved up and became a symphony of drums and hand-carved flutes, spreading so wide it finally softened to a simple, sweet sigh. Instantly the Mimbres Indians vanished from her vision as they had so many centuries before from the earth.

And now, across the eons right to the present, she saw the grayness move out of the brush and become circular movement. It was a great, shining, gray stallion who pranced with arched neck and high-tossed tail, back and forth directly across the canyon at about her level. Her scars were no longer felt, nor the stiff limbs, nor any of the lumps of the years. She was possessed with an inner feeling of permanent warmth and peace. Her eyes became so sharp she could see the nostrils of the stallion flare as he turned his head to nicker and squeal to her. She heard it as clearly as the bells of Notre Dame, and knew all its meaning as she always had and always would. She saw the stallion racing across the canyon, through space, towards her, mane and tail streaming. Then he sailed up and up above the grass the brush and the trees. She whirled agilely about, leaping down the rough terrain and then ascending sharply, racing in a soothing, golden vacuum straight towards her mate, at last.

At the very moment Pauline Healy had yelled for her father to look in the sky above the descending buzzards, an El Paso reporter, a photographer and three cowboys, who were expert ropers and trackers, were moving their pickups and gear towards the Healy's camp. If the Ranger and his daughter had been listening into the quietness, they would have heard the truck engines straining uphill.

From another direction came the *chawp, chawp, chawp* of the helicopter as it passed over Jimmy Bason's Ranch loaded with people from the Associated Press. The Healys didn't hear the sounds below because the discovery that lay before them blocked out all else.

The Ranger felt his horse's muscles tense beneath him and saw three coyotes scatter away from a chestnut carcass.

He said with an infinite loss in his voice and a painful expulsion of breath, "Ohhhh . . . nooo. We're too late! The coyotes and buzzards have already beat us to her."

Pauline's wide, wondering eyes were locked on a movement in the sky. She did not hear her father, or see the signs and activity on the ground. Three tiny clouds, each one bigger than the other, raced across the blueness to the cumulus cloud and right up on top of it. There the girl saw a stallion, a mare, and a colt playing together in the upper mists and lights of the massive formation of white moisture. They were silhouetted proudly against the sky. Forever. Anyone could see them who knew how to look.

With an imponderable smile on her suddenly beatific face, the girl said softer than the whisper of a saint, "There will never be another her. Never."

Mourning Old Spareribs

LOLO WESTRICH

LoLo Westrich is both writer and illustrator, and if her illustrations are anything like her writing, she is unique indeed. No schoolmarms and shoot-'em-ups in Main Street here. LoLo's approach to the Western story is strange and original and unclassifiable, as any good fiction should be. She's actually been published quite a bit, but she has still not received the exposure she deserves. I hope after reading this story, LoLo Westrich is a byline you'll be looking for, and maybe some publisher will help out your search by publishing her novels.

After Slim died, a victim of influenza, "in this disease-ridden year of our Lord 1918," as the newspaper obituary so succinctly put it, Anna gathered up a few of their belongings, including his old deer rifle, and her old damask tablecloth, and rode the train westward to Cholla Valley—the very place to which he'd promised, much to her chagrin, to send her an angel to keep her company. There, on the edge of the Wisdom Desert, four miles west of Needleton, where the cactus grew like garden weeds, she bought the very sort of place they'd always dreamt of owning—"nothin'

fancy, mind you, just room enough for us and them chickens we'll raise"
—and toward which, in fact, they'd saved their money for the twenty
years since first they'd seen the valley the year they were wed.

"You mustn't let my dyin' stop you from goin', Annie," he'd bid her on
his deathbed. "You gotta head on out to Cholla Valley anyhow. That's
what you gotta do."

"How could I?" she whispered, her voice breaking like twigs under the
weight of winter ice. "How could I bear to go there all by myself?"

"But you won't be alone for long," Slim hastened, taking her hand and
pressing it to his papery lips. "You think I'd allow the likes of that? Why,
Annie, honey, I never would."

"Oh?" she whispered, both brows arched. She sat forward, clutching
the arms of her rocking chair, readying herself for the words she sensed
would meet her burning ears, some nonsense or other about what he
sometimes termed "the neighborliness of angels."

She sensed rightly, for that's precisely when he told her that he planned
to send an angel all the way down to Cholla Valley, "just to keep you
company, Annie, honey." And he said it with a straight face—so that
there was no way she could pretend, as she liked to do at times like this,
that he was half teasing. She hadn't seen him so solemn since his leg was
crushed in a buggy wreck way back when they were courting.

"I see," she murmured, but she looked away, irked at the thought that
Slim would resort to *any* brand of "angel talk" at a time like this—when
they had so little time left together. Not that it was really anything new
with him. A milkman himself, nowise inclined toward the pulpit, he was,
nonetheless, the only son of Preacher Increase Harkins, the so-called "Ge-
ographer of Paradise," whose sermons on the subject of the ready accessi-
bility of heavenly spirits—to whomsoever happened to believe in them—
had rocked St. Louis at the turn of the century. As Slim himself was wont
to put it, "Why, Annie, honey, I cut my teeth on the trappings of angels."

Anna was a down-to-earth sort herself and had no time for fancies.
(Once when, in a rare show of anger, Slim had cried, "Drat it all, Anna,
you got no more imagination than an ironing board," she'd riled him
further by flatly agreeing.) Still, in the beginning she'd accepted this quirk
of his in much the same manner as she did his cowlick, his limp (wages of
that buggy wreck), and his penchant for practical jokes—of which she was
often the purse-lipped brunt. In fact, she didn't really begin to seethe
inside until after five or six years had passed, by which time he'd bent her
ear with literally hundreds of tales of incredible encounters with the most
motley crew of spirits ever conjured up.

Among those hosts of heaven in question were cherubim in saloons, seraphim in streetcars, ministering spirits masquerading as men at work—helping to load the milk trucks, of all things. There were angels who were angels in every sense. There were others who were strictly of a nominal sort—ordinary folk unknowingly expediting the devises of heaven as they went about their business. Once Slim even went so far as to aver that a one-eared tomcat who hung around the Do-Right Dairy devouring the rats that threatened to destroy the establishment's credibility was actually the Angel Bulwark acting as a cat. True, his tongue was in his cheek both before and after he said it; she could see this plainly, but the fact remained that his tales got wilder as the years rolled by. And toward the end, when they both knew he was dying, it was all she could do to keep from blurting out her feelings, from letting him know, at last, that which he ought to have surmised long ago—that she, quite frankly, had never put stock in his angels at all.

Instead, however, she asked him some round-eyed questions contrived to cloak the disbelief she feared might cast a shadow on his dying hour. (After all, she did love him, despite his quirky ways.) "But tell me, Slim, how'm I to know this angel when I see it? What's to say I won't mistake it for an ordinary mortal?"

"Just trust me," he said, his off-color eyes afire with a zeal that turned them to amber. "I'll put my mark on it somehow, Annie, darlin'. By hook or crook, I'll stamp it. Can't say just how—but believe me, I swear it; you'll know your angel when you see it, sure as fire. Only trust me, Annie, honey. Trust me—and you'll see."

"Uh-huh," she murmured, but she balled her fists and turned away. Dern him anyway! Don't he know that without him I don't give a hoot for goin' west? That I don't care beans for a house or a yard or all them dandy layin' hens we was always plottin' we'd get. Cain't he see that even if his dad-blamed angels was a dime a dozen I wouldn't want no company if I couldn't have his? Why, if he's gonna do me this way, confound it, I'll stick right here in Missouri!

She didn't stick, however. His dying wish pricked her like a burr that had somehow got stuck in her stocking. In fact, as soon as the burying was done, she packed up her trunks and took the first train west to Cholla Valley. Once there, she bought an old yellow house—such as Slim himself would have picked—and a horse and a buggy to get her back and forth from it to Needleton.

The house itself was a small frame structure on a patch of earth that seemed so wanting for livestock that she waited scarcely a week to right that wrong. (Slim would have had it no other way.) This she did with a flock of hawk-colored chickens with legs the color of old piano keys, and depthless eyes like beads of jet. She made a makeshift pen, she strewed it with straw, she arranged her days to revolve around the gathering of eggs.

Thusly situated, Anna set about the business of living alone. "See Slim?" she said one day, grinning wryly. "There ain't nobody here but me and the chickens. I guess that's a joke on you, huh—after you vowed you was gonna send me an angel to keep me company?" Alone as she was, she kept right on talking to the dead-and-gone Slim—as if he could hear her all the way from heaven.

This is not to say she talked to him incessantly. In the early mornings, as she tended the chickens, her mind was blessedly as wide and as empty as an overturned pitcher. It was at night that the stars came out and put thoughts in her head. The stars and the thoughts turned on and off, on and off, like rows of lights on an old movie house. It was then she'd talk to Slim. She'd tell him how the hens were laying, or how she felt about the weather, how she missed St. Louie, or how her arthritis had her down in the back.

But then one night a full moon appeared and lit up the land all about her in a wondrous way. She stared out the window at the silvered desert, as stunned as if she'd reckoned no moon shone this far out west. "Well, I'll be derned!" she said. "How 'bout that?"

At that moment, as if those words comprised a cue to bring it forth on stage, a coyote—a bedraggled old creature with a low-slung tail and a faltering gait—slunk up on a hillock some yards away, sat himself down on his raw-boned hunkers, and pointed a keening muzzle up toward the sky.

"How thin he is," she murmured to the ears of the night. "How hungry he looks." And then suddenly squaring her shoulders, rearing back: "Why, the dad-blamed varmint, he'll kill my chickens—if I don't get him first."

She intended, of course, to reach for Slim's old rifle. Yet she made no move. She sat with one hand holding back the curtain, the other at her throat where her palm could feel a pulsing like the rush of a sea. A *thurumpa, thurumpa,* beating time to his keening. Even as she watched him, breath sucked in, he lurched away—only to return in the midnight hours and wreak his havoc. He stole a chicken whose death-throe cackles wrenched her rudely from her sleep, a fine fat hen who was just getting broody.

After that, he came back every other night or so, drawing her toward the window with his howl or his bark or his eerie yip. Some nights he'd leave the hens unbothered; he'd lurk about the yard; he'd hunch on the hillock and howl to the moon as if to taunt her. Other times he came only to dine; he'd find a new way to break into the pen, which Anna was always struggling to secure. He was most adept. He'd dig under, break through, climb over, or—like some otherworldly rodent—he'd gnaw away at the wood to which the wire was nailed. At length, she felt as if she knew him like she knew her thimble finger. Or, perhaps it was more like she knew her *trigger finger*—the one she could never bring herself to pull, though she had that critter in her sights a dozen times over.

"Hey, Spareribs," she'd say, "you scruffy old, yellow-eyed varmint, you ain't nothin' but a bag of bones." Or "Ain't you an ugly one with your coat all lumped up like knotweeds? What a sight you are. What a sorry mess."

Sometimes she talked to herself instead of to him. "Let's see now," she'd murmur, as she jounced along on her way to Needleton to buy some staples and sell some eggs. "That's one chicken last week, two the week before." Or words to that effect. And always she had the feeling that old Spareribs was hearing every word she said. He was watching her too—she was sure of it—as his ancestors before him had watched the covered wagons once, teamsters sleepy in the afternoons, and red-skinned hunters with rutted faces seeking forever white buffalo.

One day when she was in the Needleton store, the propiretor—Peter Blant, by name—peered over the tops of his smudgy glasses and shot her a glance so intense it seared her cheeks. She surmised from the way his Adam's apple bobbed up and down, up and down, like a cork awash in a running creek, that he'd been summoning up courage for something more than buying and selling since she'd first set foot in town.

"I hear you're a widow woman," he said.

"Uh-huh," she answered, taking care that the color in her cheeks didn't tint her tone. "That's right. Sure am. Now you can help me tote in my eggs if you've got a mind to."

"Sure, sure, missus. Sure thing."

But after they were done with the business at hand, he tried again. "'Tain't fittin' for a woman to mourn too long," he said. "A woman ought to git herself out, git herself some friends."

"Yes sir," said Anna, her eyes upon his Adam's apple. "Well, now I'll see you next market day—be the good Lord willin'."

"There's gonna be a dance Saturday next," he called after her. "Town hall."

Anna didn't answer. Late sunlight was pouring in the streaked glass window in yellow rectangles, and she walked out with her eyes tearing from the glare and from sudden rage. Don't he know a widow's got her rights? A widow's gotta mourn?

As she climbed in the wagon, her face was as hot from anger as if she'd packed it with poltices to counteract some ache, and so it stayed until she was almost home. Then the afternoon yielded to the dusk that came down like chimney soot, and the coyote tuned up to howl his mournful tune.

"Now you and me, old Spareribs—we understand each other, huh?" Anna whispered. For a moment—until the impact of that statement struck her like a cuffing about the ears—she reveled in the way she felt to know how near he was. But once it struck her, the reveling was done; she was ashamed and embarrassed.

"How come?" she cried. "How come your howlin' don't turn my blood to ice? Ain't you the critter who steals my hens? How come I ain't shot you yet? Buck fever? Is that what I got? Is that why my finger freezes up every time I aim to pull the trigger?"

She caught sight of him then, hunkering down beside a yucca tree, his muzzle pointed toward those very heavens from which—according to Slim and his father before him—angels came pouring down in flocks like migrant birds. He might have been singing to those angels. And to Slim too, perhaps? At any rate, that canine jaw vibrated like the strings of a harp, giving rise first to yips and yaps ventriloquistic, and then into a wail so piteous Anna thought she might weep just from the sound of it.

"I don't understand," she whispered, and the sound of her own voice reached her ears like the hiss of snakes. "Ain't no way to understand it." Then suddenly she cried, "Hey, Slim," head tilted back, eyes rolled upward, and she shook her fists toward the great starred sky. "You up there! You tell me now, what kinda joke you pullin' on me?"

The days passed. But Spareribs didn't. He grew bolder as the time ticked by. He sang to her at dusk, but in the pitch of midnight hours he filled his bloated belly on her livelihood, on her fine plump hens, her good young pullets. The terrible cackles would pierce the chill night air, and Anna, cold with sweat, would sit at the window with her finger on the trigger like a digit of a corpse, never bending, never pulling, stiff as a bone.

And so the time passed, days into weeks, weeks into months, months into seasons, tick-ticking by.

About the time the beavertail cactus bled its purple blossom and the sand verbena sprinkled the earth with dwarf bouquets, a stranger came riding up to the chicken ranch. He had an under-forty mouth but the knowing eyes of age, a big-brimmed hat, old high-heeled boots, and a hickory shirt. He looked as if he'd come riding right out of yesterday, a drifter from the century over and done. Yet when he spoke to Anna as she stood in the doorway leaning on her broom, it seemed to her that the present moment came into focus with alarming clarity.

"Howdy, ma'am," he said.

She stared at him, at the way his shoulders sagged forward as he crooked one long, denim-clad leg around the saddle pommel with a twist that matched the curve of his wide lips turned up in a grin she adjudged presumptuously familiar.

"These your holdings?"

"That they are," she answered tautly, leaning on her broom. "And what's it you're after?"

"Well now," he said, "fact is, ma'am, I'm hungry. I could use some grub."

At once he dismounted—and set about hitching his horse to the post— as if his declaration alone had somehow earned him the right to stay for dinner. Anna glowered at him and then at the horse, one of those homely, pale-eyed, Mexican duns, flicking flies off his rear with a tail as scrawny as an old hemp rope.

"Well, I do have a bit of stew in the pot," she said, snipping each word off short as if her lips were scissors. "I was just fixin' to set down and have a bite myself. I suppose it wouldn't hurt none if I was to dish you up a bowl."

"Beef stew?" he said, rubbing his belly with the palm of his hand. "Hey, now, I'll have to say, nothing in all this world could suit me better than a bowl of stew."

He walked right in, almost brushing her shoulder as he moved through the doorway—although she'd stepped three steps backward to make way for him—and he moved with a cowpoke's sort of swagger that seemed to Anna somehow too calculatedly easygoing. He doffed his hat, ran one hand through a thatch of sand-colored hair, and fastened his likewise sand-colored eyes hungrily upon the pot of stew. She followed his gaze and saw that the sunlight through the larch tree branches was splashing golden freckles on the tabletop.

"Right pretty sight!" he said in a way she knew he meant both stew and sunlight, and not just one or the other.

He ate like a man who'd had nothing but hardtack or jerky for a week or two. But he talked like a man who'd had no one to hear him for longer than that. How he bent her ear! With no grounds whatever to think she gave a hoot, he told her about how he'd left the West and the cattle ranches some years back, how he'd settled in the East and gone to work in an office, as an accountant, "because somehow, by golly, I come to be good with figures."

"But I tell you," he said, leaning forward on the edge of his seat, "that city life weren't for me. After a while I couldn't take it no more. I quit my job, tossed all my fancy duds in an ash can, and started in shopping around for a mount to carry me in this direction. Bought that old dun horse you see tied out there to your hitching post. Dundy's no beauty, I'll grant you that, but . . . as soon as I laid eyes on him, I knew he was right for me. He was stomping and snorting and facing west. It's like he was sort of seconding my motion, if you get what I mean. When a critter does that, I'll tell you, he kinda gets you right here."

It was at that moment that Spareribs howled his mournful preface to the dusk—ever on cue, so it seemed to Anna, who was, at that very second, wondering if mourning could be thought of as a motion.

"That there's old Spareribs," she said, as if the name she'd given him could make some difference in how the stranger would perceive him.

"Well, you have to watch those coyotes, ma'am. I see you got some chickens out back. Them coyotes, they're hell on chickens."

"I know," she said, looking down at her bowl. "He's showed me."

"And you haven't tried to shoot him?"

"Let's just put it this way; I ain't *shot* him," said Anna. "Not yet, leastwise. And I'll thank you not to start preachin' to me about that critter. It's my business when I do him in."

"Well now, ma'am," he said, steepling his hands, "I'm no hand at preaching anyway. But if you don't mind me saying it, that's crazier than seven hundred dollars—letting a chicken-killer roam free like that."

The freckles of gold were fading from the tabletop. Flies were crawling in and out the empty bowls and buzzing like bees after honey.

"You can go now," said Anna, pushing back her own chair. "You've had your stew and you've had your say!"

"Well, all right," said the stranger. "But I was fixing to ask if you needed a hired man around here. I was in Needleton earlier asking around, and a feller I met says to me, 'If I was you, I'd try at the Widow Harkins place bout four miles west.' That's what he said and that's why I come."

"Well, that feller was wrong," cried Anna hotly. She stood up and began to clear the dishes from the table.

"Are you certain now?"

"Land sakes! Of course I'm certain!" she cried.

"Well then, I sure thank you for the stew, ma'am. Me and Dundy, we'll be getting on."

She kept her back to the door as he left, swallowing hard and rattling the dishes with a fury.

But when she heard the thud of hooves over the earth, she ran to the door wringing her checkered apron in her callused hands. The sky was pink as locoweed and casting a glow down over the sand, and over man and horse.

"Say—" she called, waving a hand that still clutched a fold of apron. "Say there . . ."

"Thornton's the name, ma'am," he said, kneeing the horse about.

"Well, Mr. Thronton," said Anna, "come to think of it, the chicken pens need fixin' real bad now. That's the coyote's doin's, I'll admit it—though I'll tell you right now, if you do stay on, I don't want to hear another word from you about that critter, about whether I shoot him or whether I don't. That's my business. Your business'll be fixin' things up. Like the gate out front—it's plumb off it's hinges, as you doubtless seen. Fact is, the whole dern fence, I'd say, could use some workin' over."

He stayed.

For the next meal Anna spread the damask tablecloth, all freshly ironed, and lace-edged napkins, and then she placed in the center of the table, a small bouquet of oleander flowers, in a milk-glass vase. By the time the week was over she'd served up all her specialties, from soda biscuits to chicken potpie. By the second week, she'd moved on to Slim's favorites—although she felt rather like a traitor in the process—corn pone and beans, milk gravy and bread, fried mush heaped high with strawberry jam. The third week she baked an apple pie such as she used to serve when Preacher Harkins was still among the living and used to come calling on a Sunday afternoon. No matter what she fed him Mr. Thornton would rub his belly and shoot her a glance so fraught with feeling her cheeks would burn.

But Anna was filled with emotions that warred with one another endlessly and fought their hardest at the hour of dusk when Spareribs called. She'd hear that howl and shame would sear her cheeks far more than plaudits for corn pone or chicken potpie, enough to keep her awake and fidgety half the night.

Yet in the mornings when Thornton came walking in from the barn with that swaggery sort of gait of his and his hair askew from another night's snooze in the hayloft, her heart would swell. By the time they'd sit down to together, she'd feel as if her rib cage would split wide open and pour that organ right out on the tabletop. And how it would hammer when he talked about Cholla Valley, how he took to every hole and gully that pocked it like the wallows of the long-gone buffalo. "By golly, Anna Harkins," he'd say, "I can't even tell you how I cotton to this place."

That was not all he "cottoned" to; she began to sense this a month or so after she hired him on, and by June she knew he had a question blowing in his mind like a sheet on a clothesline—just as the answer billowed out in hers. So although it pleased her so much the tears rolled in rivulets down her sunburned cheeks, it was no surprise when he mouthed it. He asked; she said yes. They found a sensible preacher in Needleton one day, a man who had nothing whatever to say about angels but who quite simply pronounced them man and wife.

Bed and Thornton were rebirth. The dark night was a new morning of Starting All Over, so that she had to stay awake floating in her pillow, listening to his breathing, thanking the stars.

It was 'long about midnight, right after a little owl hooted to the moon, that Anna heard the chickens, the horrified cries of hens taking to their flappy wings.

Thornton slept on, but Anna tiptoed to the open window with Slim's old rifle held fast in her hands. She scanned the sea of night—until there he was, right in her sights, standing on the hillock with his latest victim in the clutch of his jaws, its neck swinging back and forth like a pendulum on a clock. Her fingers shook, her palms were slippery from the eking sweat of dread, yet somehow she didn't miss; she hit her mark.

She was crying by the window, leaning on the sill with her head buried in her arms, when she heard the soft thud of Thornton's bare feet moving toward her across the creaking board floor. When she looked up, however, he hesitated, then stopped in his tracks, as if propriety demanded he keep some distance from her grieving.

"I killed old Spareribs. He was after my chickens, Thornton," she said —as if there'd ever been a time when he hadn't been. And she sobbed, "I had to do it."

"Why sure you did, Anna," he said, knuckling the sleep from the corners of his eyes, "and don't you fret now."

"It weren't easy to do," she murmured, "you gotta see this, Thornton. It was real hard to do."

"I know," he said, and he turned up the palms of his empty hands as if to cup her woes.

"It got real lonely out here before you come," she added, tears streaming down her cheeks like Missouri freshets. "I reckon, in a way, it drove me kinda quirky 'cause I got to thinkin' mournin' was my duty and I just daren't quit it. And then as if that ain't bad enough I got to thinkin' things even quirkier than that. I got to thinkin'—"

"I know, I know," he repeated, although of course—it seemed to her—there was no way he could.

He began to edge over in her direction then, ever so slowly at first, as if he felt a need to proceed with caution through an air so charged with weltering emotions. But after an instant, he quickened his pace, so as to reach her the sooner, apparently forgetting, in the process, to assume a certain way of walking, that exaggerated laid-back swagger she'd come to love, which she suddenly reckoned—dazed though she was—he must have cultivated long ago in order to cloak a certain lameness, a limp in his left leg. And when he did reach her, when he stood close enough to take her in his arms, his sand-colored eyes shone like amber in the moonlight that slanted through the window.

"Oh, now I see," she cried, her words like pent-up steam escaping. Wonder turned her knees to honeycomb, her mind to a mass of half-formed thoughts that she fancied were fanning outward in concentric circles such as a raindrop in a puddle can sometimes set in motion. She fell into his arms.

In the morning they found no dead coyote upon the hillock, but only the hapless chicken, its broken body resting by a clump of rosemary mint, its feathers ruffling in the breeze

"Gone?" Anne cried, blinking her eyes as if the whereabouts of the corpses depended on her focus.

"Well, I'll be derned," said Thornton, brows so cocked they almost met that shock of unruly hair that fell across his sun-browned forehead like a vine needing pruning. "Why, you musta only nicked him, Anna, that's what you musta done. Either that or the poor old thing just dragged himself off to die. Critters'll do that sometimes, you know—find themselves a hideaway where there's no one to see them but old Mother Earth."

Anna didn't answer. She was busy composing scenarios of another type entirely and playing them out in her mind like songs. In one of these a ministering angel in the form of an immense yellow bird had swooped down from a dappled sky and caught the chicken killer in golden talons curved like cees. She could see it; she could see it quite clearly. On this morning born for breeding fancies old Spareribs was bound for a greater

Wisdom Desert where the buffalo still wallow, antelope still graze, the sun shines down in rods of gold, and Indians with chiseled-rock faces count the coyote their brother.

The Indian Summer
of Nancy Redwing

HARRY W. PAIGE

Harry W. Paige I know very little about, other than that he teaches at Clarkson University in Potsdam, New York. And that he writes beautiful and powerful little stories like the one that follows.

It was the Moon of Falling Leaves, the white man's November. Nancy Redwing sat on the ash-gray, timeworn steps of her tarpaper shack and watched the sun drip like honey through the fragile lace of leaves that still clung to the only shade tree for six prairie miles.

It made her heart sad to see the brittle leaves waiting to be taken by the wind. She had watched her flowers close like velvet fists against the early-morning cold. She had watched the prairie turn to a stubbled yellow. She had watched the moving sky change from a turquoise blue to a cold, gray flannel. Soon the white shroud of winter would unfold itself over the empty miles and tuck itself in at the distant place where the earth and sky met. And then the long, gray time would begin and her hours would be spent by the spitting wood fire quilting for the next summer's tourists while the wind charged the hilltop cabin and snow seeped through the mud chinks and gathered delicately in the dark corners.

Her heart was heavy too because it was her thirty-fifth birthday and her husband had not remembered. She knew it was a little thing: Indians, especially poor ones, did not make the white man's fuss over the day of one's birth. She remembered that her grandmother could not even name the day she was born. It was sometime in the Moon of Cherries Reddening, in July, but the old woman with the spiderwebby lines in her dark face could not recall the day. It was written somewhere in the church records perhaps, but she had not even bothered to find out. Yes, truly, it was a little thing.

Birthdays were for children, she told herself. The little ones who wandered knee-deep in summer and did not count the falling leaves. But even as she told herself these things there was a pain that closed like a cold fist on her heart.

Summer dies slowly, she thought, watching still another leaf break from the tree and waltz to earth. A leaf at a time. Yet the sun was warm and tender on her face—like a remembered kiss from a far away time. And the breeze was gently warm as it played in the dark waterfall of her hair. It was enough to make the heart glad, this Indian summer. Even if thirty-five winters had passed and your man had not remembered to add them with you.

As she watched the nearly bare branches score the falling sky a cloud of dust rose beyond the tree and she knew that a car was climbing the hill to her home. She watched it stop and pass through the cattle gate, knowing the visitor must be a stranger when the car did not stop again to close the gate. The car was shining and new so she did not recognize it but she watched as it gleamed through the churning dust.

In a few minutes the car pulled into her yard in a hail of flying stones and a flurry of squawking chickens. A white woman, neat and attractive, got out of the car and approached her.

"Hello there," she called in a friendly drawl. "Are you Mrs. Redwing?"

Nancy Redwing rose from the step and nodded, holding out her hand shyly to the strange woman.

The white woman took the rough, worn hand in her own slim, manicured fingers. "I'm Helen Wingate from Valentine," she announced professionally. "I'm your district Gentry Lady."

"Gentry Lady?"

The white woman smiled patiently. "Maybe you've seen our ads on television—" She stopped herself suddenly, noticing that no wires ran into the tarpaper shack. She sounded a quick, nervous laugh. "Maybe you've heard of us from friends then?" She waited and when there was no answer, she continued: "The House of Gentry is your own private cosmetologist."

The dark, liquid eyes of Nancy Redwing gave no indication that they understood.

"Cosmetics," the white woman explained. "Makeup to bring out the beauty that is already yours." She pantomimed the action of applying makeup.

Nancy Redwing nodded, momentarily lost in the white woman's smell that was like a field of summer flowers on the wind. She had rubbed herself with sage a few hours before but the smell of the white woman took it away.

The white woman took a deep breath like a diver about to plunge into the water. "Now you appear to be a woman of about my own age." She giggled, running a thin scale of laughter. "Heaven knows I wouldn't tell that to anybody but a good customer." She lowered her voice and bent down secretly. "Well, I'm forty-three years old. Most people refuse to believe it, but that's what I am—forty-three. People take me to be ten years younger. And that's because I take care of myself, you know. Diet, proper exercise, plenty of sleep—and the scientific assistance that's available, especially for me at the House of Gentry."

Nancy Redwing smiled and the smile followed the hard creases in her face like gentle rain following the rough furrows in the land. She watched another leaf fall from the tree and flutter down through the branches with a lonely, scratching sound. She noticed too that a few clouds had started to gather in the west.

The white woman excused herself, went to her car and removed a suitcase and a handful of color brochures. "Do you mind if I show you a few things in our new line of products?" She held out a small jar decorated with flowers. "But first here's a free sample of our new Luxura 100 face cream that makes wrinkles vanish like magic and deep-cleanses the pores like all get out."

Nancy Redwing took the flower jar in her thick, spade-shaped fingers. She smiled and her dark eyes crinkled and were lost. "*Pilamiye,*" she said softly. Then, embarrassed, she added quickly: "Thank you."

The white woman brushed off the step with paper tissue and sat down. "Let's have our little chat out here, shall we? It's such a lovely day and there won't be many more, now will there? This will probably be my last trip to the reservation until next spring. The roads are so bad—and everything."

She lay the suitcase at her feet and opened it, her words coming faster and dripping over the display of bottles and jars set like jewels in the black velvet of the case . . .

After the woman had left, Nancy Redwing hurried into the house and looked at her new face in the cracked mirror that hung from a nail in the kitchen. She stared at her reflection as though it were a ghost. It was hard to believe that lotions, creams and paints could take away the years so! She had tried the old herbs and potions of Emma Black Bear, the medicine woman from out near Box Elder Creek. She had taken tobacco and several of her best quilts to the old woman in exchange for her knowledge of the young-looking medicines. But it had done no good. The seams of her face were still as creased as leather and the foot of many crows gathered around her eyes. Her breasts still sagged like half-empty pouches and her hips continued to spread.

She smiled at her image and the painted lips cracked and the white teeth shone against the burnished, mahogany skin. Her eyes had become dark pools shining like a fawn's against the lighter background of the eye liner. Doe eyes, she thought, looking out from a snow bush. The lashes were longer too—heavier and swept upward. The stray tufts of hair had been plucked from her cheeks and her mole had been painted over like a mistake in a picture. She smiled again. Truly, she was a different woman! She even smelled different: the perfume from behind the ears and the V of her loose, calico gown seemed to fill the room and take away the bread-frying smell and the smell of the kerosene lamp that hung from one of the exposed beams.

When she thought of the twelve dollars and sixty cents her smile faded and a worried look crossed her face like a dark shadow. Even with all of her quilt money she had taken from the coffee can she still had been forty-two cents short, but the good-smelling white woman had told her to forget about it. She said that she would make up the difference herself, out of her own pocket.

But the chill of having no quilt material for the winter showed in her face until she smiled again and there was a thawing that started in her heart. She was younger and prettier and her eyes shone where the tiredness had been. It was like looking at an old photograph and seeing the way she used to be before the loneliness and hard times had come.

And today was her birthday! It was a reason to take away some of the years with paint. It was an unexpected gift—like Indian summer. To make her know the faraway times again and throw her tiredness into a cracked mirror.

She would leave the paint on her face and surprise her husband. She would tell him about the sweet-smelling white woman with the presents called samples. But she would not speak of the quilt money that was gone and could not buy material for the winter quilting.

She brushed at a tear that had welled crystal in her eye suddenly, as though it had been squeezed from her by memory. She watched as a single tear coursed down her cheek, washing away the paint and leaving a dark delta near the corner of her mouth. She daubed at it with the hem of her gown and then touched up the streak where the tear had come down. It was strange how the sadness came even as she smiled. Even as she looked at her presents lined up on the kitchen table. Even as she smelled the smell of many flowers blowing in the wind.

She would go outdoors and wait for her husband on the steps. She would spend this last, golden day like a coin on remembering the good things—the son who was away at school, the husband who was a good man and the pains that had made her smile into a glass.

But when she stepped outside the tears came again, this time from both eyes. The weather had turned around in a cruel joke. Dark clouds boiled up in the west and the wind was a cold knife. The tree rattled and shook down its dry and wrinkled leaves. The sun was gone, swept behind a cloud. Shadows spread across the prairie like a stain, drawing dark designs. Where Indian summer had been there was only a sad, gray November day that promised a winter moon.

Nancy Redwing went back inside, shivering. She gathered up the flowered bottles, put them into a paper sack and stuffed them into the bottom drawer of her ancient sewing machine. Then she filled the washbasin, using a tarnished dipper to carry the water from a twenty-gallon oil drum. She got a fresh bar of brown soap and lathered her hands. Then she leaned over the basin like a priest at a baptismal fount and patted the harsh suds on her face. In a few minutes the strong soap took away the perfumed smell of flowers.

Several times during the washing she stopped and straightened up to listen as the blowing leaves scraped across the roof with a forlorn and desperate sound—like something trying to get in.

Winter on the Belle Fourche

NEAL BARRETT, JR.

Neal Barrett, Jr., is one original and brilliant writer, and I don't think much else needs to be said after that. Other than the fact that his story for the last volume in this series appeared in Year's Best Science Fiction, 1987, *that his novel* Through Darkest America *is out, and it's wonderful, and that the following story isn't at all what you might expect.*

He had come down in the cold from the Big Horn Mountains and crossed the Powder River moving east toward the Belle Fourche, all this time without finding any sign and leaving little of his own. There were wolf tracks next to the river and he saw where they had gone across the ice, which told him they were desperate and hungry, that they would turn on each other before long. An hour before dark he pulled the mount up sharp and let his senses search the land, knowing clearly something had been there before. Finally he eased to the ground and took the Hawken rifle with him, stood still in the naked grove of trees, stopped and listened to the quiet in the death-cold air, heard the frozen river crack, heard the wind bite the world. He looked south and saw the Black Hills veiled in every fold, followed them with his eyes until the land disappeared in the same soot color as the sky. He stood a long time and sniffed the air and the water moving slow beneath the ice. He let it all come together then and simmer in his head, and when it worked itself out he walked down in the draw and started scooping off the snow.

A few inches down he found the ashes from the fire. They had camped right here the night before, made a small supper fire and another in the morning. He ran the ashes through his fingers then brought them to his nose. They were real smart Injuns. They hadn't broken dead sticks off the trees but had walked downstream to get their wood. Cupping more snow aside, he bent to smell the earth. Six, he decided. If he dug a little more he'd find they all had mounts, but he didn't need to bother doing that. They wouldn't be on foot out here.

This close to the Powder and the Belle Fourche they could be any kind of red nigger and not any of them friends. He knew, though, this bunch wasn't Sioux or Cheyenne, but Absaroka. He'd smelled them right off. Crow warriors certain, and likely from Big Robert's camp.

He straightened and looked east, absently touching the bowie at his belt, the scalp ring next to that. That's where they'd gone, east and a little north, the way he was headed too. They weren't after him, didn't know that he was there. And that was something to chew on for a while.

The snow came heavy in the night, slacking off around the dawn. He was up before light and keeping to the river. Soon he'd have to figure what to do. It was two hundred miles to Fort Pierre on the Missouri, a lot more than that if he kept to every bend in the river. Del Gue would be waiting at the fort; he didn't need to be chasing after Crow, there were plenty out sniffing after him. Still, it wouldn't take much time to see what kind of mischief they were up to over here. The Absaroka were a little far east from where they rightly ought to be. He didn't think they'd want to keep on riding and maybe tangle with the Sioux, who would go without breakfast any day to skin a Crow.

At noon he found the answer. The snow had lightened up enough for tracks and he saw where the Crow had taken off, digging up dirt in the snow and hightailing it across the frozen river, heading back northwest into Absaroka country. Now he went slowly, keeping his eyes open for whatever had spooked the Crow. Sioux, most likely, though the Cheyenne could be around too. Hard winter and empty bellies made everybody brave, and a man might go where he hadn't ought to be.

He smelled the death before it saw it. The cold tried to hide it but it came through clear and he was off his horse fast, leading it down to cover in the draw. The dead were in the trees just ahead and though he knew there was no one there alive he circled wide to make sure, then walking into the clearing, the Hawken crooked loose against his chest.

Three men, mostly covered by the snow. He brushed them off enough to see they were soldiers, a white lieutenant and two buffalo troopers. Each had been shot and soundly scalped, then cut up some in the playful manner of the Sioux. The soldier's clothes and boots were gone; the Sioux had taken everything but long-handle underwear and socks.

A quick look around showed the Sioux hadn't taken them by surprise. They'd stood their ground and gotten off a few shots, and that was of some interest in itself. North, he found high ground and lighter snow and saw where the Sioux had walked Army-shod mounts northwest among their own. Ten or twelve riders. They'd gone back to the river with their trophies; the Crow had seen them then and turned for home. About this time the day before, the massacre a little before that.

He stopped and tried to work the thing out. What had the three troopers been doing up here? And why only three? It was maybe a hundred and fifty miles to Fort Laramie, a powerful lot to go in heavy snow and the cold maybe thirty-five below. Troopers didn't have a lot of smarts, but anyone'd know more than that.

He mounted up and crossed the river, circled and crossed again. Two miles down he found the trail. Something about the tracks caught his eye and he eased out of the saddle and squatted down. Now there was puzzle for sure. One of the horses had ridden double—*before* those boys had been hit by the Sioux. But there were only three bodies in the snow. Which meant the red coons had likely taken one alive, carried him back home for Injun fun. Nothing you could do for that chile, except hope he got to die, which wasn't real likely for a while. Del Gue had been taken by the Sioux the year before, and barely got out with his topknot intact. A trooper would get an extra measure sure, a skinning and worse than that.

He had the whole story now. There was no use following tracks back to the clearing but he did. He'd kept his scalp for twelve years in the wilds, and part of that from being thorough, taking two stitches in a moccasin when one might do as well, winding up a story like this to see how it came about.

He came upon the cabin without knowing it at all, reined the horse in and just sat there a minute and let the sign all around him sink in. The cabin was built low against the side of a ravine, nearly covered by a drift, and he'd damn near ridden up on the roof. He cursed himself for that. It was the kind of aggravation he didn't like, coming on something like this after he'd gotten the whole story put away. He could see it clear now, like he'd been right there when it happened. The troopers had ridden past this place into the trees, sensed trouble up ahead and the man riding double had ridden back, stopped at the cabin, then turned and joined his comrades again. Which meant he'd left someone behind. There were no more tracks in the snow, so whoever that'd be was still there, unless they'd sprouted wings and flown to Independence like a bird.

Snow was nearly three feet high against the door and he carefully dug it clear. Jamming the stock of his Hawken in the snow, he pulled the Colt Walker and the bowie from his belt and stepped back.

"You inside there," he called out. "I'm white an' I don't mean ye any harm, so don't go a-shootin' whatever it is you got."

There was nothing but silence from inside. Edging up close, he bent his head to listen. There was someone in there, all right. He couldn't hear them but he knew.

"Mister," he said, "this chile's no Injun, you oughter have the sense to know that." He waited, cussed again, then raised his foot and kicked solidly at the door. It was old and split and snapped like a bone. Before it hit the floor he was in, moving fast and low, sideways like a bear, coming in with the Colt and the knife and sweeping every corner of the room. Kindling and dead leaves. The musty smell of mice. A fireplace nearly caved-in. Half a chair and a broken whiskey crock. An Army blanket in the corner, and something under that. He walked over and pulled the blanket aside with his foot.

"Great Jehoshaphat," he said aloud, and went quickly to the still and fragile form, touched the cold throat and felt for signs of life he was sure he wouldn't find.

She woke to the memory of cold, the ghost of this sensation close to death, a specter that consumed her, left her hollow, left her numb with the certainty there was no heat great enough to drive the terrible emptiness away. She woke and saw the fire and tried to draw its warmth to her with her eyes. The walls and the ceiling danced with shadow. The shadows made odd and fearsome shapes. She tried to pull her eyes away but could find neither the stength nor the will for such an effort. The shadows made awful, deathly sounds, sounds she could scarcely imagine. And then with a start that clutched her heart she remembered the sounds were real; she had heard them all too clearly through the walls from the trees across the snow.

"Oh Lord Jesus they are dying," she cried aloud, "they are murdered every one!"

Darkness rose from the floor and blocked the fire. It seemed to flow and expand to fill the room, take form as a broad-shouldered demon cloaked in fur; it grew arms and a dark and grizzled beard, a wicked eye.

She screamed and tried to push herself away.

"Ain't any need for that," the demon said. "Don't mean ye any harm."

She stared in alarm. His words brought her no relief at all. "Who—who are you?" she managed to say. "What do you want with me?"

"My name's John Johnston," the figure said. "Folks has mostly took out the *t* but that ain't no fault of mine. Just lie right still. You oughter take in some soup if ye can."

He didn't wait for an answer, but moved across the room. Her heart pounded rapidly against her breast. She watched him carefully, followed his every move. He would likely attack her quite soon. This business of the soup was just a ruse. Well, he would not catch her totally unaware. She searched for some weapon of defense, pulled herself up on one arm, the effort draining all her strength. She was under some heavy animal skin. It held her to the floor like lead. She saw a broken chair, just beyond her reach. With the help of Lord Jesus it would serve her quite well. David had very little more and brought another fearsome giant to his knees.

As she reached for the chair, stretched her arm as far as it would go, the heavy skin slipped past her shoulders to her waist. She felt the sudden cold, stopped, and caught sight of herself. For an instant, she was too paralyzed to move. Frozen with terror and disbelief. She was unclothed, bare beneath the cover! Her head began to swim. She fought against the dizziness and shame. *Oh Lord don't let me faint,* she prayed. *Let me die, but don't let me faint in the presence of the beast!*

Using every ounce of will she could find, she lay back and pulled the cover to her chin. With one hand, she searched herself for signs of violation, careful not to touch any place where carnal sin resides. Surely he had done it in her sleep. Whatever it was they did. Would you know, could you tell? Defilement came with marriage, and she had no experience in that.

The man returned from the fire. She mustered all her courage.

"Stay away from me," she warned. "Don't take another step."

He seemed puzzled. "You don't want no soup?"

"You—you had no right," she said. "You have invaded my privacy. You have looked upon me. You have sinned in God's eyes and broken several commandments. I demand the return of my clothing."

He squatted down and set the soup on the floor. "Ma'am, I didn't do no sinnin' I recall. You was near froze stiff in them clothes."

"Oh, of course. That is just what you would say to excuse your lust. I would expect no less than that."

"Yes, ma'am."

"I cannot find it in my heart to forgive you. That is my failing. I will pray that our Blessed Savior will give me the strength to see you as His child."

"You feel a need fer this soup," Johnston said, "it's on the fire." With that he rose and left her, moved across the room and curled up in a buffalo robe.

He woke at once and grabbed his heavy coat and picked up the Hawken rifle, all this in a single motion out of sleep. The woman hadn't moved. He had propped the broken door back up as best he could, and now he moved it carefully aside and slipped out into the night. The world seemed frozen in sleep, silent and hard as iron, yet brittle enough to shatter into powder at a touch. He couldn't put his finger on the sound that had broken through his sleep. The horse was all right, safely out of the wind by the cabin's far wall. The ground was undisturbed. He circled around and watched, stopped to sniff the air. Nothing was there now, but something had left its ghost behind.

Inside he warmed his hands by the fire. The woman was still asleep. It wasn't fair to say that she hadn't roused him some, that the touch of her flesh as he rubbed life back into her limbs hadn't started up some fires. Not like an Injun girl now, but some. He'd seen maybe two white women stark naked in his life. They seemed to lack definition. Like a broad field of snow without a track or a rock to give it tone. An Injun girl went from one shade to another, depending where you looked. John Hatcher had kept two fat Cheyenne squaws all the time. He kept them in his cabin in the Little Snake Valley and offered Johnston the use of one or both. He had politely declined, preferring to find his own. Hatcher's squaws giggled all the time. An Injun woman tended to act white after a spell and start to giggle and talk back. His wife hadn't done that at all. She'd been pure Injun to the end but there weren't very many like that.

When she woke once again she felt sick, drained and brittle as a stick. The man was well across the room, squatting silently by the wall.

"I would like that soup now if you please," she said as firmly as she could. She would show him no weakness at all. A man preyed upon that.

He rose and went to the fire, filled a tin cup and set it by her side.

"Take a care," he said, "it's right hot." He returned to the fire and came back and dropped a bundle on the floor. "Your clothes is all dry," he said.

She didn't answer or meet his eyes. She knew any reference to her garments would encourage wicked thoughts in his head. The soup tasted vaguely of corn, meat a little past its prime. It was filling and soothed the hurt away.

"Thank you," she said, "that was quite good."

"There's more if you want."

"I would like you to leave the cabin for a while. I should think half an hour will do fine."

Johnston didn't blink. "What fer?"

"That is no concern of yours."

"You want to get dressed, why you got that buffler robe. Ain't no reason you can't do it under there."

"Why, I certainly will not!" The suggestion brought color to her cheeks.

"Up to you," he said.

"I shall *not* move until you comply."

"Suit yerself."

Oh Lord, she prayed, *deliver me from this brute. Banish transgression from his mind.* Reaching out beneath the robe, she found her clothing and burrowed as far beneath the cover as she could, certain all the while he could see, or surely imagine, every private move she made.

"Certain rules will apply," she said. "I suppose we are confined here for the moment, though I trust the Lord will release us from adversity in good time."

She sat very close to the fire. The warmth never seemed enough. The cold came in and sought her out. The man continued to squat against the wall. It didn't seem possible that he could sit in this manner for long hours at a time. Only the blue eyes flecked with gray assured her he had not turned to stone. He was younger than she'd imagined, perhaps only a few years older than herself. His shocking red hair and thick unkempt beard masked his face; hard and weathered features helped little in determining his age.

"You will respect my privacy," she said, "and I shall certainly respect yours. There will be specific places in this room where you are not to venture. Now. I wish to say in all fairness that I believe you very likely saved my life. I am not ungrateful for that."

"Yes'm," Johnston said.

"My name is Mistress Dickinson. Mistress Emily Elizabeth Dickinson to be complete, though I caution you very strongly, Mr. Johnston, that while circumstances have thrown us together, you will *not* take the liberty of using my Christian name."

"Already knew who you was," Johnston said.

Emily was startled, struck with sudden fear. "Why, that is not possible. How could you know that?"

"Saw yer name when I went through yer belongin's," Johnston said.

"How dare you, sir!"

"Didn't mean to pry. Thought you was goin' to pass on 'fore the morning. Figured I ought git yer buryin' name."

"Oh." Emily was taken aback. Her hand came up to touch her heart. "I . . . see. Yes. Well then . . ."

Johnston seemed to squint his eyes in thought. For the first time, she detected some expression in his face.

"Ma'am, there's somethin' I got to say," Johnston said. "Them soldiers you was with. I reckon you know they're all three of 'em dead."

"I . . . guessed as much." Emily trembled at the thought. "I have prayed for their souls. Our Lord will treat them kindly."

"Some better'n them Sioux did, I reckon."

"Do not take light of the Lord, Mr. Johnston. He does not take light of you."

Johnston studied her closely again. "Jes' what was you an' them fellers doin' up here, you don't mind me askin'."

Emily paused. She had kept this horror repressed; now, she found herself eager to bring it out. Even telling it to Johnston might help it go away.

"Captain William A. Ramsey of Vermont was kind enough to ask me to accompany him and his troopers on a ride," Emily said. "There were twelve men in all when we started. The day was quite nice, not overly cold at all. We left Fort Laramie with the intention of riding along the North Platte River a few miles. A storm arose quite quickly. I believe there was some confusion about direction. When the storm passed by, we found ourselves under attack, much to everyone's alarm. Several men were killed outright. It was . . . quite terrifying."

"Cheyenne, most likely," Johnston said, as if the rest was quite clear. "They kept drivin' you away from the fort. Gittin' between you an' any help."

"Yes. That is what occurred."

"Pocahontas an' John Smith!" Johnston shook his head. "Yer lucky to be alive whether you know that or not."

"The men were very brave," Emily said. "We lost the Indians the third day out, I believe. By then there were only three men left and myself. Whether the others were cruelly slain or simply lost in the cold I cannot say. We could not turn back. I think we rode for six days. There was almost nothing to eat. One of the colored troopers killed a hare but that was all."

"You got rid of the Cheyenne an' run smack into the Sioux," Johnston finished.

"Yes. That is correct."

Johnston ran a hand through his beard. "You don't mind me sayin', this end of the country ain't a fit sort of place fer a woman like yerself."

Emily met his eyes. "I don't see that is any concern of yours."

Johnston didn't answer. She found the silence uncomfortable between them. Perhaps he didn't really mean to pry.

"Mr. Johnston," she said, "I have lived all my life in Amherst, Massachusetts. I am twenty-five years old and my whole life to now has passed in virtually one place. I have been as far as Washington and Philadelphia. I had no idea what the rest of God's world was like. I decided to go and see for myself."

"Well, I reckon that's what ye did."

"And yes. I confess that you are right. It was a foolish thing to do. I had no idea it would be like this. In my innocence, the Oregon Trail seemed a chance to view wildlife and other natural sights. Soon after departing Independence, I sensed that I was wrong. Now I am paying for my sins."

"I'd guess yer folks ain't got a idea where you are," Johnston said, thinking rightly this was so.

"No, they do not. I am certain they believe I am dead. I only pray they think I perished somewhere in the New England states."

"You ain't perished yet," Johnston said.

"I fear that is only a question of time," Emily sighed.

This time he was waiting, fully awake and outside, hunched silently in a dark grove of trees. It was well after midnight, maybe one or two. There was no wind at all and the clouds moved swiftly across the land. He thought about the woman. Damned if she wasn't just like he figured, white in near every way there was, stubborn and full of her own will. It irked him to think she was stuck right to him and no blamed way to shake her loose. There wasn't any place to take her except back to Fort Laramie or on to Fort Pierre, and either way with one horse. He thought about White Eye Anderson and Del Gue and Chris Lapp, and old John Hatcher himself, seeing him drag in with this woman on a string. Why, they'd ride him for the rest of his life.

The shadow moved and when it did Johnston spotted it at once. He waited. In a moment, a second shadow appeared, directly behind the first. He knew he'd been right the night before. How many, he wondered. All six or just two? What most likely happened was the Crow ran back toward the Powder, then got their courage up when the Sioux were out of mind. One was maybe smarter than the rest and found his trail. Which meant there was one red coon somewhere with a nose near as good as his own. Now that was a chile he'd like to meet. Johnston sniffed the world once more and started wide around the trees.

Now, there was only one shadow. The other had disappeared while he circled past the grove. He didn't like that, but there was not much for it. He sat and waited. Part of the dark and the windblown striations of the snow. Part of the patch of gray light that swept the earth. He knew what the Crow was doing now. He was waiting to get brave. Waiting to get his juices ready for a fight.

When it happened, the Indian moved so quickly even Johnston was surprised. The Crow stood and made for the cabin door, a blur against the white and frozen ground. Johnston rose up out of nowhere at all, one single motion taking him where he had to be. He lifted the Crow clearly off the ground, the bowie cutting cold as ice. It was over fast and done and he knew in that instant, knew before the Crow went limp and fell away, where the other one had gone. Saw him from the corner of his eye as he came off the roof straight for him, and knew the man had buried himself clean beneath the snow, burrowed like a mole and simply waited out his time. Johnston took the burden on his shoulder, bent his legs and shook the Indian to the ground. The Crow came up fighting, brought his hatchet up fast and felt Johnston's big foot glance off his chest. He staggered back, looked fearfully at Johnston as if he knew a solid blow would have stopped his heart at once, as if he saw in that moment the widows in the Absaroka camp whose men had met this terrible sight before. Turning on his heels he ran fast across the snow, plowing through drifts for the safety of the trees. Johnston tugged the Walker Colt from his belt, took his aim and fired. The Crow yelled but didn't stop.

Johnston cussed aloud; the red coon was bloodied but still alive. He didn't miss much, and this sure was a poor time to do it. He'd counted on horses. Now the Crow would take them off. He maybe should have gotten the horses first. The Crow would go and lick his wound and come back and that was pure aggravation.

He dragged the dead body well back behind the cabin. He sat beside the corpse, cut the heavy robes away. He saw a picture in his head. He saw his woman. He saw his unborn child within her womb. The child sprang to life. It played among the aspens on the Little Snake River and came to him when he called. The picture went away. He drew the knife cleanly and swiftly across the Indian's flesh below the ribs and thrust his hand inside the warmth.

With no windows at all, with the cold outside and no difference she could see between dismal day and night, the hours seemed confused. She was often too weak to stay awake. When she slept, the rest seemed to do her little good.

She felt relieved to wake and find him gone. Relief and some alarm. His size, his presence overwhelmed her. Yet, these very qualities, the nature of the man, were all that stood between her and some greater menace still. He cannot help being what he is, she told herself. God surely made him this way for some reason, for some purpose, though she could scarcely imagine what that purpose might be.

The soup tasted good. That morning he had made some kind of bread out of corn and there was still a little left. The fire was getting low and she added a little wood. The wood caught and snapped, for an instant lighting every dark corner of the room. He had set his belongings along the wall. A buffalo robe and a saddle. Leather satchels and a pack. His things seemed a part of the man. Fur and hide greased and worn, heavy with the raw and sour smells of the wild.

She had never ventured quite this close to his things. It seemed like a miniature camp, everything set the way he liked. Her eyes fell upon a thick leather packet. She looked away and then quickly looked back. The corner of a paper peeked out, and there was writing on the edge. How very strange, she thought. Literacy was wholly unexpected. She knew this wasn't fair, and chastised herself at once.

Certainly, she did not intend to pry. She would never touch Mr. Johnston's things. Still, what one could plainly see was surely no intrusion. I should not be here at all, she decided. I must turn away at once. Should dizziness occur, I might very well collapse, and this is not the place for that. Indeed, as she turned, this very thing happened. Her foot brushed against the leather packet, and slipped the paper free.

"Now look what I have done," she said, and bent to retrieve the paper at once. In spite of her good intention, the words leaped up to meet her eyes:

> It makes no difference abroad,
> The season fit the same,
> The mornings blossom into noons,
> And split their pods of flame.

And then, from the packet, another scrap of paper after that:

> The sky is low, the clouds are mean,
> A traveling flake of snow
> Across a barn or through a rut
> Debates if it will go.

"Oh. Oh dear," Emily said aloud. "That last one's quite nice. Or at least I *think* it is." She read the lines again, frowning over this and that, and decided it was slightly overdone.

Still, she wondered, what was verse doing here? Where had this unlettered man of the wilds come across a poem? Perhaps he found it, she reasoned. Came across it in a cabin such as this where some poor traveler had met his fate.

The sound of the shot nearly paralyzed her with fear. "Oh Blessed Jesus!" she cried. The papers fluttered from her hand. She fled to a corner of the cabin, crouched there and stared at the door. An Indian would enter quite soon. Possibly more than one. They would not slay her, though, they would take her to their camp. She would tell them about

Christ. They would renounce their savage ways. They would certainly not touch her in any way.

It seemed forever before the door opened again and Johnston appeared. "Oh, thank the Lord you're all right," Emily sighed. "That shot. I thought—I thought you had surely been killed!"

"Took a shot at a deer," Johnston said. "Wasn't nothin' more'n that." He shook his coat. His beard seemed thick with ice.

"God be praised," Emily said.

Johnston set his Hawken aside. Stomped his feet and ran his hand through a bushy nest of hair. He looked down then and saw the papers on the floor and picked them up. He looked right at Emily and didn't say a thing.

Emily's heart began to pound. "I . . . I'm very sorry," she said. "I certainly had no right."

"Don't matter none," Johnston said. He stood with his backside to the fire.

"Yes, now yes it does," Emily said firmly. "It is I who have transgressed. I am clearly in the wrong. I do not deny my sin."

"I ain't never hear'd so much about sin," Johnston said.

Emily felt her face color. "Well, there is certainly sin abroad, Mr. Johnston. Satan has his eye upon us all."

"I reckon," Johnston said. He scratched and set down. Leaned against the wall in his customary manner.

Emily wondered if she dare break the silence. He didn't seem angry at all, but how on earth would one know? And they could not simply sit there and look at one another.

"Mr. Johnston, I do not excuse my actions," she said, "but perhaps you'll understand when I say I have an interest in poetry myself. As a fact, one small effort has seen the light of publication. Three years ago. February 20, 1852, to be exact. In the *Springfield Daily Republican.*" She smiled and touched her hair. "I recall the date clearly, of course, There are dates in one's life one remembers very well. One's birthday, certainly—" Emily blushed, aware she was chattering away. "Well, yes, at any rate . . ."

Johnston said nothing at all.

"You must be quite chilled," Emily said. "There is still a little soup." "I ain't real hungry," Johnston said.

This time would have to be different; the Crow was wary now and hurt, and an Injun like that was the same as any other creature in the wild in such condition, the same as he'd be himself, Johnston knew, as deadly as a stirred-up snake. The Crow would be in place early this night, out there in spite of the cold, because the first man out could watch and see what the other man would do. It was a deadly advantage, and Johnston was determined to let the Absaroka have it.

The Indian was cautious and he was good. Johnston could scarcely hear him, scarcely smell his fear. He seemed to take forever, moving when the wind rose some, stopping when it died.

Tarnation, Johnston thought, *come on and git it done, chile, 'fore I freeze these bones to the ground.*

At last the Crow struck, coming in swiftly without a sound. The hatchet fell once, slicing the heavy furs, withdrew and hacked again, and Johnston, even in the dark, saw emotion of every sort cross the Absaroka's face, saw surprise and alarm and then final understanding that the furs crouched there against the tree didn't have a man inside, that it was simply too late to remedy that.

Johnston shook the snow aside. "That war your trick, son, not mine," he said aloud. "Ye got no one to blame but yourself . . ."

She hated the boredom most of all. It overpowered fear and apprehension. Now she sorely missed being scared. Now there was nothing at all to do. Was it day outside or was it night? Sometimes Johnston would tell her. For the most part he sat like a stone or wandered out in the night. Worse than sitting in the cabin were the times when she had to go out to attend to bodily needs. It was horrid, a humiliation she could scarcely bear. She had to *ask.* He would not let her venture out alone. He would stand by the door with his weapon while she struggled as far as she dared through the snow. And the cold! That fierce, and unimaginable cold. Winter, she saw now, gave New England a fleeting glance. This terrible empty land was where it was born.

She heard him at the door and then he stepped inside, letting in the cold. "Found us a couple of horses," Johnston said, and dropped his heavy coat on the floor.

"You did?" Emily was surprised. "Why, isn't that odd."

"Ain't nothin' odd to it," Johnston said.

"Yes, well . . ." He seemed very pleased with himself. It dawned on her then that horses had meaning in her life. "Heavens," she said, "that means we can leave this place, does it not?"

"First thing in the mornin'," Johnston said. He didn't even glance her way. He simply wrapped up in his robes and turned his face against the wall.

Emily felt the heat rise to her cheeks, and this brought further irritation. Anger at Johnston, but mostly at herself. What did *she* care what he did? They certainly had nothing to talk about. No topic that would interest her in the least. Still, the man's rudeness had no bounds at all. He had no concept of social intercourse.

"You are just going to—sleep?" she said. "Right now?"

"I was plannin' on it," Johnston said.

"Well you could at least impart information. There are things one needs to know."

" 'Bout what?"

"About the trip." Emily waited. Johnston didn't answer. "What I mean, is how long will it take? I have no idea of the distance to Fort Laramie. As you know, I left under unusual circumstances."

"Ain't goin' to Fort Laramie. Goin' to Fort Pierre."

Emily sat up. "Mr. Johnston, I demand to be returned to Fort *Laramie*. I have no intention of going anywhere else."

"Fort Pierre's whar I'm headed," Johnston said.

"Whatever for?"

"Meetin' someone."

"Well who?"

"Like you're fonda sayin', Miz Dickinson, that ain't no concern of yours."

Emily tried to contain herself. To show Christian restraint. A sudden thought occurred. A woman, that was it. He was going to see a woman. Possibly a wife. The thought defied imagination. What sort of woman would this backwoods ruffian attract?

"Are you married, Mr. Johnston?" Emily asked. "I don't believe you've ever said. But of course you're quite correct. That is no concern of mine."

Johnston kept his silence. He had likely gone to sleep and hadn't heard a word she said. The man had no consideration.

"My wife's dead," Johnston said. The tone of his words brought a chill. "Her an' the chile too. Crows killed 'em both."

Emily felt ashamed. "I'm . . . terribly sorry, Mr. Johnston. Really."

"Reckon I am too."

"You are angry with me I know."

"Ma'am, I ain't angry at all."

"Yes now, you are. I do not fault you for it, Mr. Johnston. I have intruded upon your life. I am guilty of certain violations. And you are still upset about the poems."

"No I ain't."

"Yes you are. That is quite clear to me. I want you to know that I have since shown respect for your possessions. I was tempted, yes. We are all weak vessels, and there is nothing at all to do in this place. Still, I did not succumb. Lord Jesus gave me strength."

"Git some sleep," Johnston said, and pulled the buffalo robe about his head.

He awoke in fury and disbelief, clutched the Hawken and came to his feet, saw the dull press of dawn around the door, heard the faint sound of horses outside, hardly there at all, as if they'd come up with him out of sleep.

Great God A'Mighty, they'd played him for a fool, him sleeping like a chile and sure he'd got the only two. Maybe it wasn't Crow, he decided. Maybe it was Sioux coming back. And what in tarnation did it matter which brand of red coon it might be—they flat had him cold like a rabbit in a log.

The woman came awake, a question on her face. "Jes' get back in yer corner and keep quiet," Johnston said harshly. He turned to face the door, made sure the Walker Colt was in his belt. How many, he wondered. The horses were silent now.

"Come an' git your medicine," he said softly, "I'm a-waitin' right here."

"Inside the cabin," a man shouted. "This is Lieutenant Joshua Dean. We are here in force, and I must ask you to come out at once unarmed."

Johnston laughed aloud. He decided he was plain going slack. A man who couldn't tell shod horses in his sleep was a man who maybe ought to pack it in.

"I am grateful for what you have done," Emily said. "I owe you my thanks, Mr. Johnston."

"Nothin' to thank me for," Johnston said. The troopers had stopped fiddling about and seemed ready to depart. He wondered why a soldier took an hour to turn around. The lieutenant had eyed the Indian ponies but didn't ask where their riders might be. If he recognized Johnston or knew his name he didn't say.

"We have had our differences, I suppose," Emily said.

"I reckon so."

"God has a reason for what he does, Mr. Johnston. I am sure this adventure serves a purpose in His plan."

Johnston couldn't figure just what it might be. "You have a safe trip, Miz Dickinson," he said.

"I will do just that," Emily said. "I expect Massachusetts will seem dear to me now. I doubt I'll stray again."

She walked away through the snow and the lieutenant helped her mount. Johnston watched till they were well out of sight then went inside to get his things.

As he rode through the flat white world with the slate-dark sky overhead, he thought about the Bitter Root Mountains and the Musselshell River. He thought about the Platte and the Knife and the Bearpaw Range, every peak and river he'd ever crossed clear as glass in his head. He thought about Swan, eight years dead in the spring and it didn't seem that long at all, and in a way a lot more. Dead all this time and he still saw her face every day.

Before dark he found a spot near the Belle Fourche and staked the horses out safe. One Crow pony had a blaze between its eyes. He favored an Injun horse with good marks. He wondered if Del Gue was still waiting at Fort Pierre. They'd have to get moving out soon to get some hides. He thought again how he'd waited too long to get in the trapping trade, the beaver near gone when he'd come to the mountains and hooked up with old Hatcher. Just bear and mink now and whatever a man could find.

Scooping out a hole in the snow, he snapped a few sticks and stacked them ready for the fire, then walked back and got his leather satchel and dipped his hand inside. Johnston stopped, puzzled at an unfamiliar touch. He squatted on the ground and started pulling things out. There was nothing but an old Army blanket. His paper was all gone.

"Well cuss me fer a Kiowa," he said aloud. That damn woman had filched the whole lot. He was plain irritated. It wasn't like he couldn't spark a fire, but a man fell into easy habits. A little paper saved time, especially if your wood was all wet. Came in handy too if you had to do your business and there wasn't no good leaves about.

She'd gotten every piece there was. He hadn't ever counted, but there were likely near a thousand bits and scraps, rhymes he'd thought up and set down, then saved for the fire. This was by God pure aggravation. He grumbled to himself and found his flint. A man sure couldn't figure what was stewing in a white woman's head. An Injun wasn't like that at all.

ABOUT THE EDITOR

Joe R. Lansdale is the author of *The Magic Wagon* and the editor of *The Best of the West* for Doubleday. He is also the author of the wildly imaginative science fiction novel, *The Drive-In,* the new suspense novel *Cold in July,* and scores of short stories. He lives in Nacogdoches, Texas, with his wife and two children.